CLOSE KNIT KILLER

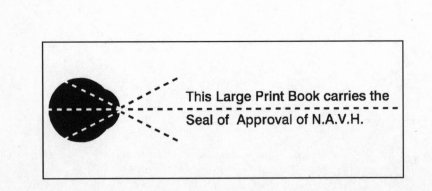

CLOSE KNIT KILLER

MAGGIE SEFTON

THORNDIKE PRESS
A part of Gale, Cengage Learning

Detroit • New York • San Francisco • New Haven, Conn • Waterville, Maine • London

GALE
CENGAGE Learning®

LIBRARY OF CONGRESS CATALOGING-IN-PUBLICATION DATA

Sefton, Maggie.
    Close knit killer / by Maggie Sefton. — Large print edition.
        pages ; cm. — (A knitting mystery) (Thorndike Press large print mystery)
        ISBN 978-1-4104-6013-4 (hardcover) — ISBN 1-4104-6013-4 (hardcover)
    1. Flynn, Kelly (Fictitious character)—Fiction. 2. Knitters (Persons)—Fiction.
    3. Dressmakers—Crimes against—Fiction. 4. Murder—Investigation—Fiction.
    5. Large type books. I. Title.
    PS3629.E37C56 2013b
    813'.6—dc23   2013020388

Published in 2013 by arrangement with The Berkley Publishing Group,
a member of Penguin Group (USA) Inc.

Printed in the United States of America
1 2 3 4 5 6 7 17 16 15 14 13

ACKNOWLEDGMENTS

I want to thank Martha Martin of Snyder, Texas, for the novel's title, *Close Knit Killer.* I'm still using some of the wonderful title suggestions that were sent to me in late December 2009 and January 2010 for my "Name a Kelly Flynn Mystery" contest.

There were nearly two hundred e-mails and literally several hundred title suggestions. There are about ten title suggestions remaining, so I have lots to choose from for Kelly's future adventures. Of course, all titles have to pass muster with my editor, too.☺

The three short recipes included with this book are also contest winners. I had an Appetizer Contest awhile ago on the Cozy Chicks blog, where I post weekly with six other mystery authors (www.cozychicks blog.com). There were two categories: Hot Appetizers and Cold Appetizers. Last year's *Cast On, Kill Off* included several of the winners of the Hot Appetizer contest. This year for *Close Knit Killer,* several of the winners of the Cold Appetizer contest and their names are included along with their recipes. Again, thanks to all who participated.

CAST OF CHARACTERS

Kelly Flynn — financial accountant and part-time sleuth, refugee from East Coast corporate CPA firm

Steve Townsend — architect and builder in Fort Connor, Colorado, and Kelly's boyfriend

Kelly's Friends:

Jennifer Stroud — real estate agent, part-time waitress

Lisa Gerrard — physical therapist

Megan Smith — IT consultant, another corporate refugee

Marty Harrington — lawyer, Megan's husband

Greg Carruthers — university instructor, Lisa's boyfriend

Pete Wainwright — owner of Pete's Porch Café in the back of Kelly's favorite knitting shop, House of Lambspun

Lambspun Family and Regulars:

Mimi Shafer — Lambspun shop owner and knitting expert, known to Kelly and her friends as "Mother Mimi"

Burt Parker — retired Fort Connor police detective, Lambspun spinner-in-residence

Hilda and Lizzie von Steuben — spinster sisters, retired school-teachers, and exquisite knitters

Curt Stackhouse — Colorado rancher, Kelly's mentor and advisor

Jayleen Swinson — Alpaca rancher and Colorado Cowgirl

Connie and Rosa — Lambspun shop personnel

ONE

Kelly Flynn bit into her last slice of pesto pizza. *Yum.* "This is so good, I feel like baking another one," she said to her friends who were seated around Megan and Marty's backyard patio table.

"Hey, put in another pepperoni and cheese, would you?" Greg asked.

"Why don't you try something different for a change?" Lisa prodded her boyfriend. "I bought one of those Hawaiian pizzas."

Greg's pizza-eating cohort Marty screwed up his face across the table, which was completely covered with pizza pans and bottles of craft beers. "Pineapple on pizza? *Heresy!*" red-haired Marty declared.

Kelly took a sip of her favorite ale and leaned back into the cushioned patio chair. "Marty, you're eating barbecued chicken on your pizza now. Why not give ham and pineapple a try?"

"Marty doesn't take risks when it comes

to food," Megan said, grinning at her husband as she rose from her chair. "I'll put in more pizza. One pesto and one pepperoni and cheese. Is that it?"

"Make that two pepperoni and cheese," Greg advised. "Otherwise there won't be any left for Steve after Marty gets through with it."

Kelly sipped her Fat Tire, listening to her friends tease Marty as she glanced around Megan and Marty's backyard. Thanks to her boyfriend Steve's generous wedding gift of a reduced price, Megan and Marty were able to move into one of the empty houses in Steve's struggling housing development on the north edge of Fort Connor. They'd had their eye on it for months, because it was only two doors down from Lisa and Greg's home. The sounds of laughter and backyard barbecues rose up from the neighboring yards surrounding them. It was late May, and the early summer weather was hot already. Temperatures were in the nineties during the days, coupled with that Colorado staple — sunshine, sunshine, sunshine.

"When's Steve coming?" Jennifer asked after she wiped pizza sauce from her cheek. "Aren't the guys playing their old rival Greeley tonight?"

Kelly glanced at her watch. "I thought

10

he'd be here by now. He's got his gear with him, so he may have stopped at the house to change."

Marty checked his watch. "We're gonna have to head for the ball fields in about twenty minutes. He can always meet us there. We'll need Steve's big bat to beat those guys."

"How're you liking Steve's rental house, Kelly?" Pete asked as he took the last slice of pesto pizza. "It's a three-bedroom, right?"

"Yeah. I love the layout. It's got lots of room."

"Have you finally unpacked?" Megan asked as she snuggled against Marty.

"Finally," Kelly said, then took a deep drink of her ale. "It wasn't a hard move because I didn't have that much furniture in the cottage. And Steve never bought much, either, since he's been working in Denver."

"That dark cherry bedroom set of yours sure weighed a lot," Marty teased. "My back still hurts."

"Don't forget the sofa, dude. That was a killer. It was all I could do to finish my ride the next day."

"Get Lisa to rub out the kinks in those muscles," Kelly suggested to mountain biker Greg. "After all, she's a physical therapist."

11

"Are you going to bring some of your cousin Martha's antiques you've got in storage? There were some beautiful pieces there," Megan said.

"To tell the truth, I haven't even had time to think about it yet. So, they'll have to stay in Wyoming for a while longer, I guess." Kelly took another sip of ale.

"Well, you could add a few pieces a little at a time," Lisa suggested. "We'll be glad to help."

"I dunno . . . Antiques sound heavy," Greg added. Lisa gave him a playful jab.

"That's true, and do we want to fill up that house with furniture when someone might buy it this year or next year?"

"Or next is right," Jennifer said with a weary sigh. "This housing market is still depressed."

"Sorry we couldn't help with the move," Pete said, sipping his beer. "We had back-to-back catering jobs that weekend. Man . . . this feels so strange not to be working on a Friday night."

"Amen to that," Jennifer agreed.

"It's great to have you guys join us tonight. Those catering jobs during the school year really kept you busy," Marty said.

"Amen, again," Jennifer echoed, lifting her cola can. "Yesterday, I took some clients

12

into the three-bedroom house a block from here. It's a little smaller than Greg and Lisa's, but the bedrooms are good-sized, and the kitchen is spacious. Living room and dining area are good-sized, too. It's got lots of light and is really nice."

"Well, let's hope someone buys it," Kelly said, then drained her Fat Tire. "There are still three unsold houses left in the development. That one plus a four-bedroom at the entrance road, and the three-bedroom Steve and I are living in."

"It was a smart idea to move to that house and eliminate Steve's apartment rent," Marty said, stacking empty pizza pans as Megan approached with a freshly baked pizza.

"And it's great having you guys over here," Megan added as she reclaimed her chair.

Pete turned his beer bottle on the chair arm. "Do you have any idea what that smaller three-bedroom would rent for? I mean, in case it doesn't sell to that couple."

Kelly shrugged. "Haven't a clue. You'll have to ask Steve, whenever he gets here. Why? Do you know of someone looking for a place to rent?"

"Actually, yes," Jennifer answered. "Pete and I are. Neither his place nor mine is big enough for all our stuff together. We need more room."

"Yeah, we were talking today about maybe asking Steve about renting one of his houses until it sells. We figured we could swing it with what Jen and I are both paying for rent."

Megan jumped up in her chair. "Hey, that's fantastic!"

"It would be great to have you two over here with us," Lisa said.

Kelly thought she detected the sound of Steve's truck's engine at the front of the house. "You can ask him yourself. I think I just heard his truck."

Greg checked his watch. "Boy, he's cutting it close."

"You guys have enough time. Let Steve take a few minutes to swallow some pizza," Lisa admonished.

"Hey, guys," Steve said as he slid open the glass door to the patio.

Megan jumped up from her chair and beckoned to Steve. "Come on over, Steve, and have some pizza. Marty, you and Greg can take another few minutes for Steve to eat."

"Sit down, buddy." Marty directed Steve to a chair. "You're already changed, so we've got a few minutes."

Steve stopped by Kelly's chair first. "Hey,

there." He leaned down to give her a kiss. "Sorry I'm late. Mimi asked me to stop by before she closed shop."

Kelly reached up and put her arm around Steve's neck, pulling him closer for the kiss. "Hey, there, yourself. What'd Mimi want?"

Steve settled into the chair beside her and snatched a slice of pepperoni pizza. "Some suggestions for remodeling. She and Burt have been kicking around ideas. Man, I'm starving." He devoured the slice in two bites.

"There you go, buddy," Marty said with his big grin as he placed the familiar brown bottle of ale in Steve's outstretched hand.

"What are they planning to remodel?" Kelly asked. "The shop is perfect the way it is."

Steve gulped down half the bottle before answering. "Ahhhh. It's not the shop. They want to do something with that older building that used to be a garage. Mimi's used it for storage ever since she started the shop." Another slice of pizza disappeared almost as fast as the first.

"Why don't you ask him now?" Greg gestured to Pete and Jennifer.

"What's that?" Steve took another deep swig of ale.

"Let the starving man eat," Jennifer teased. "We'll talk later. Pete and I are coming to watch your game."

"Hey, that's great," Kelly said. "Thank goodness for end-of-semester breaks when the university goes quiet for a while, and the catering slows down. You two deserve some weekend nights when you're not working."

"Got that right," Greg added. "Why don't you two go up into the mountains tomorrow. Get some high-country air in your lungs." He took in an enormous breath and exhaled loudly. "Do you good."

Pete laughed and sank back into the cushioned chair. "Boy, that sounds great. But I'll probably go down to Denver and visit my grandfather Ben and my niece Cassie. I try to go every month, but it's been so busy here that six weeks have passed by. So, I'll be driving to Denver after lunch finishes tomorrow afternoon."

"And I'll be doing floor duty at the real estate office. Pray that some deep-pocketed customer walks in looking for a home. Preferably someone with a stellar credit rating and lots of money in the bank," Jennifer said, then finished her pesto pizza.

"Wow, you guys are always working," Marty observed as he leaned back in his chair, hands behind his head.

"How old is your niece again?" Lisa asked.

"Eleven, going on twelve. Cassie's a real sweetheart. Grandpa Ben and my grandmother Mary raised her from the time she was a baby. Mary died a couple of years ago." His normal smile disappeared as a somber expression appeared. "My sister Tanya has never been able to take care of Cassie. She's just not stable enough. Got into drugs early in college and has never stayed away for long. Been in and out of rehab. Will work one job for several months until she starts oversleeping and missing work, gets laid off, or fired. She did okay for the first few months after Cassie was born, but then she started bringing the baby over to my grandparents' every night so she could go out to the bars. Tanya always liked to sing and was drawn to musicians, so she'd just live with one guy after another who wanted to party all the time like she did."

"What about the baby's father?" Steve asked as he took another slice of pizza.

"Tanya can't remember which guy it was. Some college student," Pete said sadly.

"Whoa." Lisa leaned back in her chair.

Jennifer toyed with her cola can. "Yeah, it's sad. Last time we were in Denver at Ben's house, Tanya stopped by to announce that she'd 'found her man.' He's a musician with another band that's starting to get popular in the area. Tanya says she's going to travel with them and do their publicity online."

"What about Cassie?" Kelly asked, reading between the lines of what Jennifer was saying.

"Yeah, what about the little girl?" Marty asked, leaning forward now.

"That never seems to come up on Tanya's radar screen." Pete rubbed his forehead. "Tanya said she's trying to build a life with this musician, which means she'll be traveling around the country with Hank and the band. Then she gave Cassie a kiss and told her to be good and do what Grandpa told her." Pete closed his eyes and shook his head.

"Poor kid," Megan said with a frown.

"Yeah, that's why I try to get down there once a month and take Cassie out to places, do stuff with her. That gives Ben a break."

"We took her to the mall last month, and her eyes nearly popped out," Jennifer said, smiling. "She'd never been to that big mall in south Denver. So she was looking in every window, I swear. I thought we'd never pull her away from the computer store. Ben's got an ancient desktop computer, so Cassie has never seen the newer laptops and

18

stuff except on television."

"Hey, Steve, are you full now, because we're gonna have to tear outta here to get to the ball fields?" Greg popped up from his chair.

Steve drained the last of his ale. "Yeah, I'm good. Let's go."

Kelly quickly rose from her chair, as did her friends. "Knock it out of the park, okay?" she said, giving Steve a quick kiss.

Steve grinned. "I'll do my best. See you guys at the game."

Two

Kelly walked across the driveway separating her cottage office from the knitting shop that was a larger version of her beige stucco, red-tile-roofed cottage. The former farmhouse–turned–successful fiber shop was the center of her beloved aunt Helen's life while she was alive. Helen's murder was the reason Kelly had returned to her childhood home in Fort Connor, Colorado, several years ago. As Helen's only relative, Kelly came to bury her aunt and handle the small estate the talented knitter and quilter had left. But Kelly found herself staying — drawn to the warmth and friendship that surrounded her once she entered the knitting shop, Lambspun.

An over-the-shoulder briefcase banging her hip, empty coffee mug dangling in one hand, Kelly followed the flagstone path that ran through the backyard patio and garden area behind the shop. Located at the rear of the knitting shop, Pete's Porch Café spilled out into the patio. Wrought-iron tables with umbrellas and chairs were sprinkled here and there among the shady trees and greenery. Surrounded by a stucco wall on two sides and a decorative iron fence on the other, the café was a popular breakfast and lunch spot, so most outdoor tables were usually filled during good weather.

Glancing across the garden, she drank in the colors of the spring flowers that had already burst into bloom. Then she spotted Mimi's husband Burt sipping from a takeout cup as he strolled though the garden toward the parking lot. "Hey, Burt," she called, hoping to catch the retired Fort Connor police detective's attention.

Burt gave her a big smile and waved as he headed her way. "Hi, Kelly. Jennifer told me the guys won their ball game last night."

"By the skin of their teeth. It was Greg's hit to left field that drove in the winning two runs. It was the bottom of the ninth with two outs."

"Whoa, that must have been exciting. Mimi and I will have to catch one of those games this summer."

"Oh, it was exciting, all right. But there'll be no living with Greg this weekend," Kelly teased.

"Well, that's true," he said with a laugh.

"By the way, Steve said he talked with Mimi yesterday about remodeling the garage." She gestured toward the older stucco-and-red-tiled structure that occupied the corner between the garden and the parking lot.

"Yeah, Mimi and I have been thinking about doing something with this garage we've been using for storage. We thought about turning it into a combination classroom and storage where we could teach bigger spinning and weaving classes. Weaving looms and spinning wheels take up a fair amount of room. Now we have to limit the size of our classes, since the classroom in the shop is only so big. It would be nice to spread out and be able to teach more people."

"That's a good idea," Kelly said, slowly accompanying Burt back down the pathway toward the old garage. "I know you guys are cramped for space with those classes. Sometimes you have to break them into two sections because there're so many people. But what will you do about the stuff you've got stored here?" She pointed toward the bolted door on the side of the structure.

Burt smiled. "Well, we think we've come up with an innovative idea. Most of what we've stored are fleeces we've bought from local spinners, and some other fibers. Mimi and I thought we might have shelves built along the walls inside and offer some of the fleeces for sale, plus allow area spinners to put their fleeces up on consignment. Offer them a larger customer audience. It would be a win-win, we think."

"That's a great idea, Burt," Kelly agreed as she eyed the aging structure. "This garage is pretty old. I remember Uncle Jim using it for farm equipment when I was a kid. Are you going to tear it down and start from scratch or what?"

"Oh, no, we don't want to tear it down. Mimi and I both love all the old stucco outbuildings. We're hoping that Hal Nelson will be able to reenforce the exterior, then totally rebuild the inside. That's another reason we bought the shop and outbuildings from the property owner. We wanted to make some changes of our own."

"And a smart idea, it was. This Hal Nelson is a local builder, I take it. I don't recall Steve ever mentioning his name."

"Yes, he's been working with some larger construction companies for several years and started doing small jobs on his own. Branching out. We found him through Jayleen. She's been working with the Mission's rehab program and helping some of the men who're moving from homeless back into the work force. The Mission program allows them to apprentice in various construction jobs with local companies. That way they kind of ease their way back into society. They qualify to rent a room in a shared house that offers dormitory-style sleeping quarters until they can hopefully land a permanent job, even if it's part-time."

"Boy, that's the hard part. This recession has eliminated so many jobs."

"You're right about that, Kelly. But Curt told us there are some job boards that are posting various day jobs, hard labor mostly. Clearing out demolished buildings and tear-downs or some farm work. That's hot summer work, but it pays."

"I'm not surprised Curt started getting involved at the Mission with Jayleen. He's got connections to ranchers, farmers, and builders. There are plenty of opportunities there for someone who's willing to work." Kelly checked her watch. "Well, I'm going to take a break and knit for a little bit before I head back to work."

Burt chuckled. "You mean before you head back across the driveway. I'm so glad you decided to turn the cottage into your office, Kelly. It wouldn't feel right not to see you pop into Lambspun every day."

"I feel the same way, Burt. Steve and I had to move out last fall because we were bursting at the seams inside the cottage. So it made perfect sense for us to move to one of his empty houses and make the cottage my office. Steve can use the extra bedroom in the house for his home office. And I've still got a mortgage on the cottage. Besides, Carl doesn't have any squirrels to chase in the new yard."

"Well, we're just happy to see you regularly. We've gotten addicted to that." Burt started toward his car. "I'd better head out on errands."

"Talk to you later, Burt." She gave Burt a good-bye wave, slowly walking along the sidewalk leading to the knitting shop's front entry. Passing by the newly planted clay flower pots and enclosed gardens, she admired the young impatiens and daisies pushing their bright faces upward, overtaking the remnants of springtime's tulips.

Looking out to the golf course that bordered the other side of the shop driveway, Kelly observed how many golfers had already progressed this far on the links. With Colorado's gorgeous sunny summer weather beckoning, how could any self-respecting golfer resist an early tee time?

Just then, a black pickup truck rumbled down Lambspun's gravel driveway. Red lettering on the driver's door read NELSON CONSTRUCTION. Kelly only glimpsed the man driving the truck, but figured it had to be Hal Nelson, the builder Burt mentioned who would do the garage remodel. She paused on the sidewalk, curious to meet him. Somehow Kelly felt she should "oversee" any changes to the property that once belonged to her uncle Jim and aunt Helen.

The sprawling knitting shop had once been their farmhouse when Helen and Jim raised sheep. The beautiful rolling greens where golfers now chased errant balls were once sheep pastures where sheep chased one another and munched far less lush grasses. Kelly remembered walking with her uncle in the sheep pastures when she was a child. Hard economic times had forced Helen and Jim out of raising sheep, so Jim took a job with the State of Colorado Transportation Department. Helen continued to spin the fleeces from her former flock and knit beautiful creations for Kelly and others.

After Uncle Jim's death from a heart attack several years ago, Helen sold the large farmhouse to an investor who rented most of the space to Mimi Shafer, who operated a popular knitting shop in Old Town and wanted to expand. Pete had created his café from the remaining space. Helen moved into the small cottage, a look-alike version of the farmhouse right across the driveway. It had been a guesthouse and Helen's quilting refuge for years. Situated between the driveway and the golf course, it sat beneath two large spreading cottonwood trees. The views of the Front Range of the Rocky Mountains in the distance were beautiful — the "foothills," as the locals called them. Kelly never tired of gazing at them. Also, bordering the city-owned golf course were the familiar outlines of the turn-of-the-century buildings in Old Town Fort Connor. Thankfully, some things hadn't changed.

A tall, middle-aged man with sandy brown hair stepped down from his pickup truck, so Kelly figured she might as well introduce herself. As she walked up to him, she noticed another, older-looking man get out of the passenger side of the truck.

"Hello, there," she said, approaching the sandy-haired man. "Are you Hal Nelson? Burt Parker told me you'll be remodeling the garage." She extended her hand. "I'm Kelly Flynn. My aunt and uncle used to own all this land years ago."

The man's broad face broke into a smile. "Yes, I'm Hal Nelson. Glad to meet you, Ms. Flynn," he said, shaking Kelly's hand. "I remember your aunt and uncle. They used to raise sheep. Good people."

"Yes, they were. And both were taken far too early," Kelly said.

Nelson's smile disappeared. "I was really sorry to hear about your aunt, years ago. That was just a shame. I certainly hope that man is still serving his time. He deserves to, that's for sure."

Kelly usually didn't allow old angry memories to claim her attention. Good people could do bad things. Her aunt's killer had committed an awful act of violence — and now he was paying for that reckless choice in the state penitentiary.

"I'm sure he is, Mr. Nelson. And I'm sure he's had plenty of time to regret his actions." Switching subjects deliberately, Kelly gestured to the garage. "This building is pretty old. I remember Uncle Jim keeping his tractor inside. Burt said he and Mimi want to preserve this old exterior. Boy, that's going to be a challenge. I'm curious how you'll do it."

"You're right about that. It'll be a challenge for sure," he said walking toward the garage. "We're going to see how bad the rot is inside and go from there. We're hoping to be able to preserve most of this exterior, but we'll have to see."

As Nelson moved away from his truck, Kelly could finally get a good look at the older man who had been standing on the other side. He was not as tall or as broadly built as Hal Nelson and had a medium-length beard that edged his thin face. It was hard to tell how old the man was, but as he walked closer to where Kelly and Nelson stood on the sidewalk, Kelly did notice something. She recognized that thin bearded face. She'd seen him before, but where?

"Well, you gentlemen have your work cut out for you, that's for sure. I'll come over and check on your progress because I work over there in the cottage." She pointed across the driveway. "Aunt Helen left me the cottage in her will, along with the mortgage," she added. Both men smiled.

"You should keep that property, Ms. Flynn. This is a choice piece of land, as you know. I bet your aunt Helen wouldn't want you selling it off."

"No, siree," the older man spoke up.

"I agree," Kelly said, then turned to the bearded man. She finally remembered where she'd seen him. "Excuse me, but I think I've met you before. Isn't your name

Malcolm?"

The bearded man flushed slightly and a smile appeared. "Yes, ma'am. I recognize you, too. You came into the Mission one day a couple of years back with Miss Jayleen and Jerry. You asked me questions about that young girl who was found dead on the trail beside the river."

"That's right!" Kelly exclaimed. "You were really helpful. No one else had seen that girl except you. Thank God you spoke up."

Malcolm flushed deeper and gazed down at the driveway. "Well, I wanted to help out Mr. Jerry and Miss Jayleen. They'd been really good to me. And they still are."

"You know, I remember that story in the paper," Nelson said, turning to Malcolm. "Did you see that girl being killed, Malcolm?"

Malcolm looked horrified. "Oh, no, sir! I never saw any of that. I just saw someone, looked like a man to me, walk that girl down the trail and leave her sitting on a rock."

"That's exactly right," Kelly said. "If it weren't for Malcolm speaking up, the killer would have gotten away with murder."

Hal Nelson smiled at Malcolm and put his hand on his shoulder. "Good for you, Malcolm. You really stepped up. I'm proud of you."

Malcolm looked down at the ground again, clearly embarrassed. "Thank you, Mr. Nelson. That's good of you to say."

"It's the truth, Malcolm. You provided the clue that led to solving the case. If you don't believe me, ask Burt Parker. He'll tell you," Kelly chimed in.

Hal Nelson laughed as he walked toward the back of his truck. Several toolboxes sat inside along with ladders and other gear. "That is the truth. Burt was a detective here for many a year."

"And he's still detecting," Kelly added as she turned back to the sidewalk. "It was nice meeting you two. You'll see me going back and forth from my office to the shop. Eduardo's coffee keeps tempting me."

"Take care, Ms. Flynn," Malcolm called over his shoulder as he went to help Nelson lift the toolboxes from the truck bed.

"You, too, Malcolm," Kelly said as she sped down the sidewalk. She should really get inside and see how much work she could accomplish before lunch. Kelly skipped up the brick steps to the Spanish colonial–style farmhouse and heaved open the heavy wooden front door.

Stepping inside the Lambspun foyer was always a delight, a visual treat for the senses.

31

It never disappointed. Baskets and chests, spilling over with fat balls of thick yarn or skinny twists of whisper-thin fiber. Tables were stacked with twisted coils of hand-dyed mohair and silk, a rainbow of colors. Kelly couldn't resist stroking the sensuous softness.

Knitted, crocheted, and woven creations were everywhere. Hanging from open doors of an antique dry sink. Draped along the walls above tables and shelves. Old steamer trunks and wide wicker baskets bulged and spilled over with colors and textures. With her one free hand, Kelly succumbed to the yarn's siren call — *touch, touch.* She indulged herself as usual, touching everything in sight. Mohair and silk, alpaca, bamboo, baby alpaca, merino wool.

Walking from the foyer into the central yarn room, Kelly found even more temptations. Wooden bins lined three walls, floor to ceiling, filled with every type of fiber — wools, mohair, cashmere, alpaca, baby alpaca, and combinations. Pudgy round balls of yarn as fat as Kelly's little finger. Small, delicate coils of silken twists no thicker than a single strand of hair.

"Good morning, Kelly." Mimi's voice broke into Kelly's fiber indulgence. "You're coming in for a coffee break, aren't you? I can see your empty mug."

"You're right. I've finished my pot of fresh coffee and decided to combine a coffee break with starting a new project." Kelly smiled at Lambspun's attractive owner.

In her early sixties, blondish, blue-eyed Mimi Shafer was still pretty and youthful-looking. Mother Mimi, as Kelly and her friends called her, was also the in-house expert on All Things Fiber. Knitting, crochet, spinning, weaving, felting, dyeing, no matter — Mimi knew about it and had done it many, many times. Any question you had, Mimi could answer. Which Kelly found reassuring, since she always had lots of questions.

"A new project, how exciting." Mimi's smile spread. "Have you picked out something?"

Kelly trailed her fingers along the delicate silken fibers of a coiled skein. "Nothing is calling me yet."

"Well, in that case, you can help me out by knitting a baby hat for our knitting guild's charity contribution to the hospital pediatric wards. There's a continuing need, not just for babies going in for cancer treatment, but also newborn and premature infants need hats to help their little bodies retain warmth. We lose most of our body

33

heat through our head, you know."

"Oh, yes. All you have to do is lose your hat while you're going down a ski run to discover how cold it is. The last time that happened, I thought my ears would drop off. They were nearly frozen by the time I reached the bottom of the run." Kelly shivered dramatically, even though it was hot outside.

"Well, then, why don't you help out the guild by knitting one of those baby hats while you're deciding on your next project for yourself."

"Hmmmm. I've never knitted a baby hat before, but I assume it's exactly like knitting a regular hat. Only smaller."

"Precisely. You'll use much smaller needles, but it's still exactly the same."

"Smaller needles, huh?" Kelly looked at her skeptically. "I foresee problems. I'm not sure I could work on those teeny-weeny needles. I'd never be able to manage them. I've seen Lizzie work with those, and it's fascinating. But I'm much too clumsy."

Mimi gave one of her dismissive waves. "Oh, pooh. You're much better than you think, Kelly. You could work on the larger needles, if you wish. There are plenty of older babies who need hats, too."

"Sounds good. You and the experts can

handle the preemie newborns. What are you using for yarn?"

"Cotton yarns. Come over to the next room, and I'll show you." Mimi beckoned Kelly as she walked through the main room with its long library table. Knitters and fiber artists of all persuasions gravitated there every day to work on their projects.

Kelly dumped her briefcase onto one of the chairs as she followed Mimi to the adjoining workroom and classroom. Floor-to-ceiling wooden bins lined the walls here as well, but half of the yarns here were of the softer pastel shades. Adorable baby and child-sized sweaters and dresses and other knitted outfits dangled from the walls.

"Here're all the cottons that would be suitable for baby hats," Mimi said, gesturing to one large section of bins. "You'll have plenty to choose from."

Kelly looked at the variety of beautiful balls and coils of yarns stacked neatly into the bins — but she never got to choose. Jennifer came rushing into the room from the hallway that led to the café in the back of the shop.

"There you are, Mimi. I've been looking for you." Jennifer hurried to them, breathless. Her face was flushed.

"What's the matter, Jennifer? You're all

flushed," Mimi said, clearly concerned. "Are you sick, dear?"

"No, no, I'm fine," Jennifer said, waving away the suggestion. "Pete just got a call from his grandfather Ben's neighbor in Denver. Ben had a heart attack this morning. The neighbor came out to get into her car and saw Ben lying on his driveway across the street. The neighbor called nine-one-one right away."

Mimi gasped, her hands at her face. "Oh, no!"

"How's he doing? Did the neighbor say?" Kelly asked.

"The neighbor doesn't know." Jennifer paused to catch her breath. "The paramedics said Ben was still breathing but his pulse was very weak. She followed them to the hospital, but the staff couldn't tell her anything since she's not family. All they said was Ben's condition was serious. They may be taking him in for heart surgery. And they suggested she notify Ben's family. Thank God, she had a key to Ben's house. Ben keeps important phone numbers on his fridge."

"Oh, that's awful!"

"I imagine Pete must be panicked," Kelly said. "It sounds like he and his grandfather were very close."

"Oh, they are. When Pete's mom and dad were killed by the drunk driver years ago, Ben and Mary were the only family Pete had left."

"Has Pete already left for Denver?"

"Yes, he drove off a few minutes ago. He'll go straight to Methodist Hospital. That's where they took Ben."

"Oh, goodness, what about Cassie? Pete's niece?" Mimi asked, worry lines appearing.

"The neighbor told Pete that she put a note on the door telling Cassie to come over to her house when she comes home from school."

"That's good. You don't want to take her out of school. That would probably scare her even more," Kelly said.

"Absolutely. Pete will be staying down there in Denver, right?" Mimi added with a maternal nod.

Jennifer nodded. "Yes, he'll stay at the house with Cassie and make sure she's taken care of and gets to school. Then he'll be at the hospital all day. Who knows when Ben will go into surgery. Maybe he already has."

"Can you and Julie and Eduardo handle the café all by yourselves?" Mimi asked.

"We'll need help. Pete told me to call the part-time cook we use when we have bigger catering events. Frank can fill in while Pete's gone. Who knows how long it'll be?"

Kelly watched the worried expression on her friend's face and sought to reassure. "Don't worry, Jen. Doctors have so many more life-saving procedures now. I'll bet they can take care of Ben."

Jennifer looked a little dubious. "I hope so. Ben wasn't in the best kind of shape to begin with. That's the problem."

"Well, we'll say a prayer and then keep thinking the best," Mimi added. "Meanwhile, is there anything I can do for you, my dear?"

Jennifer shook her head. "No, thanks, Mimi. But I've already called the real estate office and told them I wouldn't be in for a few days. Thank goodness I don't have any clients in the active phase of looking or buying right now. I didn't think I'd ever say that. But I'm needed here at the café every day through lunch and for the prep work afterwards. I may have to help Frank, too."

"Well, just let us know if you need anything, Jen," Kelly said.

"Don't worry, I will. Thanks, guys," Jennifer said, then hurried back down the hallway.

THREE

Kelly looked up from her laptop computer screen. The breakfast rush at Pete's Porch Café was in full swing. Waitresses Jennifer and Julie, ever-present coffeepots in hand, were efficiently moving between customers' tables and the counter where grill cook Eduardo placed plates of scrumptious breakfast orders, fresh from his hot grill. The divine aroma of bacon and eggs, pancakes, and homemade sausage and gravy drifted on the air. Kelly inhaled the heavenly flavors. It was enough to make her want to order a second breakfast.

That was the danger of working at the café during the morning, Kelly found. She didn't have to go out and look for temptation; it drifted right past her nose while she was trying to concentrate on accounting spreadsheets.

"More coffee, Kelly?" Julie asked as she paused by Kelly's small corner table beside the back door that led into the patio.

Eyeing the amount remaining, Kelly held out her large ceramic mug. "Perfect timing, Julie. You have radar instincts."

"I just know you, Kelly. I know your routine. When you're working here in the café, you drink more coffee. So do I. It's because Eduardo's coffeepot is always brewing and sending out coffee aromas."

"True, and we eat more of Eduardo's delectable food, too," Kelly said, watching the grill cook smoothly transfer a perfectly done omelet from pan to plate. "How does he do that?" she said, pointing. "That's one of those unbelievable veggie and cheese creations. It's three inches thick. I tried making it at home once, and it wound up half in the pan and the other half on the counter. Carl, of course, was doggie-on-the-spot and snatched it off the counter before I could rescue it."

Julie laughed lightly. "I hear you. I can't flip those omelets, either. Eduardo says it's all in the wrist."

"Yeah, sure," Kelly scoffed, then took a sip of hot, hot coffee. *Ahhhh.* Eduardo's nectar. Black and strong. That woke up her brain cells in charge of worrying. "Has Jennifer gotten an update from Pete yet? His grandfather went into surgery over an hour ago."

Julie's smile disappeared. "Not so far. Jen's got her phone in her pocket so she can feel it vibrate. That way she can't miss it."

"I guess no news is good news." Kelly tried to find something positive to say. "Aren't those temp waitresses coming in soon?"

"Bridget will be in midmorning till lunch, then Doreen works through lunch. Listen, that spreadsheet you made for us is great, Kelly. It's so helpful to have something like that posted on the wall with everyone's schedule and availability right there."

"Well, I wanted to help out. You're all working so hard. And since I'm positive you wouldn't want me cooking anything, I figured a spreadsheet was the best way to help. Jen told me to add space for the temps. After all, that's what I do every day." Kelly moved her laptop around so Julie could see the screen filled with a spreadsheet detailing client Arthur Housemann's real estate investment expenses.

Julie briefly scanned the spreadsheet, then rolled her eyes. "Wow, Kelly, how do you do that stuff every day? All those numbers would drive me crazy."

"Numbers are where I live." Kelly grinned.

"Let me know if you want something else for breakfast," Julie said as she moved away. Other customers were waiting.

"I already ate one of Eduardo's yummy omelets. That will hold me until lunch," she said as Julie moved to the adjacent table where other coffee cups were extended to the waitress and her coffeepot.

Kelly gazed through the large windows that lined two walls of the café. Customers filled every available table outside in the spring green of the patio garden. Daisies and irises, gold and purple, burgundy and orange, gently waved on their tall green stalks, boldly flaunting their royal colors. Colorado's gorgeous spring weather made it easy to dine alfresco for all three meals of each day if someone chose. Sunny weather and that bright Colorado blue sky beckoned. It was hard to resist.

A tall, heavyset, middle-aged woman appeared, entering the garden from the parking lot. She was followed by a short older woman who carried a large fabric bag over her shoulder. Kelly recognized the tall woman who hurried along the garden's flagstone path, not taking time to glance at the riot of springtime color on either side of her. The older woman, however, slowed her pace, obviously admiring the bright display.

Kelly recognized the tall woman as Barbara, one of Mimi's part-time knitting and fiber arts instructors. Kelly had gotten to know Barbara nearly two years ago when she was teaching at Lambspun. Barbara's son Tommy was dating the young woman who first appeared on Kelly's doorstep one night, high on drugs. The girl, Holly, straightened her life out with Mimi's help, only to wind up dead from an overdose on the Poudre River Trail one morning. That was the girl Kelly had questioned then-homeless Malcolm about at the Mission. Malcolm had been sleeping in the leaves along the Poudre River Trail. Everyone assumed the girl had lapsed into her former drug habits. But Kelly kept asking questions until she found the truth . . . as well as the girl's killer.

Noticing Barbara approach the steps leading to the café's back door, Kelly jumped up from her chair and pushed the metal door open. Barbara was carrying two bags of what looked like fleeces in her arms.

"Hey, there, Barbara. You've got your arms full, for sure," she said as Barbara walked inside the café.

"Thanks, Kelly. That's my mom, Madge,

behind me. She's come to help with a spinning class." Barbara pointed toward the older woman who was coming up the stairs.

Kelly stepped out and reached for the woman's fabric bag. "Here, ma'am, do you want me take that for you? It looks pretty heavy."

"Oh, no, I'm fine, dear. But thanks anyway," the little woman said with a smile as she strode into the shop. "I'm stronger than I look."

"Are you going to teach a spinning class, Barbara?"

"No, no. Mom's the spinner. She's here to help Burt with one of his classes," Barbara explained, taking the fabric bag and slinging it onto her broad shoulder. "Mom, this is Kelly Flynn. She's the one I told you about. She's Helen's niece who settled here after her aunt's death."

"Oh, yes, yes." The older woman smiled up at Kelly with clear blue eyes and extended her hand. "I'm Madge Bennett. Helen and I knew each other well. It was such a shame to lose her."

"Yes, it was," Kelly replied, shaking her hand. She felt a fleeting reminder of her aunt's absence. This woman looked to be in her midseventies — the same age her aunt would have been had she lived. She had a kind face, like Helen's.

"Kelly's the one who helped take police suspicion away from Tommy when she found the person who really killed Holly."

"Ohhhh, yes! That was simply dreadful! Poor little Holly. It just broke my heart when I learned she'd been killed." Madge wagged her head sorrowfully. "Why do people do such things?"

A good question, Kelly thought to herself. She still hadn't figured it out, and she'd helped solve several murder investigations since she returned to Fort Connor four years ago.

"No one knows, Madge," Kelly replied. "People always seem to find a reason to kill. They manage to justify it to themselves, though. I agree with you. It is hard to understand how their minds work."

"Well, I'm just glad you were there to help out, Kelly. Listen, Mom, why don't we chat with Kelly for a few minutes then I'll get the classroom all set up." She slung her mother's fabric bag into the wooden café chair.

"Whatever you say, dear." Madge settled into a chair beside her daughter.

Kelly pulled out the chair across the table from them. "Do you need any help setting up the class, Barbara?"

"No, no, I'm fine. Burt said he couldn't make his class today because his doctor's appointment was rescheduled. So, I told him we'd be happy to fill in. Rather, Mom will be. I'm simply carrying the luggage."

Kelly laughed. Barbara was a no-nonsense, take-control sort, a head nurse at a local doctor's office, so Kelly knew her natural tendency to "get it done" would surface sooner or later. "Will you be spinning all that fleece, Madge? If so, you'll be here all day."

"Oh, no. Burt bought some of my fleeces for the class," Madge said. "That was nice of him to do so. Every little bit helps."

"Mom has some of the best Rambouillet flocks in northern Colorado," Barbara said proudly. "She regularly takes ribbons at the Estes Park Wool Market every June."

"I was noticing that lovely shade of gray," Kelly said, pointing to one of the plastic bags Barbara held. "Is that one of your prize-winning fleeces, Madge?"

Madge straightened and her pale cheeks colored. "Yes, it is. That fleece is from Montclair Blue, my prize ram."

"It's certainly lovely. I may just have to move my coffee and laptop to your classroom if it's not too full. I'd love to see you spin this one." She sank her hand into the bag of smoky gray wool. Softer than soft. "Oh, my, that feels divine."

Barbara laughed. "Well, come on in and join us, Kelly. I think there are only six people signed up for this class. So there will be plenty of room."

"Burt told me their plans for remodeling the storage building into a larger classroom. So someday you may have bigger classes to teach, Madge."

"That would be nice. But the best thing is that Mimi and Burt are allowing me to sell some of my fleeces there once the building is remodeled. That will be wonderful. Lamb-spun has so many customers, my fleeces will be seen by many more people. I am so grateful they offered me that opportunity."

"Barbara, you should create a website for your mom's fleeces," Kelly suggested.

"I set up a website for her three years ago, but the amount of vendors online now . . ." Barbara gave a dismissive wave of her hand. "It's almost impossible to call attention to yourself. Of course, she has found devoted buyers who love the quality of Rambouillet fleeces."

"I had no idea," Kelly said, stepping out of the way as Jennifer scooted past them, a tray filled with breakfast dishes balanced on her shoulder. "Well, I'm glad Mimi and

Burt are giving some of our local spinners a chance to show what beautiful fleeces they have."

Just then, Kelly noticed Jennifer waving to her from the hallway section behind the grill. "If you ladies will excuse me, it looks like Jennifer wants to tell me something. But I think I will take you up on that offer to sit in on your class. Watching spinners always relaxes me."

"We'll be glad to have you," Barb said.

"What have you heard from Pete?" Kelly asked as she rushed over to her friend.

"The surgeon just came out to talk to him. Ben had five arteries clogged, so that's why it's taken so long."

"*Five!* Yikes!" Kelly whispered.

"Yeah, that's what I said. The surgeon told Pete they've fixed all five, but poor Ben is in pretty bad shape. Pete said they're taking him to recovery in the Intensive Care Unit." Jennifer exhaled a long breath.

Kelly watched the worried expression on her close friend's face. "Well, Ben made it out of surgery, Jen, so that's good news."

"You're right. We'll have to focus on that. Meanwhile, Pete will be staying down in Denver for the next few days until Ben's condition stabilizes."

"That's understandable. How's his niece

doing? Cassie, right?"

"She's a real trooper, Pete said. She's helped Pete a lot by finding where Ben kept all his legal papers and stuff. I haven't had a chance to talk to her yet, but I thought maybe tonight when Pete's back with her at the house, we can all three talk. She must be pretty scared with Ben in the hospital."

"Jen, your order's up," Eduardo said from the grill.

"Listen, I've gotta get back, but I'll keep you posted. Oh, do me a favor and tell Mimi, okay?" she said as she reached for a tray.

"Will do. I'll be working here at the shop or at the cottage if you need me for anything. Errands, whatever."

"I may take you up on that," Jennifer said as she headed toward the counter.

Kelly closed the cottage's front door behind her and walked down the narrow cement pathway that led from the cottage to the driveway. The unexpected business call with client Arthur Housemann had taken most of the morning. Glancing at her watch, Kelly noted the time. Madge's spinning class was scheduled for eleven. That left enough time for another coffee refill.

As she walked across the driveway, the

activity around the old garage drew her attention. The front garage doors had been removed and leaned against the back of the structure. The side door was propped open wide, and Kelly thought she saw Hal Nelson inside, measuring a wall width. Then Malcolm came out the side door, carrying some lengths of old lumber. At least, that's what it looked like to Kelly.

Curious, Kelly changed direction, walking toward the structure rather than the knitting shop. "Hi, there, Malcolm, you guys look busy. How's it going?"

Malcolm jerked his head around quickly, and his thin face spread with a smile. "Why, hey, Kelly. You been working over there in your little office?"

"I sure have. I started out working at the café this morning, but when I get a client phone call I need more peace and quiet."

Malcolm made a face as he tossed the old wood into the back of Nelson's truck. "I used to work with numbers years ago. Seems far away now. But I do remember how you could get all twisted around with numbers."

Intrigued by his comment, Kelly couldn't resist prying. "Were you an accountant, Malcolm? Because that's what I do. I handle clients' financial accounts and statements and their taxes."

Malcolm brushed both hands together, then rubbed them on his worn denim shirt. "Well, I wasn't a CPA like you, Kelly. But I was a financial planner. Feels like another lifetime ago."

"Really? Did you work here in Fort Connor?"

"Yes, I did." He looked off toward the Big Box shopping center across the busy avenue that ran beside Lambspun and the golf course. "I was with a local investment group. Colorado Investor Associates."

Really curious now, Kelly wanted to follow up on Malcolm's statement, but hesitated to do so. She could sense Malcolm's reticence when he spoke. Clearly this had been Malcolm's earlier life — his life before he began to abuse alcohol and start on that downward spiral her friend Jayleen had described for her. Jayleen was a recovering alcoholic herself. "Fourteen years sober," she would proudly proclaim when telling others about her former life in Colorado Springs.

Wondering what had happened in Malcolm's life to start him on that downward path, Kelly made a mental note to ask Jayleen what she knew of Malcolm's earlier years.

Hal Nelson stepped outside the structure, carrying another piece of board he'd obviously removed. "Hey, there, Kelly. You going over for another coffee break?" he greeted her.

"You got it, Mr. Nelson. I need caffeine to keep the numbers straight on those spreadsheets."

"Now I know why I don't miss that work anymore," Malcolm said with a little smile.

"You can call me Hal, Kelly," he said good-naturedly as he walked over to the truck and tossed the piece of wood inside.

"Rotted wood?" Kelly pointed to the truck. "Is there a lot inside?"

"There's enough. It's the support beams that will be the real problem. We're gonna have to replace most of them. Aren't we, Malcolm?"

"Yes, sir. Several of the ones I checked so far today are rotted."

Remembering to check her watch, Kelly turned toward the knitting shop entrance. "Well, I'll leave you gentlemen to the rotted wood, and I'll return to my spreadsheets. I'll check in with you again. Oh, my boyfriend Steve Townsend is coming into town tonight, so I bet he'll stop by as well. Builders can't resist."

Nelson smiled. "You tell Steve to drop by

anytime. I've worked with Steve on a couple of his projects over the years. He's a good guy and a damn good builder, too. I'm really glad to hear he's done well in Denver. Maybe he'll be able to start up here in Fort Connor again once this recession lets go of us."

"I'll tell him, Hal. Meanwhile, you two have fun with the rotted wood. I'll play with the numbers," Kelly said with a smile, and she headed for the back door of the café. There was just enough time to grab a quick shot of caffeine before she relaxed with the spinners.

"That's it, nice and easy," Madge said as she watched a young woman slowly ease the drafted wool through her fingers and onto the turning wheel. "Find a rhythm with your feet, nice and easy, that's it."

Madge stood beside the beginning spinner, not hovering, but close enough to help if an extra hand was needed.

Kelly watched the young spinner's face. She had an expression of intense concentration. That seemed typical for most beginning spinners, Kelly had observed over the four years she'd been visiting Lambspun. The spinners' craft had always attracted Kelly. She loved sitting with them while she knitted or worked on her client accounts. She found it soothing and relaxing, almost as if the atmosphere around the spinners was peaceful. She wasn't sure whether the spinners created that peacefulness with their ancient craft or gravitated to it like she did. Kelly had found the same peaceful feeling while knitting quietly by herself at the shop — that relaxed state where ideas seemed to pop into her head more quickly and easily. "Knitting meditation," someone had once called it.

The relaxation she experienced sitting with the spinners was also conducive to getting her work done. Kelly found that even the numbers on her spreadsheets seemed to be more ordered, and fewer errors appeared. Strange, Kelly had often thought. But she didn't have to understand why it occurred; she was simply glad it did. Co-operative numbers were always easier to work with.

"That's good," Madge encouraged again. "You're doing good, dear." She sat down in her chair in front of the five spinners and started drafting more of the wool fleece from the plastic bag, turning it into "batten" or "roving," as spinners called it.

Kelly watched Madge do what she'd seen Burt do countless times — take a handful of cleaned and carded fleece and stretch it between both hands, gently pulling the fibers apart, just enough to make the fleece easier to slide between his fingers and join with the yarn twist that was already wound around the wheel. Feeding the drafted yarn onto the wheel so that it wound around and around and onto the spindle. The spindle fattened as the wheel turned and more yarn wound onto it. Fatter and fatter as the wheel turned.

"Did any of you see that article in the paper this morning?" asked another spinner. A more experienced spinner, Kelly surmised, watching her rhythmic movements, feet and fingers working together, batten sliding smoothly between her fingers and onto the hungry wheel. "This guy's in town to teach a financial seminar or something. But the paper said that he'd been in prison for financial fraud."

"Oh, yes, I saw that article," a gray-haired older woman spoke up, her movements a bit more hesitant than the other woman. Still, the spindle on her wheel was fattening with Madge's prize-winning gray wool. "He's the thief who cheated all those people out of their money years ago. What was his name?"

"Rizzoli," Barbara spoke up from her chair

along the wall where she sat knitting a lime green shell.

"Rizzoli, that's it," the gray-haired woman said. "Now I remember. He ran an investment firm and he cheated all his clients out of their money."

"Oh, I remember that," a middle-aged woman beside Barbara commented. "He was convicted and sent to prison if I'm not mistaken."

Kelly looked up over her laptop screen, drawn to the conversation. "What was this? Who's this Rizzoli guy and what did he do?"

"Rizzoli was an investment advisor who worked with several financial agencies and banks around town. He handled all sorts of securities and had lots of clients. No one suspected he was also running a Ponzi scheme until people began losing money."

"It was terrible. I remember one of the women in my church lost her life savings! She had to sell her house here and go live with her children in Kansas."

"Lots of people lost money," the middle-aged woman added, the gray wool sliding through her fingers faster than some others.

"Many people lost more than that," Madge's soft voice spoke.

Kelly glanced to Barbara's mother, sitting quietly, drafting the gray wool fleece in her lap. Curious, Kelly asked, "What do you mean, Madge?"

Barbara's firm voice spoke up instead. There was an edge to it, Kelly noticed. "My mother means that some of us lost more than money. We lost cherished loved ones. My father killed himself when he learned his clients' investments were wiped out. He'd trusted Jared Rizzoli. And Rizzoli had cheated them."

Kelly stared at Barbara, appalled by what she'd heard. Barbara's strong features had hardened, as if chiseled in stone. Resentment and anger were etched into her face. Kelly glanced around her and noticed the other spinners sat and stared as well. Even the wheels stopped turning.

"Good Lord, Barbara . . . that's awful," Kelly spoke at last. "I'm so very sorry."

The other women added their soft commiseration. Then Madge's soft voice sounded. "Others lost loved ones as well. It was a long time ago. Over ten years."

"Twelve, to be exact," Barbara's hard voice came.

Everyone was quiet, Kelly noticed; then, one by one, the wheels began to turn until their gentle hum was the only sound in the room.

Four

Kelly shifted her briefcase over her shoulder as she held the cell phone to her ear. "I just e-mailed the draft of May's revenues and expenses to you, Don. Only two more working days left in May, so most of those numbers will stay firm," Kelly said into her phone as she walked across the driveway heading to Lambspun. Spotting Malcolm working beside the storage building, Kelly returned his wave.

"Oh, yeah, I see your e-mail now," her client Don Warner said. "Excellent."

"I'll finish up on the thirty-first and send the final statements then. Meanwhile, don't make any plans based on the draft, okay?" Kelly warned as she sped up the wide brick steps to the knitting shop, pausing right outside the door.

Warner chuckled. "Don't worry, Kelly. I know how you hate to send drafts, so I promise to be good. Listen, my other line is ringing. Gotta go. Talk to you later."

Kelly clicked off her phone and shoved it into her pocket, about to open the front door, when she spied a familiar truck turn down the driveway. She spotted the blond woman driving and recognized her friend Jayleen Swinson.

Kelly watched as Colorado cowgirl Jayleen stepped down from the truck and approached Hal Nelson and Malcolm, exchanging greetings. Jayleen glanced Kelly's way and waved toward her. "Hey, Kelly," Jayleen called out.

Kelly gave her friend a thumbs-up sign before she heaved open the heavy front door to the knitting shop and stepped inside. Hopefully she could settle at the knitting table and start her account work. Kelly had spent practically all day working at the shop yesterday, and planned to be here again today. That way she could be close at hand in case Jennifer needed her to run an errand. And she'd be close by whenever Pete called with an update on Grandpa Ben's condition.

The only time Kelly had seen someone close to her hospitalized was years ago when her dear father was dying from lung cancer. Both Uncle Jim and Aunt Helen had died while she was back East, working at a

Washington, DC, corporate accounting firm. Although Pete's grandfather was a stranger to her, Kelly felt connected because Jen and Pete were dear friends. She recognized the worry and anxiety she saw on Jennifer's face. Kelly remembered how that felt, and how alone she'd felt. She didn't have a close network of friends back in Washington, not like she did here in Colorado. She wanted to be able to support her friends any way she could.

Trailing her fingers across some of the tempting yarns, Kelly headed for the main room and set her briefcase on the long library table that dominated the room. Floor-to-ceiling shelves lined one wall and were filled with magazines and books dealing with fiber in all its forms and all the ways it could be used — knitting, crochet, spinning, weaving, felting, dyeing, all manner of manipulation. Both walls surrounding the archway entrance to the room were lined with wooden bins, stacked with yarns, yarns, and more yarns. Sometimes Kelly felt overwhelmed by it all. There was so much she didn't know. But the comforting thought was that Mimi knew everything about all things fiber.

Kelly pulled out her coffee mug and was about to head to the café for a refill when she noticed Megan walking toward the knitting table, Jennifer in tow. Literally in tow. Megan had her hand around Jennifer's arm, guiding her toward the table. Kelly stepped aside. She wasn't about to get in the way of Megan on a Mission.

"See, Kelly's here. This is a perfect time for you to take a break," Megan declared, releasing Jennifer's arm before she pulled out a chair.

"I see Megan decided you needed the break," Kelly said, smiling at her friends.

Jennifer looked over at Kelly and rolled her eyes. "I was going to come over in a few minutes, but Megan had other ideas."

Megan pulled out a chair for Jennifer to sit. "I've been knitting in the café, waiting for you to take a break for nearly an hour. If I hadn't dragged you out, you'd never have left." Megan plopped two knitting bags onto the table and sat in the chair beside her. "I brought your bag, too."

Kelly pulled out a chair and joined her friends. "Megan did you a favor, Jen. I know how easy it is to get so caught up in work that you forget about yourself. I recognize it because I do it, too." She pulled her laptop from her briefcase. "Eduardo and Julie and Frank can spare you for ten minutes."

"Fifteen," Megan decreed, pulling out a

royal blue yarn from Jennifer's bag. It looked like a top that was halfway finished.

"All right, all right," Jennifer said, picking up the yarn on her knitting needles and giving it a shake. Now it looked to Kelly like a lacy-patterned sleeveless top was being created.

Kelly slid her laptop computer several inches away and reached into another pocket of her briefcase, withdrawing the small circular needles with the beginnings of the yellow and white baby hat she'd started.

"Have you heard anything from Pete?" she asked Jennifer. "You said he was going over to the hospital after he took Cassie to school."

"Yes, he called about twenty minutes ago —"

Megan turned to her with a shocked expression. "You didn't tell me that!"

Jennifer gave Megan a long-suffering look. "I was about to, Miss Bossy, when you grabbed my arm and dragged me out of the café."

"I did it for your own good," Megan said, in her familiar self-righteous tone, fingers moving at their usual warp speed. Kelly never could understand how someone could knit that fast and be that accurate. Amazing.

"What did Pete say, Jen?" Kelly asked, putting her concentration on her friend rather than the yarn in her lap.

Jennifer's bantering expression changed to a more somber look. "He said it really shook him up to see Ben this morning. Ben's still not conscious because he's taking so many painkillers following surgery. Plus, he's hooked up to all sorts of machines keeping track of everything. Pete said it really sank in how serious Ben's condition is. I could tell just from Pete's voice how worried he is."

"Oh, Jen, I'm so sorry," Megan said.

Kelly stared at her friend. "What did the doctor say?"

"The doctor explained why Ben's hooked up to all of the machines. His condition is *very* serious. Ben has been so weakened by the heart attack that it's going to take a long time for him to recover."

"Wow, that sounds like he's going to be in the hospital quite a while," Megan said. "How long will Pete stay in Denver?"

Jennifer let her knitting settle into her lap as she stared off. "I don't know. We haven't had a chance to talk about it yet. But he can't stay there indefinitely. We'll need him back here at the café. Frank said he could work for two weeks max. That's all. He's got a conflict on dates."

Kelly could feel Jennifer's worry coming across, so she reached over to give her friend's arm a squeeze. "I'm sure Pete will be coming back soon, Jen."

"What about his niece, Cassie?" Megan said. "She can't be left down in Denver all by herself. Do you think Pete's sister will be able to stay with her?"

Kelly was going to follow up on that comment when Jayleen strode into the room. "Hello, there, gals. It's good to see you," she cheerfully announced, then grabbed a chair and spun it around backward so she could sit. "How's Pete's grandfather, Jennifer? I heard from Rosa what happened."

"Not good," Jennifer answered.

"I'm going to have to run, guys," Megan said, shoving her blue knit top and needles back into her bag. "Jen, keep me posted, okay? Why don't you join us tonight over at Kelly and Steve's house. You need to relax with friends, not sit home alone and worry."

"That's a great idea," Kelly said. "Don't worry about dinner. We're ordering Indian food. You'll probably know more from Pete by then, so you could tell us all at the same time."

"Gotta run," Megan said, waving at everyone as she hurried out.

"How bad is Pete's grandfather's condition?" Jayleen probed.

"Five arteries were clogged, so the surgery was pretty intensive," Jennifer said, starting to put away her own knitting. "The doctor told Pete that Ben would need a long time to recover. Months, he said."

Jayleen screwed up her face. "*Damn.* That's gonna be hard on you folks. Didn't Pete say he has a niece in Denver? What's going to happen with her? Are there any other relatives in Denver she could stay with?"

Jennifer shook her head. "Nobody that Pete or Ben would trust. Listen, I'd better get back to the café." She rose from her chair. "But I think I will stop by at your house tonight, Kelly. It'll be good to be with all of you. I don't feel like being alone."

"That sounds like a good idea," Jayleen said with a big grin. "Better to be with friends at times like these."

"Come on over as soon as you're free, Jen," Kelly said.

"Thanks, Kelly. Good to see you, Jayleen. Talk to you later," Jen said with a smile and walked away through the central yarn room.

"My, oh, my, are we all glad Jennifer and

Pete have each other. Hard times are easier to bear when you're not alone," Jayleen said, shaking her head full of blond curls. Silver was darting through the blond hair now.

"That's for sure. By the way, I saw you talking with Hal Nelson and Malcolm outside. It looks like they're making good progress on that old garage. Malcolm says there's a lot of rotted beams."

"Yeah, there sure are. Hal showed me what they were dealing with. They're gonna have to replace a lot of those support beams. You don't want to have the roof cave in on one of those spinning classes."

"You know, it took me a few minutes, but I finally realized where I'd seen Malcolm before," Kelly said. "I was surprised that he remembered me."

"Sure, he does. Malcolm didn't think he'd done much, but Jerry over at the shelter and I made sure we kept heaping the praise on him for stepping up. He really made a difference." Jayleen smiled. "Malcolm's a good guy, and I'm proud of the progress he's made. You'd already met Malcolm over at the Mission, so you knew he was in our counseling program and has been coming with me to AA. It's been over a year now."

"It looks like he and Nelson work well together. I made sure I told Nelson how important Malcolm had been in that investigation. Without his help, the killer would have gotten away with murder," Kelly added with a smile.

Jayleen grinned. "That was mighty good of you, Kelly-girl. That really helped boost Malcolm's self-confidence — you can bet on it."

"You know, I'm curious about something, Jayleen," Kelly said, remembering her conversation with Malcolm the previous day. "When I was talking with Malcolm yesterday, I mentioned that I had to work with numbers all the time since I was an accountant. And Malcolm said that years ago he used to work at a financial office here in the city. Then he kind of gazed off and didn't say any more. I wondered if he'd ever mentioned that to you or Jerry over at the Mission."

Jayleen nodded. "Oh, yes. Malcolm's got quite a story. Seems he worked for one of the many financial firms in town that went belly-up when that crook's Ponzi scheme went bust. Malcolm lost everything when his company went bankrupt. His job, all his savings, which he'd invested with them of course, even his home. Couldn't make the payments on that pricey real estate once the paychecks stopped coming in. Hell, even

Malcolm's wife left him. Walked out and took whatever she could find. Poor devil. That's what started Malcolm on that dark road that leads only one way . . . *down.*" Jayleen gestured.

"Whoa . . . would you believe that's the second time I've heard a story like that? Barbara's father owned one of those financial firms in town that lost everything, too. All their clients' money was lost with that guy's phony investments. What's his name?"

"Rizzoli. Jared Rizzoli. Yeah, I read in the paper that he's back in town giving a financial seminar." Jayleen gave a disgusted snort. "Paid his debt to society, he says. *Hummph!* There's no way that low-down thief can repay all the damage he's done to lives of people all over this city. People killed themselves because of that son-of-a-snake! Paid his debt?" Jayleen added some colorful expletives Kelly hadn't heard from her friend in quite a while.

"Wow, he really does sound like a piece of work."

"That, he is. Curt and I had to take a ride to cool off after we read that article in yesterday's paper. And today's." She screwed up her face again. "He said he wanted to offer his apologies to the people in Fort Connor who suffered losses. Well, a

free financial seminar won't put back together the families that were destroyed by
his schemes."

"Barbara's mother Madge is helping with
one of the spinning classes. I sat in with
them yesterday, so I heard all about Rizzoli.
Every person in that class had a story, I
swear."

"Hundreds all over town have stories. Not
just Fort Connor, either. All over northern
Colorado." Jayleen pushed herself out of
the chair forcefully, swinging her leg over.
"Listen, I'd better get back to the canyon
and my chores. I need to get out in the fresh
air after talking about that low-down dirty
snake."

Kelly rose from her chair as well and
grabbed her empty mug. "I promise I won't
mention it again, Jayleen," she said, following her friend into the central yarn room.

Jayleen paused on her way to the front
door. "Make sure to keep Curt and me
posted about Pete and his grandfather,
okay? We want to help any way we can."

"You bet. Say hi to Curt for me," Kelly
said, heading toward the hallway, the aroma
of fresh-brewed coffee beckoning her.

"See you tomorrow, Rosa," Kelly called to
the knitting shop clerk in the front room. "I

have to finish some work across the driveway."

"You mean your 'office'?" Rosa teased as
she sat at the yarn winder.

Kelly waved as she pushed open the front
door. Then she suddenly stopped because
she almost ran into a man who was about
to enter the shop.

"Oh, excuse me!" she apologized, stepping away.

"No problem, miss," the man said, moving aside. "The door didn't touch me."

"My friends all tell me I move too fast,"
Kelly joked.

"Do you work here, miss?" the man asked.

"Oh, no, I just come here a lot," Kelly said
with a smile. "Did you need to buy some
yarn or fiber? One of the shop assistants is
inside, so she could get anything you need."

"No, no, I don't knit," the middle-aged
man said, smiling. "I just wanted to ask a
question about the building that's being
remodeled. Over there." He pointed to the
garage.

"The owners are doing some renovations.
They're enlarging that old garage and turning it into a classroom and storage area."

"Do you happen to know the builder in
charge of it? I'm looking for a Hal Nelson
and was told by his office that he was work-

ing at this location."

"You're right, he is." Kelly scanned the parking lot. "But he must have finished for the day because I don't see his truck."

The man frowned as he stared at the driveway. "I was really hoping to speak with him. I'd heard from someone that he had property in the Poudre Canyon that he wanted to sell. I'd hoped to speak with him about it."

"Well, I'm working right across the driveway, so if I see him before I leave this evening, I'd be glad to tell him you wanted to speak with him. Do you have a card?"

"That would be very kind of you," the man said, reaching inside his jacket. His *expensive* suit jacket, Kelly couldn't help noticing as he handed her his card.

Kelly stared at the card as the man's name registered. *Well, well, well.* " 'Jared Rizzoli, Financial Expert,' " she read, deliberately changing her tone of voice to sound impressed. "I think I read about you in the newspaper. You're that financial authority on avoiding investment scams. The article said you were in town to give two financial seminars."

Rizzoli's handsome face spread with a wide smile. "Yes, that's right. And you are?"

Kelly extended her hand. "Kelly Flynn.

I . . . uh, I own a small business. Bookkeeping."

"Ah, a small business owner. The very backbone of our economic system. I hope you're managing to weather this brutal recession?"

Kelly adopted a guileless expression and deliberately downplayed her success. "I'm doing my best. It's really hard, though. But I'm hanging in there."

Rizzoli's smile widened as he focused on her, leaning forward just a little. "Well, don't forget your financial future, Ms. Flynn. There are ways to protect your hard-earned savings so they'll be there when you retire. Of course, you're so young, retirement must sound far away. But I assure you, you have to prepare now. In fact, you would benefit from attending my free seminar here in Fort Connor tomorrow night. I also have a book coming on the ways to avoid being caught in financial scams. You don't want to work hard to save and then have someone steal it away, right?"

Kelly had to plant both feet firmly on the concrete porch in order not to be blown over by the force of Rizzoli's energetic sales pitch. For that was exactly what all of his encouraging and reassuring words boiled down to: *a sales pitch.* Kelly was fascinated by Rizzoli's transformation from regular guy into a smooth-talking salesman. She had no doubt that he had been very successful convincing clients to invest in his financial scheme.

"Well, maybe I'll do that, Mr. Rizzoli."

"Call me Jared." He beamed.

"Jared," she said, careful not to allow her smile that lurked inside to escape. Just then, Kelly spotted Hal Nelson's black truck rolling down the driveway. "Well, Jared, I think this is your lucky day. That's Hal Nelson now."

Rizzoli jerked his head around. "Wonderful. That's perfect timing. Thank you so much, Ms. Flynn."

"I'm happy to help, Jared," Kelly said with a winning smile as she started to walk away. "And I may take you up on your offer to attend the seminar."

"I'll look for you, Ms. Flynn," Rizzoli said as he turned toward Hal Nelson, who was parking his truck.

Don't look too hard, Kelly said to herself as she headed for the cottage.

"Wow, Pete's grandfather sounds in really bad shape," Marty said, leaning forward in the deck chair.

"How long will Pete be down in Denver,

do you think?" Greg asked, tipping back his beer bottle.

Empty white take-out boxes lay scattered on the round glass tabletop. The aroma of Indian food still hung in the early evening air.

Jennifer had sunk back into the chair cushions on the shaded outdoor patio, so Kelly answered for her tired friend. "Not too long. Jen said that the replacement cook has a schedule conflict so could only work two weeks."

"What about Pete's niece?" Lisa asked in concern. "Will her mom be able to take care of her?"

Megan gave a disgusted snort. "It doesn't sound like you'd want her taking care of Cassie, would you, Jen?"

"I think it's kind of unlikely Tanya would leave her boyfriend and the band to come back to Denver and take care of Cassie. Frankly, I don't think Pete would trust her, either. And I wouldn't want Cassie put in that situation."

Kelly looked around at her friends, seated on the spacious patio in the back of one of Steve's unsold Wellesley development houses. She and Steve had lived there only two months, but she was amazed how quickly she'd adjusted to having more

74

space. Living in the cottage had been fun and convenient, but it had also been cramped. After both of them had been living in apartments and smaller quarters for years, she and Steve reveled in the extra space.

Kelly decided to ask what she knew the rest of her friends wondered as well. "Have you and Pete talked about his bringing Cassie here to Fort Connor to stay with you guys while Ben's recovering?"

"Actually, we talked about it just this afternoon," Jennifer said. "I told Pete I'd feel better if Cassie were up here with us. He thought so, too, but had hesitated to mention it at first."

Steve smiled as he balanced his bottle of Fat Tire on the arm of his chair. "Sounds like Pete. He was probably worried you wouldn't want her here."

Jennifer nodded. "I told him I'd be more worried if we *didn't* have Cassie here with us. I wouldn't want her back in Denver with some neighbor or, God forbid, her spacey mother."

The sound of a cell phone's music interrupted. Kelly recognized Jennifer's distinctive selection. Jennifer reached for her phone. "Hey, it's Pete. He must have gone to see Ben again. Let me put him on speakerphone. Hey, Pete. I'm over here at Kelly and Steve's with the gang, so I'm gonna put you on speaker, okay?" She propped the phone against an empty container of Indian vindaloo chicken on the patio table.

"Hey, guys," Pete's voice sounded.

Kelly joined her friends as they greeted their absent member. "How's Ben doing?" she spoke up louder than normal.

"He's the same. Which is to say, not too good. He still needs help breathing and is still unconscious. I brought Cassie in after school, only because she hadn't seen him yet." A long sigh sounded. "It really shook her up. I didn't want to do it, but she insisted."

"That's okay, Pete," Lisa spoke up. "It's good for kids to see their loved ones in the hospital recuperating. They need to know that they're still alive and are trying to get better. That way they don't wonder about what's happening to them or if they'll ever come back."

"Speaking of coming back, when will you come back, buddy?" Marty asked.

"Well, Cassie had her last day of school today. I'd like to stay through the weekend to see Ben. I'm hoping he'll wake up a little."

Steve leaned forward in his patio chair.

"Listen, Pete. Why don't you and Cassie plan on coming back to Fort Connor in a few days, depending on how Ben is doing. Meanwhile, the rest of us can use this weekend to move all the stuff from your apartment over to the house around the corner here. You know, the one we talked about. We can help Jennifer pack up all your stuff. With all of us helping, we'll get you two packed up, moved, and unpacked by the end of the weekend. That way, you and Jen and Cassie can move into a house that's big enough for all of you."

Kelly leaned over and kissed Steve on the cheek as all her friends loudly echoed Steve's suggestions.

FIVE

"Can you give me a refill, Eduardo?" Kelly asked, dangling her mug over the café counter. "Both Julie and Jennifer are way busy with customers." Glancing around the crowded café, Kelly didn't spot one empty chair. Great for business. The accountant lobe of her brain did a little happy dance. Small business successes always made Kelly happy.

"Sure thing, Kelly," the genial grill cook said, taking her mug over to the coffee machine. "We've been swamped since seven this morning."

"Did you turn on those fans that blow all the good breakfast smells towards the golf course?" she teased. "I see more people wearing golf shoes in here than normal."

Eduardo grinned as he returned her mug. "Naw. I had to stop doing that. Jen said it was cruel to tempt them in the midst of their round."

The black nectar's aroma drifted to Kelly's nostrils. *Ahhhh, caffeine.* Not spotting the temporary cook, she asked, "Isn't Frank the temp cook here? I usually see him helping."

"Oh, he is. He's downstairs doing the baking. Good thing he made extra loaves yesterday because we've used them all up today. Plus, we're all out of pies, so he'll be doing those the rest of the morning before the lunch rush."

"Well, I'd offer to help, Eduardo, but I don't think you'd want any pie I'd bake. The customers might run screaming out of the café."

"Ahhhh, Kelly, if you can bake your aunt Helen's gingersnaps, then you can bake a pie."

Changing the subject, Kelly leaned over the counter, watching Eduardo return to the grill, turning the sizzling bacon slices, then placing a metal plate on top of them. "Has Jennifer heard anything from Pete this morning? I didn't want her to take time away from her customers."

"Yeah, she did," Eduardo said as he poured what looked like beaten eggs from a pitcher onto the hot grill. Kelly watched the mixture bubble up as Eduardo deftly flipped and turned the yellow liquid with his metal spatula until it turned into scrambled eggs.

"Ben's still unconscious, but his breathing has stabilized, the doctor said, which is good." He wielded the spatula again, scooping up the scrambled eggs and expertly sliding them onto a plate all in one smooth movement.

"Well, that's something," Kelly said, noticing Hal Nelson enter the café. "I'll let you get back to work, Eduardo. I'll be in the shop until this breakfast rush dies down."

Eduardo gave her a thumbs-up and a grin as he buttered Pete's signature whole wheat toast, placing the slices beside the scrambled eggs and bacon.

Kelly walked toward the front of the café, where Nelson stood. Julie had already spotted the dangling coffee mug in his hand and was in the process of refilling it.

"Hi, Hal. I see it didn't take you long to discover Eduardo's strong coffee," she said, raising her own mug.

"Morning, Kelly," he greeted with a smile. "You're right about the coffee. I have to admit, it's some of the best. Strong and black."

"I think Eduardo's secret is the nails and shoelaces he throws in when we're not looking." She took a sip while Nelson laughed. "How's that remodeling going?"

"Pretty good. We've got the rotten beams

replaced and any other pieces that needed replacing. And we've only lost a few places on the original stucco, which isn't too bad. We're going to keep working on the interior today. Put in some insulation and the dry-wall tomorrow."

"Wow, you two are moving right along." Kelly couldn't help adding, "I'm so glad to see Malcolm doing as well as he is. Jayleen stopped in yesterday, and I got to hear more about his background."

"Thanks, miss," Nelson said as Julie handed him his mug. "I appreciate that." He handed her some bills. "Yeah, Malcolm has had it kind of rough. Some people can handle those rough spells life throws in better than others. Some folks get beaten down." He looked away as he took a sip, then blew on the hot liquid.

"Jayleen told me some of what happened to Malcolm to send him on that downward trajectory, so to speak. It sounds like everything kind of piled up on him. Losing his job, his career, his home, even his wife . . ." Kelly wagged her head. "I don't think there's many of us who wouldn't be dropped to our knees by all that onslaught."

Nelson gave her a wry smile. "You're right about that, Kelly. That's kind of the reason I got involved with the Mission's program a few years back. I wanted a way to help some people who've been knocked down learn how to get back up again. Give them some work to do, and get them on a path to feel good about themselves again."

Kelly looked at Hal Nelson, sizing him up anew. "That's really admirable of you, Hal. Not many people would make the effort during these bad economic times to help other people find a job. Jayleen mentioned you have your own construction company to run. How do you manage all that?"

"Well, I've got two good people who work for me. One's an older guy, Dutch, who's been supervising construction crews for a lifetime. So he and the other guy, George, can handle anything. I try to split my time between sites when I'm doing a Mission job, but it's a challenge."

Remembering yesterday afternoon's visitor, Kelly said, "By the way, I spoke with that man who stopped by the shop yesterday afternoon looking for you. We chatted for a few minutes before you drove up. Rizzoli was his name."

"Yeah, Rizzoli." Nelson nodded. "He wanted to see this parcel of land I've got up in Poudre Canyon. I thought I'd give Jennifer a heads-up. She listed it for me last year, but nothing was selling then, so it's been sitting."

"Well, Jennifer is a personal friend, but I've also used her as an agent, so I know how good she is. Poudre Canyon is one of my favorite places. I almost bought some land up there a few years ago, but . . . it wasn't meant to be, I guess. I let someone else buy it."

Nelson looked at her briefly, then glanced out into the café. "I know what you mean, Kelly. I'm not sure now if I want to sell the land or not. But my wife insisted I show it to him anyway." His mouth twisted into a smile. "Susie reminded me we haven't had a serious offer on this property yet because of the real estate market collapse."

"I hear you," Kelly sympathized. "Jennifer's told us how brutal it is. There are so few sales right now. Not many people can qualify. Thank goodness Jennifer works at the café. And you know that Steve lost his business in the downturn. If this Rizzoli can qualify, you might want to take his offer seriously. They are few and far between."

Nelson's smile widened. "You sound just like my wife Susie. And you're both right. We can use the money, for sure. That's why I called him and said to contact Jennifer so she can take him to the canyon to see the property."

"Hey, that's great," Kelly enthused. "I hope he falls in love with it. Apparently this guy can afford it. I read in the paper he's giving all these free financial seminars here in town. So, he must be doing okay."

"Ohhhh, yeah. He made it a point to tell me he'd be paying half in cash. And the balance upon closing."

"Whoa, take the money and run, Hal," Kelly said, laughing.

"That's exactly what Susie said."

Jennifer quickly walked over to the two of them. "Hal, Julie's watching my tables, so why don't we take a few minutes now." She turned to Kelly. "Bridget is coming in earlier this morning so I can take off."

"Hey, if you need me to help with anything or run errands, let me know."

"Thanks. I think we've got it covered for now." Turning back to Nelson, she said, "Hal and I have already done all the paperwork on the listing last year. We've raised the price a little, so we'll wait to see if he wants to buy."

"Listen, Kelly, I'll talk with you later," Hal said as he walked toward the front door, Jennifer following.

Kelly headed through the back of the café toward the hallway that led to the knitting shop. As she approached the classroom and workroom, she spied Barbara and her mother Madge.

"Good morning, ladies. Another class today, I take it," she greeted them.

"Yes, indeed," Barbara answered, pulling a spinning wheel into place beside two other wheels. "Burt and Mimi decided to take an extra-long weekend in the mountains."

"Ooooh, that does sound nice," Kelly said as she walked toward the main room. "I'd love to get away, but this weekend is already booked. A bunch of us are moving Pete and Jennifer from their small apartment to one of Steve's unsold houses in Wellesley."

"Oh, my, are they buying a house?" Madge asked, eyes widening in interest. "How brave of them in these difficult times."

"I'm amazed they were able to qualify," Barbara commented as she pulled a fourth wheel into place. A rough approximation of a semicircle was forming.

"They're renting, not buying," Kelly replied. "And for the same reason you mentioned, Barbara. Even people with good credit have trouble getting a bank loan to buy a home nowadays. Jennifer has told me how bad it is out there."

"That's nice of Steve to rent the home," Madge said as she pulled a large plastic bag

85

of fleece closer to her chair. The wool was golden colored, drawing Kelly closer.

"He thinks it's better to receive money from renters while waiting for the housing market to improve. Better than letting it sit there empty." She set her coffee mug on a nearby worktable and dropped her briefcase on the floor. "This is beautiful, Madge." She fingered the golden softness. "Is this another of your sheep?"

Madge's thin cheeks colored in obvious pleasure. "Yes, it is. This is from my prize-winning ram Jason."

Kelly had to laugh. "Jason and his golden fleece. I love it. Well, I may have to sit in with you and your class again, Madge. I've always wanted to see someone spinning gold."

Kelly looked up from her laptop screen where she was squirreled away in the comfy armchair in the corner of Lambspun's front room. Three customers were lined up at the cash register counter where Rosa was handling questions and purchases. Connie, the other shop assistant, sat at the winding table, removing a fat ball of hot pink fluffy wool and mohair from the winding spindle.

"Ah, you're finished," Barbara's big voice sounded as she entered the front room.

"May I use the yarn winder, please?"

"Sure, Barbara, be my guest," Connie said as she vacated the chair. Scooping up four fat balls of the hot pink yarn in her arms, she cleared the table.

Barbara sat down and loosened the fluffy loop of smoky gray spun yarn. She arranged it on the yarn holders of the skein winder, then stretched one yarn strand and wound it around the spindle of the ball winder on the other side of the table. Slowly, she started to turn the ball winder handle, and the luscious gray yarn wound slowly from the skein winder holders to form a ball around the spindle.

"Is that Madge's prize-winning yarn?" Kelly asked.

"Yes, indeed," Barbara replied. "Mom's Montclair Blue."

"That is such a gorgeous gray. I might be tempted to actually knit a winter sweater even though it's summer, and hot outside."

"Sure you can, Kelly," Barbara encouraged as she turned the handle, looking outside.

Kelly was about to return to her spreadsheets when she caught sight of Jennifer standing beside the fence bordering the garden patio and the driveway. She appeared to be talking to a man who had some papers in his hand. Kelly focused on the man and recognized him as Jared Rizzoli. *Well, well.* Maybe Jen would make a sale this month when she didn't expect it. Extra money was always good, especially when someone was moving.

"Who's Jennifer talking to outside?" Barbara asked, glancing to Kelly.

Remembering Barbara's family's financial disaster caused by Jared Rizzoli's Ponzi scheme, Kelly hesitated to answer honestly. "Uhhhh, I'm not sure," she deliberately hedged.

Connie stopped stacking fuzzy balls of azure blue mohair and glanced out the window. "Oh, that's the guy who's doing the free seminars. Rizzoli. He's the one who went to jail. I saw him on the local TV news last night. They interviewed him."

Barbara suddenly went ramrod straight as she stared out the window. Then she jumped out of her chair, sending it backward. "That *bastard!*" she cried, and stormed from the room, her face thundercloud dark.

"Uh-oh," Rosa said, brown eyes wide in obvious concern. "Barbara's family lost everything because of him."

"Yeah, I know," Kelly said, quickly leaving her cozy arm-chair to follow after Barbara. Kelly had seen the banked fury on Barbara's face when she related Rizzoli's cheating and manipulation. No telling what Barbara might do if she was face-to-face with the man responsible for her family's ruin.

Kelly sped through the adjoining room dominated by the Mother Loom and into the foyer. Barbara was already outside, heading toward the garden patio. A tall woman, Barbara had a long stride and covered ground fast while walking. Kelly pushed through the shop front door and raced down the steps. Barbara was already down the sidewalk and entering the garden. Jennifer and Rizzoli were still talking beside the fence, completely unaware of the approaching storm in the form of Barbara.

"YOU!" Barbara yelled up ahead. "You're a thief and a *murderer*! My father is dead because of you!"

Kelly raced down the path and into the garden, noticing the startled café customers sitting at nearby tables, staring at Barbara. Jennifer stared at Barbara as well, clearly amazed by her outburst. Rizzoli, however, stood absolutely still, his face reddening as Barbara continued her accusations.

"We lost everything because of you and your . . . your Ponzi scheme! My father was an honest man. And he bankrupted himself to repay all his clients. We lost everything because of you! And we lost him, too! He shot himself in despair when he couldn't pay them all!"

Barbara was fairly shaking in her white-faced fury. Rizzoli, however, was getting redder and redder, Kelly noticed as she drew beside Barbara. She sensed an explosion.

Instead, Rizzoli's voice came out cold as ice. "I paid my debt to society. Ten years in prison."

Barbara drew herself up even taller than her six feet, and her features twisted with a sneer. "*Ha!* Don't hand me that! You were in a minimum-security prison doing administrative work. That's not a real prison! You should be out on the highway picking up trash in the hot sun every day. *You're* a piece of trash!"

Rizzoli's eyes narrowed on Barbara. "And you are a sick woman. You need therapy." He turned away from her and spoke to Jennifer. "Call me when you've drawn up the contract offer." Then Rizzoli stalked away toward a sleek, expensive-looking car.

"People lost their lives because of *you!*" Barbara yelled at him, her arm raised as she pointed.

"Get over it!" Rizzoli yelled over his shoulder. Then he jumped into his car and gunned the motor. Spitting gravel, he sped down the driveway toward the busy avenue running alongside.

Kelly stared at Barbara, who was still shaking in anger and swaying on her feet now. Barbara's face was nearly purple, she was so angry. Kelly noticed a blood vessel throbbing in Barbara's temple and feared for her heavyset friend's health.

She reached out and touched Barbara's arm. "Let's go back inside, Barbara. You need to sit down."

Jennifer interceded then, reaching for Barbara's other arm. "Come over here in the shade, Barbara. There's an empty table. I'll get you some iced tea. Would you like that?"

Barbara didn't answer, just kept staring after Rizzoli's car. Kelly followed Jennifer's direction, guiding Barbara toward the shady table beneath a large cottonwood tree, its branches spreading wide enough to shade half the patio. She glanced around and noticed the café customers returning to their lunches. She also glimpsed Malcolm standing beside the storage building, watching them.

"Here we go," Jennifer said, directing Barbara to a wrought-iron chair. "Let me get you something to eat along with that iced tea. Would you like one of Pete's bran muffins or banana nut ones?"

Kelly helped Barbara into the chair. She seemed less steady on her feet now, as if her outburst of anger had drained all her energy away. She leaned against Kelly. Fortunately Kelly was strong, because Barbara was a big woman.

"I'll take one of those banana nut muffins, Jennifer," Kelly said, glancing to Barbara. "Let me get you one, too, Barbara. You need something. It's lunchtime."

"I . . . I'm not hungry," Barbara mumbled.

"Then just nibble on it, okay?" Jennifer coaxed. "You need some food. I'm a waitress, so I recognize hunger. And you've just been through a stressful situation, Barbara. You need to take it easy now."

"Jennifer's right. Let's just sit here and cool off in the shade. We're getting summertime heat already. That iced tea should taste good." Kelly reached over and patted her arm. Glancing up at Jennifer, Kelly added, "I'll join Barbara and have some iced tea, too."

Jennifer blinked. "You're going to have iced tea? Well, now I've heard everything." She smiled as she headed toward the café steps.

"First time for everything," Kelly teased, vowing to choke it down if it helped Barbara relax. Glancing up, she spotted Barbara's mother Madge hurrying down the café steps and headed their way.

Kelly waited for Jennifer to join her in Lambspun's foyer.

"How's Barbara doing?" Jennifer asked as she followed

Kelly out the front door. "Julie and I were swamped with the lunch rush, so I never got to see her before she and her mom left."

"She's calmed down. That's good," Kelly said as they both walked toward the driveway. "Of course, I was as worried about Madge as I was about Barbara. She was white as a sheet when she came running out to us on the patio. Clearly, she was petrified that Barbara had confronted Rizzoli."

Jennifer shook her head. "I tell you, I was afraid Barbara was going to blow an artery when she was out there. I'm trying to remember if Mimi ever mentioned Barbara's health. Mimi has known both Barbara and her mother for years."

"Are you heading back to your office? It sounds like Rizzoli is serious about Hal Nelson's property."

"It sure looks like it. I took him up there this morning and he really loved it. I could tell. We walked around for about twenty minutes, then left. I swear, that was the shortest canyon showing I've ever had."

"Well, that's good because I know you were pressed for time."

"Yeah, but Julie was able to handle it, thank goodness. I asked Rizzoli if he wanted to use a buyer's agent to draw up the offer, and he said he understood contracts so he trusted me to handle the entire transaction." She shrugged. "Rizzoli didn't blink an eye at the asking price when I showed him the listing. So, we'll see what he does."

"Well, I wish both you and Hal good luck. You can use a real estate sale right now, and Hal said he needs the money, too. And Rizzoli will be putting fifty percent down in cash. You can't beat that."

"That definitely makes it easier." Jennifer clicked the door locks on her car. "Oh, yeah, I didn't get a chance to tell you. Pete called right before lunch and said Ben's finally awake. That's the best news for today."

"Wonderful news. So Pete will be able to spend some time with him and maybe come back home after the weekend, you think?"

Jennifer shrugged, then slid into her car. "We can hope. Meanwhile, I've already checked and both our temps, Doreen and Bridget, can come in and help Julie and me this weekend. With the weather as gorgeous as it is, everyone wants to dine outside. We'll probably put up extra tables."

Kelly gave her a thumbs-up. "Excellent idea. You and Julie need the help. Meanwhile, the rest of us will get you all moved from the apartment and into your new house."

Jennifer closed her eyes. "Ohhhh, that reminds me. I still have stuff to pack in those boxes tonight. I can at least clear out the desks and the bedroom dresser drawers."

"Don't worry if you can't get to it. You're so tired, you'll probably fall asleep as soon as you get home. Which wouldn't be a bad idea. Take it easy, Jen, and call me if you need anything."

"I promise," Jennifer said with a smile, then revved her car engine and aimed her car down the driveway.

Kelly gave her a good-bye wave, then turned toward her cottage office. Unfinished spreadsheets were waiting. This had been a very weird day.

Six

Kelly slid open the glass door and stepped out onto her cottage backyard patio, a large water pitcher in her hand. "Hey, Carl, here's some fresh water, boy," she called to her Rottweiler.

Carl paused in his sniffing of the fence perimeter for signs of Brazen Squirrel and his myriad relations — brothers, sisters, cousins, Colorado cousins, Wyoming cousins — and glanced Kelly's way. For a second only; then he returned to sniffing about the fence. Recent scents were still on the grass, no doubt. *Drat!* He'd missed the nimble-footed trespassers by minutes.

Noting Carl's lack of interest if it wasn't in his food dish, Kelly refilled his large metal water bowl anyway. "You'll need this, Carl. It'll be really hot today. In the nineties," she warned, watching the clear cool stream pour downward and splash into the metal bowl.

Carl trotted over and slurped up some water. Kelly rubbed his shiny black head. "You miss those squirrels when you're over at the new house, don't you, Carl? Maybe we can persuade one of the neighborhood cats to come visit you."

At the mention of the Magic Word, Carl's head jerked up. *A cat? Ohhhh, devoutly to be wished!* Kelly could almost read his thoughts.

She laughed and gave Carl another head rub. "I'm not sure I'm that persuasive, Carl. But I'll give it a try. You be good. I've got to get back to work. Spreadsheets are waiting," she said as she slid open the patio door and stepped inside. Carl trotted off toward the garden and began snuffling about the plants. The next item on his morning itinerary, separated by naps.

Checking her ceramic mug, Kelly saw that it was empty, so she headed toward the cottage kitchen and her old familiar coffeepot sitting on the counter. Steve had brought his fancier coffeemaker to their new Wellesley house, but she didn't think the "bells and whistles" made the coffee taste any better. If she remembered, she'd bring an old one from the garage storage to replace it.

Draining the last of the coffee from the pot, she found that it barely filled an inch.

Rats! She'd forgotten that she'd already refilled her mug during the long morning phone call from her Denver client, Don Warner. She glanced at her watch. Only ten thirty. Well, time for a coffee break anyway, she decided as she snatched up her portable mug from the counter and headed out the cottage front door.

Passing by the flower beds bordering her front walkway, Kelly leaned over and inspected the young plants. Pink, white, deep rose impatiens, purple and gold violas, and blue and white lobelia. Shade-loving plants. Her front yard had just enough sun for them to thrive but maintain their delicate colors.

Kelly started across the driveway, glancing toward the remodeled garage in progress, and saw Malcolm, not working on the garage but standing, talking to someone behind the building. Talking loudly, she noticed.

Curious, Kelly angled that way, and suddenly saw the man Malcolm was talking to. It was Jared Rizzoli. And from the expression on Rizzoli's face, he was not enjoying the conversation.

Uh-oh, Kelly thought, and walked closer, remembering Jayleen's comments that Malcolm had also "lost everything" because of Rizzoli's Ponzi scheme. Not wanting to witness another angry confrontation, Kelly feared Rizzoli's temper wouldn't hold back if a man confronted him. Kelly stopped beside a van, Malcolm's angry voice capturing her attention.

"You got a lotta nerve coming back to town," Malcolm accused, voice louder, jabbing his finger at Rizzoli. "You think holding those free seminars will wash away your crimes? Well, they *don't*!"

Once again, Kelly noticed Rizzoli's face darkening with anger. Yesterday, Rizzoli had clearly held himself back, despite Barbara's threats. Kelly guessed that was because Barbara was a woman. But this time, with Malcolm, Kelly sensed Rizzoli wouldn't show the same restraint.

"Back off, creep!" Rizzoli sneered, knocking Malcolm's hand aside. "I went to prison to pay my debts."

Malcolm's face reddened, clearly enraged himself now. "Don't you brush me off like I'm some piece of trash! You lost me *everything*! My job, my wife, my home, everything! *You* did, you son-of-a-bitch!" This time Malcolm jabbed his finger right into Rizzoli's chest.

The explosion Kelly had feared erupted. Rizzoli shoved Malcolm back hard. So hard, Malcolm stumbled and fell backward onto the driveway. "Get your hands off me, you piece of crap!" Rizzoli yelled. "Don't blame me for what you've become!"

Just then, Hal Nelson ran over from the parking lot. "Back off, Rizzoli!" he yelled. He shot Rizzoli a glare as he helped Malcolm up from the gravel.

"You tell *him* to back off!" Still furious, Rizzoli pointed toward Malcolm. "I've been to prison, but *you're* the one down a rat hole! Nobody's to blame for what you've become! You did it to yourself!"

Kelly watched a silent Malcolm stare at Rizzoli, stricken.

"You better leave now, Rizzoli," Nelson said in a cold voice.

"You bet I will. Tell your agent to call me when the contract's signed," Rizzoli snapped, then turned and stalked off to his car. The tires squealed this time in Rizzoli's haste to leave the driveway.

Kelly ran over to Malcolm, who still stared — white-faced and shaking — after the departing Rizzoli. "Are you okay, Malcolm? Did you hurt yourself?" she asked, grasping his arm. Nelson still had hold of the other arm.

"No . . . I'm . . . I'm okay," Malcolm answered, in a hushed voice.

"Why don't we go inside the café and get

you a cup of coffee and something to eat?" Nelson said, guiding Malcolm toward the garden patio.

"That's a good idea," Kelly said, following Nelson's lead and guiding Malcolm toward the garden pathway leading to the café. She couldn't help noticing the stares from customers who didn't expect drama to accompany their breakfast alfresco.

Waitress Julie walked over to them as they approached the steps leading to the café back door. "I swear, if that man ever shows up here again, I'm going to accidentally pour hot coffee all over him," she said with an uncharacteristic scowl, lifting her coffeepot in defiance.

Wow, Kelly thought as they climbed the steps. Jared Rizzoli seemed to ignite universal animosity. Even good-natured Julie was mad at him.

Jennifer pushed open the door and held it for all three of them to enter. Kelly followed Nelson and Malcolm, and Jennifer muttered none-too-softly to her, "I tell you, that Rizzoli is a piece of work. I almost wish Hal and I weren't doing business with him."

"Hey, hold your nose and take his money," Kelly said in a rasping whisper as she passed. "You can use it, and so can Hal. He told me so."

Hal ushered Malcolm over to a small table for two around the corner and helped him into a chair. Clearly, Nelson was making sure Malcolm got settled. Glancing toward the grill, Kelly noticed Rosa standing in the back hallway watching everything.

"Brother, this morning's confrontation had an even bigger audience than yesterday's with Barbara," Kelly said.

Rosa hastened their way. "That man is a menace. I can't wait until he leaves town. All he's done is rile up all the people he cheated years ago. You've seen those stories in the newspaper, right?"

"You couldn't miss them," Jennifer said, picking up her tray as she headed around the grill to load breakfast orders.

"Is Barbara all right?" Kelly asked, suddenly worried that Barbara's fiery outburst yesterday had triggered a health problem.

Rosa's brown eyes grew larger as she leaned closer to Kelly and lowered her voice. "Madge came in this morning to teach Burt's class all by herself. When I asked where Barbara was, she said that Barbara took a day off. Madge said that last night, Barbara was still so mad at Rizzoli she went down to the hotel where he was holding one of his seminars. And she confronted him right there in front of everyone!

Then Rizzoli's security guards took Barbara away and threatened to call the police! Can you believe that?"

"Oh, no! Please tell me Barbara went home."

Rosa nodded. "Yes, thank goodness. But still, can you imagine down-to-earth, practical Barbara doing something like that?" She shook her head.

"No, I can't, Rosa. I tell you, I was really concerned about Barbara yesterday. I was afraid she might blow an artery or something after that confrontation outside. Mimi's known her for a long time. Has she ever mentioned any health problems?"

"Yes, I remember her saying Barbara has high blood pressure and is on medication for it," Rosa said. "So you were right to worry about Barbara. I was, too, and keeping my fingers crossed nothing would happen."

Kelly looked out toward the café and watched Jennifer walking toward the grill where Eduardo had placed more breakfast orders. "Well, let's hope that episode with the security guards was a wake-up call for Barbara. She needs to calm down and leave Rizzoli alone. He's a scumbag, from what I've heard about him and seen for myself. And he's certainly not worth risking her health over."

"You're so right, Kelly. Let's hope Barbara can put the past to rest. Oooops, I hear the shop phone. Talk to you later." Rosa hurried back around the corner into the shop.

Kelly walked over to the grill where Jennifer was loading up her tray. "Sounds like Rizzoli has already made an offer on the land."

"Yep, and at the asking price, too. And accompanied by a cashier's check for half the purchase price. With the balance to be paid at closing in ten days. Naturally, Hal accepted the offer and signed it immediately." She gave a wry smile.

Kelly let out a low whistle. "Wow, he really must be rich. The papers weren't exaggerating, I guess."

"Actually, the gossip in the office is his wife's the wealthy one. She and he knew each other years ago, before he got into financial trouble with the law. Anyway, she inherited a bundle when her first husband died, while Rizzoli was in prison. Apparently he found out and started writing her. Love blooms in strange places, I guess." Jennifer lifted the tray to her shoulder. "Listen, I've gotten all the bedroom stuff packed or into garment bags. So the only things left for you to pack tomorrow will be stuff from our desk drawers and then the kitchen, of course."

Kelly gave a dismissive wave. "Piece of cake. We'll be finished before dinner tomorrow, I predict."

Jennifer grinned. "Pete says to tell you guys he's gonna make everybody their favorite pie when he gets back."

"Ooooh, make mine pecan."

Jennifer started to turn away, then stopped. "Oh, yeah. Pete finally got in touch with Tanya. She claimed her cell phone wasn't working. They're over in Omaha, can you believe? Anyway, Pete said she 'panicked' when he asked her if she could come back to Denver to help take care of Cassie. Tanya says the band is starting to get recognition now. So, she can't come back. She's singing backup with them and doing their publicity." Jennifer rolled her eyes. "So Pete told her that he was going to bring Cassie up here to Fort Connor to stay with us. Ben's going to be recovering and in rehab for months."

Kelly gave her a rueful smile. "I'll bet Tanya was relieved to hear that."

"Ohhhh, yeah." Jennifer nodded. "And that made Pete feel even better about bringing Cassie here. Tanya clearly wants no responsibility for her daughter, so Cassie will be better off here with us."

"Sounds like it. Listen, stop by Megan and Marty's tonight, why don't you? Lisa and Greg will be out, so the rest of us are relaxing with pizza. It's too hot to sit outside for dinner."

"Pizza's good. I'll be there," Jen said, then returned to her waiting customers.

"Want some coffee, Kelly?" Julie offered, pot at the ready.

"I sure do," Kelly answered, suddenly realizing she no longer had her mug with her. "You know, I think I dropped my mug in the driveway when Malcolm and Rizzoli were getting into it. Let me retrieve it. Hold that offer."

"Will do."

Kelly left through the café back door and ran down the steps, still unable to forget the stricken look on Malcolm's face.

SEVEN

Kelly leaned against the faux granite kitchen counter and looked out into what would soon be Jennifer and Pete's great room. Jennifer was right. The living and dining rooms were more spacious than normally found in most smaller three-bedroom houses. Another tribute to Steve's architectural ingenuity.

Right now, the entire great room was filled with boxes, boxes, and more boxes as her friends unpacked books, files, decorative objects, framed pictures, maps, and more books. A sofa, love seat, two chairs, and several bookcases were barely visible beneath the boxes.

"Okay, for drinks I've got three super-sized iced coffees, two diet colas, and one lemonade," Kelly read from the small memo pad in her hand. And six super burritos, two Mexicali, two beef and cheddar, two veggie. Did I forget anything?"

"Yeah, bring one of Pete's pies, preferably blueberry." Marty looked up from the box of books he was unpacking.

"And don't forget vanilla ice cream," Greg added, as he pulled a framed map of the United States from a packing box.

"You guys," Lisa chided, lifting a large garment bag from the sofa. "Can't you wait till dinner tonight for dessert?"

Marty looked at her, horrified. *"Blasphemy!"*

"We need sustenance for the last laps," Greg added, setting the map against the wall.

"You better not drip any berry juice on the furniture," Megan warned as she pulled out a desk drawer, then placed several files inside it. "I'll be checking."

"Will she really?" Greg asked Marty.

"Oh, yeah."

"Dude, how do you stand that?"

Marty grinned. "She looks so cute when she's annoyed. Sometimes I drip stuff on purpose."

"What!" Megan stared at him, aghast.

"That's cute?" Greg pointed to Megan's half-annoyed, half-shocked expression.

"Oh, yeah."

Greg shook his head, opening another packing box. "You two are seriously strange." He lifted some hardcover books from the box. "Hey, they've got a collection of Charles Dickens classics. I may ask to borrow one of these."

"Better check the title page," Steve advised as he lifted two metal bed rails to his shoulder. "Pete collects old books with original engravings. I don't think he'll lend you those."

Greg flipped to the title page of the hardbound book and his eyes widened. "Whoa, eighteen seventy-six!" He turned the page. "Wow, look at this." He pointed to a surrounding page with an engraved picture.

Steve paused on his way to the master bedroom. "I told you. Be careful with those. Now, who wants to help me set up the queen bed?"

"I will," Lisa volunteered, following Steve. "Now that you mention it, I didn't see any other beds at their apartment. The kid needs a bed."

"Ooooh, good catch," Megan said, glancing around. "We have a fold-up cot in the garage. But a bed would be better."

"I've got one in storage," Steve called from the bedroom. "We can bring it tomorrow."

"I'd better go get the food," Kelly said as she grabbed her car keys and cell phone. "We don't want Marty keeling over from hunger."

"You need any money, Kelly?" Lisa asked, from the door of the bedroom.

"Naw, my treat," Kelly said, walking toward the well-lit foyer.

"Why don't you call in the order before you leave?" Marty suggested. "My stomach's growling already."

Kelly laughed as she headed out the door. Once outside, however, she scrolled through her phone's directory and punched in the café's number. She might as well give the grill cooks a head start on those burritos.

She settled in her car, which was parked in front of the cozy and comfortable ranch-style house on the corner of Steve's Wellesley development. It was only two blocks from the house where Steve and Kelly lived and one block from both Lisa and Greg's home and Megan and Marty's.

The phone at Pete's café rang several times. Saturday lunch crunch, Kelly surmised, and waited. Finally she recognized Julie's voice answer. "Hey, Julie. Kelly, here. I've got a big order for the gang. We're moving Jen and Pete today, remember? We started at seven this morning, and we've been living on donuts. Time for some real food."

"Oh, that's right. Sure, Kelly. Tell me what

you've got, and I'll get Eduardo and Frank right on it."

Kelly recited the lunch order. "I'm in Wellesley now, so I should be there in ten minutes or so. Depending on traffic, of course. On a gorgeous summer Saturday, there's usually lots of people and lots of cars."

"All right, I'll tell them to get right on it. Oh, you'll have to enter through the Lemay Avenue driveway. Police have blocked off the Lincoln Avenue entrance entirely. Customers from the café and the shop are parking along the Lemay driveway and onto the grass. It's a mess."

It took a few seconds for Julie's words to sink in. "Why did police block off the Lincoln entrance? Is there a marathon going along that route or something?"

"I wish it were. Some guy died in his car last night, I guess. He was parked next to the trees across the driveway from Lambspun's front door. I haven't had time to even go look outside, we've been so slammed with customers. But early this morning, one of the temp waitresses said she talked to police when she walked over from the bus stop. It must have been six o'clock."

"Good Lord! Did he commit suicide or something? Who would park in our driveway and do that?"

"Who knows, Kelly. I gotta get back to work. See you in a few minutes." Julie clicked off.

Kelly tossed her phone to the adjoining car seat, then revved her car's engine. What on earth would possess someone to end it all in a parking lot?

"I'll be back in a few minutes, guys," Kelly told the busy grill cooks. "I've gotta go see what's happening outside."

"Nothing to see, Kelly," Eduardo said, deftly sliding a veggie-stuffed omelet onto a plate. "Frank checked a few minutes ago, and the cops have taken everything away. Ambulance came for the guy's body over an hour ago, I think."

"Yeah, and the tow truck was hooking up to take the car away," the thin, bearded man said as he turned sausages on the grill. Pete's homemade sausage patties sizzled, emitting a savory sage-and-herb aroma into the air. Kelly's nostrils twitched. Breakfast temptations started warring with the lunch aromas floating through the café.

"Well, I'll see if Rosa or Connie know anything," Kelly said, as she headed for the hallway that led to Lambspun.

As she neared the classroom area, she

spotted Rosa supervising a woman working on one of the small portable looms. She must be teaching a Saturday class, Kelly decided, and veered back toward the yarn rooms at the front of the shop. She skirted around the Mother Loom and the shelves filled with cones of colorful threads and trims and lacy ribbons of yarn. Through the opening into the front room, Kelly spotted Connie behind the counter helping a customer. Four more customers waited patiently in line. Two of them stood staring out through the large, multipaned front windows.

Kelly gave Connie a wave and walked to the window to look out. Three police officers were outside, along with two suited men, whom Kelly figured were detectives. She didn't recognize either man. But she did recognize something else. A tow truck was sitting at the end of the driveway, which opened to Lincoln Avenue. The driver obviously was waiting for a policeman to remove all the orange-and-white traffic cones that had blocked the entrance.

Kelly stared at the dark car that was being towed by the truck. It was a familiar design. A popular and expensive road car. A high-performance European road car. Exactly like Jared Rizzoli's car. She stared at the license plate and glimpsed the last three digits — 592 — before the truck pulled the car around the corner onto the street. Kelly couldn't remember ever noticing Rizzoli's license plate, but something about those three digits looked slightly familiar.

Kelly glanced back at Connie, choosing her words carefully. "I think I recognize that car, Connie. How about you?"

Connie looked up from the skein of bright daffodil yellow yarn she was holding and met Kelly's gaze. She nodded. "Ohhhh, yeah. So do I. It's him."

"Who's 'him'?" a woman in line asked Kelly.

"Just some guy who showed up here in the shop looking for someone who owned a piece of canyon property. He wanted to buy it, from what I heard," Connie replied.

The woman glanced to a younger woman standing in front of her. "I wonder if he was killed over a piece of land?"

The young woman shrugged. "It wouldn't be the first time. This is the West. People fight over land and water."

Kelly zeroed in on their conversation. "Uh, excuse me, but did you say 'kill'? I thought it might be suicide."

"Nope," the young woman said authoritatively. "I was walking through the garden trying to get into the shop by way of the café. And I heard one of the cops talking on his cell phone. I distinctly heard him say the guy was killed."

Another woman who was browsing among the assortment of knitting needles and crochet hooks turned around. "And I saw the medics removing his body to the stretcher. There was a lot of blood on the front of his suit."

Kelly simply stared at them as those images formed in her mind. It was clear that Jared Rizzoli had enemies. He'd cheated scores of people in town. Many lives were ruined. But, still . . . "Why would someone kill him in the Lambspun parking lot? It doesn't make sense."

"Look around," the younger woman said, gesturing outside to the driveway and golf course adjacent. "Lots of trees and bushes over in that spot. Later in the day, not that many people are playing golf. It's not full summertime light yet. Someone could have killed him that evening when everyone here and in the café was gone. No one would see them or find him."

The older woman standing beside Kelly shivered visibly. "That sounds awful."

Kelly watched the policemen and detectives conferring. "Have the police asked you and Rosa anything?"

"They sure did," Connie said as she handed a package with a Lambspun sheep logo to her customer. "They came in around nine o'clock this morning and questioned Rosa and me. I told them I didn't even notice the car when I came in because I drove in through the Lemay Avenue entrance. And Rosa did, too. So, neither of us saw anything. And once we opened the shop, it's been nonstop busy with customers, so we haven't had time to look out the windows." Connie picked up the skein of yarn the next customer in line handed her.

"Don't be surprised if they come again with more questions," Kelly advised. "From my experience, police detectives keep asking questions as they investigate and learn more."

"Have you ever been questioned by the police?" The older woman next to Kelly stared, clearly apprehensive.

Kelly had to smile. "Only as a witness, not as a suspect, thank heavens." She declined to go into detail. "Incidentally, have you called Mimi and Burt to tell them?" she asked Connie.

Connie made a face. "Not yet. I really hate to spoil their mini-vacation, but I guess I have to. I'll wait till five o'clock, right before

116

we close up."

"That's a good idea to wait until later, Connie. Otherwise Burt would be itching to drive back here right away."

"Don't we know it," Connie said, totaling the bill. "Once a cop, always a cop."

Jennifer leaned around the corner that led to a back way into the café and beckoned to Kelly.

Kelly caught her gaze and walked over to the counter. "Excuse me, Connie. I want to catch Jen up on the moving project." She scooted behind Connie, who was still working the customer's yarn purchases.

Jennifer stood around the corner in the passageway that opened to the rear of the café and grill. "Julie told me she updated you on what happened this morning. I would have called you, but I misplaced my phone somewhere around here yesterday. I looked all over the café but couldn't find it, then I had to run to the office. I used the phone there. We've been so busy since I got here this morning, I haven't even had a chance to check the shop yet."

"I'll take a look around before I leave. By the way, I glimpsed the car being towed out of the parking lot. That was Rizzoli's car, wasn't it?"

Jennifer glanced over her shoulder toward

the grill. Eduardo was talking to tall, skinny Frank. "Yeah, it was Rizzoli's, all right. I finally had a second and went into the shop to look out the window, and I recognized his car. I didn't have time to watch what the cops were doing, but I spotted the ambulance when it turned out of the Lemay driveway toward the hospital."

"A woman in the shop said she saw his body come out on a stretcher and there was a lot of blood on his suit front."

Jennifer grimaced. "Please, no details. I've been unfortunate enough to be around two dead bodies. I don't need any more gruesome images in my mind."

"Sorry, I forgot." Kelly stared out into the café alcove where Julie was serving a table of four. "Wow. That guy had a lot of enemies in town. You know all those stories in the newspapers, interviewing people who'd been cheated by Rizzoli. It's gotta be someone like that, don't you think? Someone who was still holding a grudge."

Suddenly two images flashed before Kelly's eyes. Barbara confronting Rizzoli in the garden patio. So angry she was shaking. And Malcolm, yelling at Rizzoli in the driveway, furious, blaming Rizzoli for ruining his life. Two people she knew and cared about. Two people who hated Rizzoli, whose hatred still burned bright after twelve years.

Kelly looked at Jennifer and read the same concern in her eyes. "Oh, no, Jen! Barbara and . . . and Malcolm. Both of them confronted Rizzoli. In front of other people!"

"That's exactly what I'm thinking. Barbara was enraged. And she even went down to his seminar. I don't know what to think."

"Were you guys questioned? Connie said they were."

"Yeah, a cop came in and asked each of us if we saw anything when we opened up this morning. Of course, we didn't. We're in the back of the building. We can't even see that part of the driveway. Plus, we were busy cooking and serving customers. I don't think any of us has even had a break this morning."

"What else did they ask?"

"They wanted to know if we had seen anything last evening. And I explained to the cop that we aren't open in the evening, so no one was here to witness *anything.*" Her voice underscored the word.

Kelly could tell her friend was on edge, understandably, so she switched topics slightly. "So what happens now with the sale of Hal's property?"

Jennifer exhaled a breath. Familiar territory. "The contract will have to wait until

Rizzoli's estate is settled. Any closing would have to wait until then. Who knows? Maybe the widow will want to keep the property. Maybe she'll want to sell it because it brings bad memories of Fort Connor." She shrugged. "One thing's for sure. The closing will be postponed."

"Jen, your orders are up," Frank said over his shoulder.

"Thanks," Jennifer said as she turned away. "Gotta go. By the way, how's the move going?"

"A piece of cake. We'll be finished by midafternoon. So why don't you come over after you've closed up here. You'll need to relax. Listen, I'll take a quick look around the shop for your cell phone while they're finishing my order."

"Thanks," Jennifer said as she headed for the counter.

Kelly walked back down the hallway leading into Lambspun. She'd start with the workroom. There were lots of tables and shelves where it was easy to place a cell phone — or a coffee mug — when you were in a hurry. Kelly was an expert in hurried behaviors. Since this was a busy Saturday, there were plenty of shoppers there, so Kelly slowly made her way around the room, scanning every surface. Shelves, tables, boxes, work counters. No phone to be found.

She rounded the corner into the main knitting room. The long library table had several knitters clustered around the edges, working on various projects and comparing yarns.

"Hey, folks, don't mind me," she said as she approached. "I'm checking for a misplaced cell phone. Just ignore me."

"Oh, brother. I hope your luck is better than mine," one woman said, glancing up from the royal blue yarn she was working. "Whenever I've misplaced my phone, it never appears again."

Kelly started checking under some of the assorted items that always seemed to clutter the long table. Skeins of yarn, books, patterns, magazines, teacups, teapot, plates of cookies, and various other edibles.

"Good luck finding anything in all the clutter," an older woman observed. "I'm always amazed at how much stuff accumulates on this table."

Kelly picked up cups and saucers and teapot. No phone. "You're not the only one. I wonder how Mimi and the staff find anything here." She lifted a stack of magazines, then picked up a fluffy ball of pink-and-white yarn. No phone.

"I swear, I have to put my phone in my jacket pocket after I use it or I'd lose it for sure," a younger woman with blond hair said. She was knitting what looked like the beginning of a sweater with that same pink-and-white yarn.

Kelly moved toward the middle of the table, where the "odds and ends tray" sat. The tray contained an ever-changing collection of scissors, different-sized knitting needles, stitch markers, tape measures, gauge measures, and various other important and necessary-to-knitters items.

"Is that why you always wear a jacket?" another woman asked the blonde.

Kelly joined the other women as they laughed. She pushed some of the napkins to the side and thought she felt something hard beneath them. She lifted the napkins and spotted a black cell phone. And it looked exactly like Jennifer's.

"Hey, I found a phone! Quick, everybody check your cell phones. See if you have them. Maybe this is one of yours." She held up the phone for the others to see.

"Nope. Mine's in my pocket," the blonde said with a grin.

"Mine's got a blue case."

The older woman rifled through her purse. "Nope, mine's here."

The other woman held up her phone. "Got it. Today's your lucky day."

"Thanks, everyone. And good luck with all your projects," Kelly said as she headed for the hallway once more. She pushed one of the phone's buttons and saw the view screen. A message was waiting. No name.

As Kelly rounded the corner into the café, she spotted Jennifer at a nearby table, serving coffee. "Hey, I found your phone, Jen."

Jennifer spun around and grinned at her friend. "You're kidding! Where was it?"

"Buried beneath all the stuff on the knitting table, of course." Kelly handed her the phone. "You've got a message. No surprise there."

"I'll check it later." Jennifer pocketed the phone. "Thanks a bunch, Kelly."

"Kelly, your order's been up for five minutes. It's gonna get cold," Eduardo warned, spatula in hand.

"Oooops, better get back before Marty faints from hunger," Kelly said, and hurried over to the grill.

"When's Jennifer coming?" Greg asked, sipping from a brown bottle with the familiar colorful label.

Kelly leaned back into the plastic webbed patio chair and looked past her friends who were reclining in an assortment of outdoor chairs they'd all brought as housewarming presents. The backyard of this house was smaller than the one where she and Steve lived. But it also had a pretty tree that was bigger than most in the development.

She took a sip of her Fat Tire ale and noticed the late-afternoon sun had started its downward path. "She should be here soon. So why don't we do some brainstorming before she comes? You know, thinking of ways we can help out Jen and Pete with Cassie."

"Yeah, I've been thinking about that," Lisa said, taking a potato chip from the open bag in the midst of their semicircle. "School's out now, so Cassie will need supervision during the daytime. At least in the mornings because Jennifer and Pete are working in the café, seven days a week, early morning until two or three o'clock when they close up. Then Jen goes to the real estate office."

"How old is Cassie again?" Marty asked, and tipped back his beer.

"Eleven, but she'll be twelve in July," Jennifer's voice came from behind them.

"Hey, Jen," Megan greeted. "There are more chips on the kitchen counter. There's cola, too. We're going to have Chinese delivered for dinner."

"When's that food coming?" Marty asked, checking his watch.

"By five o'clock. You can last," Lisa teased.

"We were starting to brainstorm some ideas for helping with Cassie while you and Pete are working every day," Kelly said as Jennifer sank into a patio chair between Lisa and Greg. "And I was thinking that maybe Cassie would like to come with me to the softball clinic a couple of mornings each week. I've agreed to teach a kids' class this summer. Ten- to twelve-year-old girls, so she'd fit right in. We'll meet two times a week for eight weeks."

"Hey, that sounds like a great idea," Megan said. "Do you know if she's ever played before, Jen?"

"I haven't a clue. She's never mentioned anything like that when we've gone to visit them in Denver. I know Ben took her around to concerts with him in Denver. She reads a lot. Pete said Ben used to read to her from the time she was a baby. Oh, and I remember her telling us about Girl Scouts. She really liked the campout."

Marty perked up. "Hey, I was a Boy Scout."

"So was I," Greg said, balancing his beer

bottle on his knee. "In fact, I was an Eagle Scout."

"Hey, so was I!" Marty grinned. "Betcha I had more badges."

"Dude, don't even go there. I got you beat."

"Oh, no . . . not another contest." Megan rolled her eyes.

"Then you guys can talk badges with Cassie. Common interest," Kelly teased. "And I've got all my favorite books from when I was a kid. They're finally on the shelves."

"Thank God, we finally live someplace we can *have* shelves." Steve laughed. "You had most of those books in storage for four years."

"Still don't know how you guys lived in that cottage for as long as you did," Lisa said, snatching another potato chip.

"Greg, I know something else you and Cassie can share," Jennifer said. "She loves looking up stuff on the computer. Ben limits her time, of course. He doesn't want her grades to suffer."

"Good grades?" Lisa asked.

"Oh, yeah. She's smart as a whip, in Ben's words. But Ben's computer is an old, old desktop and slow as molasses. I don't know how Cassie puts up with it."

Greg leaned forward. "Heck, I've got a

couple of used laptops in the computer lab at the university in case someone needs a loaner. One's only a couple of years old. She could have that."

"Wow, Cassie ought to love that," Megan said. "It'll be way faster."

"Oh, yeah. Warp speed compared to her granddad's ancient one," Greg added.

"Greg, you're a doll," Jennifer said. "You know, Pete and I were there one weekend when she tried to 'fix' Ben's old desktop. She had the back off and asked us what she could replace to make it faster." She laughed softly. "Of course, Pete and I were clueless."

"All riiiiight," Greg said, nodding. "Sounds like she might enjoy coming over to the computer lab with me sometime. We've got trays of circuits and mother-boards. I could show her how to make something. Something easy. She may get a kick out of it."

"Okay, now you've got me thinking," Megan piped up, reaching for a chip. "There are a lot of hours in a week. Kelly's taking her to softball two mornings. Greg's gonna tear apart computers with her. I think she needs more outdoor time. How about I take Cassie to tennis with me? Parks and Recreation have tennis classes for kids every week. I try to play every afternoon in the summer, so I can play over at those courts."

"Fantastic," Kelly said, delighted at her friends' suggestions.

"My turn." Lisa held up her hand. "Why don't I ask the clinic director if Cassie can hang around with me once a week? There's a lot going on in the clinic. People doing physical therapy, doctors coming in and out and talking to the therapists. Lots of great machines there. She can learn all about working out." Lisa smiled.

Jennifer looked around the group. "Wow, you guys are amazing, you know that? I can't thank you enough for offering to help."

"Hey, it'll be fun," Megan said, then drained her cola.

"Amazing, that's us," Greg said, then jerked his thumb toward Marty. "All except for him. He didn't volunteer because all he does is talk all day. How boring is that?"

"It's the quality of conversation that counts," Marty said, leaning back in the patio chair, hands behind his head. "Besides, I've been pondering what's the best way for me to help, and I think I've got it."

"What? You're gonna take the kid to the courthouse and show her some criminals?" Greg taunted.

Marty didn't even look fazed. "Naw, I

decided this is a job for Spot, the Wonder Dog."

Megan put her hand over her eyes and sank back in her chair. "Oh, no! Not Spot!"

"Stop him now, Jen, before he lifts a leg in your new backyard," Greg warned.

"Better be a good dog, Spot." Jennifer shook her finger at Marty. "Or Pete and I will take you to the vet's to be fixed."

At that, everyone erupted in laughter, including Spot.

EIGHT

"Look, Carl, squirrels are waiting for you," Kelly said, watching her dog race across the cottage backyard.

Brazen Squirrel and family members skittered in all directions — along the chain-link fence top, leaping into overhanging branches of the cottonwood tree, and sprinting down to the grass and onto the golf course greens. Sunday golfers were easier to escape than Big Dog. Undeterred, Carl barked furiously in each squirrel's vicinity. Doggie threats of: *Next time!*

The cottage yard was still Carl's favorite. The new house may have a bigger backyard, but it lacked the towering shade trees that only the passage of years can provide. New housing developments usually had smaller, or starter, trees. And without big trees, squirrels were hard to find. They were happily living in the larger trees along the older streets that bordered the new development.

Kelly slid the patio screen door closed. The temperatures would be in the nineties again today, not the typical early summer weather. She decided to let what light breeze there was inside the cottage while she went for some of Eduardo's coffee. Since Steve, Marty, and Greg were playing an away ball game, she and Megan and Lisa were going to indulge in a Sunday dinner in Old Town tonight. Their ball game was in midafternoon.

Grabbing her coffee mug, Kelly headed out the cottage front door. She had just crossed the driveway when she spotted a familiar SUV turning in — Mimi and Burt returning from the mountains. She watched them pull into a parking spot beside the café patio garden and walked over to their car.

"Hey, there," she greeted them as they both exited the SUV. "I'm sorry you cut your vacation short."

"That's okay, Kelly," Mimi replied, her extra-large knitting bag over her arm. "We had five glorious days."

"I'm glad you're here, Kelly. Connie only told us that a man was found dead inside a car parked in our driveway. Over there beneath the trees." Burt gestured toward the tall cedar trees that shaded the driveway and the tall spruce trees on the side. "She didn't know if it was a suicide or . . ."

"Don't even say it, Burt," Mimi ordered, hand up in 'stop' position. "I don't want to think about another murder being committed near our shop." She gave a very visible shiver.

"I understand, Mimi. Why don't we grab one of these outside café tables and order something yummy. I can fill you in while we're eating."

Burt gave her a slight smile. "That's a good idea, Kelly. I've been hankering for some biscuits and some of Pete's sausage gravy."

"Well, I might as well join you," Mimi joked. "I have certainly been ignoring my diet all week. Why start now?"

"Why, indeed." Kelly grinned. "In fact, we can make that an order for three. I'm sure temp cook Frank is using Pete's gravy recipe. C'mon," she beckoned, leading the way along the flagstone path into the garden. One empty table was within their reach.

"Oh, my, oh, my, oh, my," Mimi chanted softly as she stirred cream into her Earl Grey tea. "Why did that horrible man have to come over here to Lambspun? I'm *so* glad I wasn't here to see him. He's caused so much heartache and misery to so many fine people."

"It's just one of those things, Mimi. He heard about Hal Nelson's canyon property being for sale and came over to ask about it." Kelly rearranged the knife and fork on her plate, which was spotless. All traces of Pete's delicious homemade sausage, biscuits, and gravy were wiped clean. Their table was completely shaded, which Kelly welcomed because the sun was at its zenith. She'd be playing softball in the sun all afternoon, so the shade felt good now.

Burt leaned back in the wrought-iron chair and sipped his coffee. "It's unfortunate that Jared Rizzoli was murdered, but the man had cheated so many people here in Fort Connor that, as much as I hate to say it, I'm not surprised someone took revenge on him. Especially if he was flaunting his now-wealthy lifestyle."

"Well, what really disturbs me is Barbara's involvement. Merciful heavens! I cannot believe Barbara would confront that man out here in . . . in our own garden. But, then, to go to the hotel and confront him again in front of all those *people*!" Mimi closed her eyes, obviously not wanting to picture the scene.

"I have to admit that surprised me, too,"

Burt added. "Barb's always been such a solid, no-nonsense gal. Bossy, yes. But never would I picture her doing something so . . . so brazen as a public confrontation."

"I agree, Burt. Of course, if it turns out that Rizzoli was actually murdered, then I'm afraid the police will be turning their sights on Barbara. Once they hear about her confrontations with him." Kelly looked out toward the golf course and golfers. "And I'm also worried about Malcolm. He confronted Rizzoli, too. Right over there in the driveway. I was here to witness it, along with the entire patio filled with breakfast diners."

Mimi pinched her forehead. "Who's Malcolm, again? That name sounds familiar."

"He's the formerly homeless guy at the Mission who's been working with Hal Nelson on our remodeling," Burt explained, then turned to Kelly. "What exactly did you see, Kelly?"

"I was walking from the cottage to the café when I saw Malcolm yelling at Rizzoli. Rizzoli looked like he was going to explode, so I walked over to them in time to see Malcolm accuse Rizzoli of ruining his life. Rizzoli swatted Malcolm's hand away and started calling Malcolm names. Malcolm yelled back and jabbed his finger into Rizzoli's chest. That's when Rizzoli shoved

Malcolm so hard he fell backward onto the ground. Then Rizzoli started yelling more names at Malcolm. Hal Nelson ran over then to help Malcolm, and Rizzoli stormed off. Hal and I took Malcolm inside the café so he could calm down. But, once again, Rizzoli was confronted in public with a lot of people looking on. Not good."

Burt glanced toward the garage being remodeled. "Well, the guys will be back to work tomorrow. Let's see how Malcolm is doing. I'll talk with Hal and see what he knows."

"You might want to talk to Jennifer, too. She was the agent handling Nelson's sale. She told me that Rizzoli and Hal had a signed contract and a cashier's check from Rizzoli for one half the purchase price. Of course, everything's in limbo now that he's dead."

"Oh, goodness." Mimi frowned. "This horrible situation keeps drawing more people into it. Now Jennifer is involved."

That reminded Kelly that Mimi and Burt were unaware of the changes about to occur for Jennifer and Pete. "Speaking of Jennifer and Pete, you guys have missed what's been happening. You were still here the day Pete's grandfather Ben had a heart attack in Denver, then you left."

"Yes, yes! And Rosa's been giving us updates on Ben's condition when she calls every day. Five blockages! Terrible!" Mimi wagged her head.

"Thank goodness doctors were able to repair them. I'm not surprised Pete's still down there. It sounds like his grandfather's condition is really serious," Burt added.

"Oh, it is," Kelly agreed. "Doctors said he'll be bedridden for months and will probably need to go into a wheelchair afterwards."

"Good Lord. What about the little girl, Pete's niece?" Mimi asked. "She can't stay there, surely."

Burt frowned. "Has her mother finally shaped up and come to take care of her?"

"Nope," Kelly said with a rueful smile. "Cassie's coming to stay with Pete and Jennifer for the near future. Certainly during the summer. Pete's coming back home either today or tomorrow and he'll bring Cassie with him."

"Really?" Mimi's eyes got wide as saucers. "Are they going to try to live in that apartment?"

"Nope. Steve is letting them rent his smaller three-bedroom house that's still unsold. So the gang spent all day yesterday moving Pete and Jen's stuff from the apartment to the house. Jen has her hands full trying to handle the café and supervising the staff."

"Well, now." Burt leaned forward, folding his arms on the table. "Looks like Pete and Jennifer have suddenly acquired a family."

"I think it's wonderful that they're opening their home to that little girl," Mimi said, with the first smile Kelly had seen since they returned.

Kelly had suspected that "Mother Mimi" would be particularly pleased that Cassie would be visiting in Fort Connor this summer. After all, Mimi lost her only child, her son, to a teenage accident. Consequently, Mimi would never have any grandchildren of her own. Kelly had always noticed that Mimi was delighted whenever Burt's grandchildren came to visit or when she and Burt took them on a weekend excursion. Kelly figured that Mimi and Burt might like to join in the "Cassie Project" and maybe invite Cassie to join them when they visited Burt's grandkids. Kelly wasn't sure whether the old saying "the more, the merrier" was true, but it might be.

She decided to prime the pump, anyway. "Yeah, we all think it's a much better idea that Cassie stay up here in Fort Connor with Jen and Pete than bounce around

Denver with neighbors and her erratic mom. Of course, Pete and Jen work seven days a week through the morning and afternoon, so we all figured out ways to help them out by supervising Cassie this summer. I'm going to see if she'd like to join the kids' softball clinic I'm teaching this summer. It meets two mornings a week. Megan's going to take her to tennis classes, and Lisa's taking Cassie to the sports clinic with her. Show her what therapists do."

"What about the guys?" Burt asked, a twinkle in his eye.

"Greg's going to take her to the university computer lab with him, because Cassie is fascinated with computers, according to Jennifer. And Marty . . ." Kelly grinned. "Marty volunteered Spot, the Wonder Dog. So, there's no telling what he'll do."

Burt threw back his head and laughed. "Oh, Lord . . . I'd forgotten about Marty's dog impersonation. What a riot. I can't wait to see that again. Good old Spot."

Mimi laughed. "Goodness, me. Well, Burt and I certainly want to do our part, too. And I just got an idea, listening to all that, Kelly. Cassie could come over here every morning when Pete and Jennifer open the café. Burt and I are up way early every morning anyway. We can come over to the shop before it's open for business. That way Cassie will have something interesting to do while Pete and Jennifer are taking care of customers and before her activity schedule starts."

Kelly could tell from the way Mimi's eyes danced that Mother Mimi was delighted with the idea of "helping" with the Cassie Project. "That's a wonderful suggestion, Mimi," she enthused. "Not only will it help out Jennifer and Pete but it will also give Cassie a chance to explore the shop. Lots of fascinating stuff in Lambspun."

"I'll say." Burt nodded. "Who knows? Maybe she'll get interested in yarn. Maybe knitting. Aren't you teaching a kids' class this summer, Mimi?"

Mimi smiled. "I am, indeed. A knitting class for ages nine to twelve. That would be perfect for Cassie."

Kelly noticed Jennifer walking toward their table through the garden patio. "Hey, welcome back, Mimi and Burt," she greeted them with a big smile. "I take it Kelly has filled you in on everything that's been happening."

"Goodness, yes," Mimi said, gesturing. "But I don't even want to talk about the gruesome death in our driveway. What I want to know is when's Pete returning to

Fort Connor with little Cassie?"

Jennifer grinned. "Well, she's not so little anymore. She's gotten taller but she's still skinny as a rail. But more importantly, Pete just called and said they'll be here about three o'clock. So if you and Burt would like to meet Cassie, this afternoon might be a good time. By the time they get here, the lunch crowd will have left. So, it will be peaceful and quiet."

Mimi perked up. "Really? Why, that would be wonderful! We'd love to meet Cassie this afternoon, wouldn't we, Burt?"

Burt gave her an indulgent smile. "You bet. I'm looking forward to it. I'm already thinking about ways we can get Cassie together with my grandkids."

Mimi fairly sparkled, Kelly noticed. Her eyes danced. "Oh, yes! *Yes!* What a wonderful idea, Burt!"

Jennifer looked over at Kelly. "Pete and I are thinking we'll introduce you guys to Cassie slowly. We'll start off with Mimi and Burt. Then maybe you next, Kelly, since you stop in the shop every day. Then we'll have Megan drop by, then Lisa. We'll save Greg and Marty and Steve for last." She grinned.

"Definitely. Save the best for last," Kelly agreed, laughing. She checked her watch. Twelve fifteen. "You know, I'd better check

140

in with Megan and Lisa. We're playing Greeley here in Fort Connor at three o'clock this afternoon. But I'm thinking that we should stop by your new house, Jennifer, and make sure Cassie's bedroom is set up. We put up the bed last night, but there are no sheets or anything. So I'll go by our house first and get some. Steve bought a lot of stuff in Denver that he never even opened."

"Kelly, you're an angel," Jennifer said, beaming. "I won't be able to get off to go shopping, and I wouldn't want Cassie to walk in and find nothing in her bedroom except a bed."

"Well, we have plenty of bed linens at our house if you need more," Mimi said. "Just let us know."

"Since you ladies are setting up the house, I'm going to call my old partner Dan. See if he knows anything about this." He glanced at Mimi and smiled. "This unfortunate incident in the driveway."

Mimi made another waving motion with her hand. "I don't even want to think about it. I'm going to think about Cassie coming. That's all. In fact, I'm going into the shop right now and check that class schedule. I want to make sure everything's all ready for this week."

Kelly caught Jennifer's glance and they exchanged smiles. Mother Mimi was definitely excited.

"Hey, Kelly, did I get you at a bad time?" Burt's voice came over her cell phone.

"No, no, I'm driving back from our game. Steve and the guys are still playing Longmont." Kelly slowed her car and turned into a shopping center to park. "How'd it go with Cassie? What's she like?"

"She's a sweetheart, just like Jennifer described. Tall, skinny, with dark brown hair down to her shoulders, and the biggest blue eyes you've ever seen. Huge. I swear, I thought her eyes were going to pop out when she came into the shop." Burt's warm chuckle sounded. "She was staring in every direction and touching everything in sight."

Kelly could easily imagine that scene. "That sounds like me the first time I set foot into Lambspun. I bet Mimi was pleased at Cassie's reaction. I could tell she was hoping Cassie might like to join her knitting class."

"Ohhhh, yeah. She took a real shine to Cassie, just like I thought she would."

"What's she like? When you talk with her, I mean?"

"Well, she was real quiet when she first

came into the shop with Jennifer and Pete. She stayed right between them when Mimi and I were talking with her. Then we started to show her around the shop, and her eyes just kept getting bigger and bigger." He laughed softly again. "Of course, Mimi was in her element, showing Cassie everything, as you can imagine."

"I figured as much. I told Jennifer yesterday that I had a feeling Mother Mimi would really appreciate having some time with Cassie. Some one-on-one time. Mimi's so good at that. She's been mothering all of us, now she'll have a chance to mother someone who actually needs it."

"I feel that same way. Listen, I also wanted to let you know that I did get to talk with Dan. And he said he'd heard about Rizzoli's murder but wasn't involved in the investigation. He promised he'd look into it and get back to me with more details."

"So it definitely was murder?"

"It looks that way, but the medical examiner hasn't made his report yet. All Dan heard was Rizzoli was stabbed in the throat with a knife."

Kelly had no trouble picturing the gruesome method of murder. She had walked in on a similar crime scene years ago. The first year she was here in Fort Connor. A woman in Bellevue Canyon had her throat cut. Kelly didn't think she'd ever forget the gruesome sight.

"Stabbed in the throat. That's a pretty angry way to kill someone. That kind of fits with everything we've heard about Rizzoli and his past misdeeds. There were certainly plenty of people angry with him. Now police will have to narrow it down and find the one who did it."

"That about sums it up, Kelly. The tricky part will be the narrowing-down process. Brother . . . that could take a long time. Like we've both said, Rizzoli made a lot of enemies here."

"Did Dan say what kind of knife was used? That would be a clue."

Burt's chuckle came over the line. "Right as usual, Sherlock. Dan hadn't heard any details. I imagine more will come out with the examiner's report. Who knows? Maybe police found the weapon already."

"Well, if so, maybe there will be some fingerprints." She revved the car's engine.

"We can only hope, Sherlock. We can only hope."

NINE

"I e-mailed those financial statements through five minutes ago, right before you called," Kelly said to her Denver client, Don Warner. "They look really good, Don. I think you'll be pleased."

"Music to my ears, Kelly." Warner's voice came over her cell phone. "I'm kicking around some new ideas. I'll run them by you next time you're in Denver. Maybe on Wednesday when you're here for the staff meeting."

Kelly watched Carl roll on the ground in the cottage backyard, legs in the air, scratching his back. *Ahhhh, the life of a dog.* "Sounds like a plan, Don."

"There goes my other phone. Talk to you on Wednesday, Kelly."

"See you then," Kelly said, and clicked off the same time as her client.

Another hot, sunny day beckoned to her outside. Summer temperatures would be in the high eighties and nineties. And no rain in the forecast. Even the sparse April showers had ceased in May. All of Colorado was dry. Bone dry. And that was not a good thing in the mountains, especially heading into summer. Wildfires were too easily started in tinder-dry forests.

Kelly shoved her laptop into her briefcase. Maybe she could work outside in the café patio garden, she thought, as she grabbed her coffee mug and headed for the cottage front door. First she wanted to check on Malcolm, then go into Lambspun and meet Cassie.

She spotted Hal Nelson's truck as soon as she walked toward the driveway. Nelson was measuring a large sheet of fiberboard that was balanced on two sawhorses beside the driveway. Kelly glanced around but didn't see Malcolm.

"Hey, Hal," she greeted as she approached. "I imagine you heard the awful news over the weekend."

Nelson looked up from the fiberboard. "I sure did, Kelly. The newspaper only said a man was found dead in his car. But when I read it was 'near the corner of Lemay and Lincoln avenues,' I called Burt to see what he knew. Burt filled me in."

"I hate to say it, Hal, but it sounds like

someone took their revenge on Jared Rizzoli."

Nelson stared at her solemnly. "You're right, Kelly, and I think he had it coming."

Although a little surprised by Nelson's blunt comment, Kelly had to agree. "After everything I've read and heard for the last week, I think you're right. It isn't hard to imagine one of Rizzoli's many victims taking revenge on him." She glanced toward the garage. "Is Malcolm working inside? I was wondering how he was doing. I confess when I first learned that Rizzoli was murdered, I thought about Malcolm. And that angry confrontation he had with Rizzoli the other day."

Nelson looked away. "Well, that is a problem, especially now. I just learned this morning that Malcolm fell off the wagon the same night Rizzoli was killed. Apparently Malcolm was found drunk Saturday morning on the river trail over there." He pointed across the golf course to the stretch of the Poudre River Trail that Kelly knew so well, having run along that same trail countless times since she'd come to Fort Connor.

"Oh, no!" she said, shocked. "It was all because of their argument. It's gotta be. Malcolm looked so . . . so beaten down after that."

Nelson's mouth twisted. "That's because he was. Beaten down and kicked to the side like a piece of trash."

"Good Lord," Kelly worried out loud. "Have the police questioned Malcolm yet?"

"Not yet. I went over to see him at the Mission this morning before I came here. Apparently the guy who found Malcolm Saturday morning took him to the Mission, and they called the folks at AA that had been counseling him. They came over to take care of him."

"Thank goodness for that. But it's only a matter of time before someone tells the police they saw Malcolm in an argument with Rizzoli. Think about all the people who witnessed it when they were sitting outside." She gestured toward the garden patio. "The detectives will be crawling over poor Malcolm once they find out about his argument with Rizzoli."

Nelson glanced toward the garden. "Yeah, you're right about that. I guess anybody who had a disagreement with that bastard will be questioned."

That comment brought the other unpleasant image from the back of Kelly's mind. "And that means my friend Barbara will be questioned, too. She had an angry argument with Rizzoli in front of a whole bunch of people out here. And if that wasn't bad enough, I heard that Barbara went to Rizzoli's seminar that night and confronted him again! In front of a couple hundred people. Security guards had to remove her and threatened to call the police." Kelly frowned. "Brother, now that I'm repeating all of that, it sounds like Barbara may be in worse trouble than Malcolm. She confronted Rizzoli *twice*."

The sound of a vehicle coming down the driveway caught her attention, and Kelly turned to see a blue van pull into a parking spot on the gravel only a few feet away from them. The van's door slid open, and Malcolm stepped out.

"Well, well, I was hoping that he would come in today," Nelson said, with an approving nod. "I told Malcolm that he still had a job with me if he wanted it. Looks like one of the Mission staffers dropped him off. Hey, Malcolm." Nelson beckoned him over.

Kelly started to back away, not wanting Malcolm to feel any more uncomfortable than he probably already did. She waved at Malcolm as she turned toward the sidewalk. "Hey, there, Malcolm. Hal told me you guys are coming into the final stretch on this project. It's looking good."

Malcolm caught her glance and sent Kelly a little wave as he walked to meet Nelson. Kelly hurried away down the sidewalk, wanting to give the two men some time to talk in private. She ran up the steps and into Lambspun, pausing as she entered the foyer.

New yarns peeked out from wicker baskets. Strawberry reds, lime sherbet green, blueberry blue, cotton candy pink, and lemon pie yellow.

Stroking the silky fibers in one basket, Kelly moved into the central yarn room. New yarns were here as well, begging to be touched. Silks, cottons, bamboo.

As she moved farther into the room, Kelly glimpsed Mimi and a young girl at the other end of the knitting table. *Cassie.* It had to be, Kelly thought. And it looked like they were knitting. Or rather, Mimi was watching Cassie knit. Kelly moved around the round maple table in the middle of the room, stroking several soft skeins of pink bamboo yarn. However, her attention was focused on the library table in the main room and the instruction taking place there. Mimi was speaking quietly to Cassie, so Kelly couldn't really hear what she was saying. Kelly assumed Mimi was telling Cassie the same things she'd told Kelly when she was struggling through her first efforts.

Kelly tried to get a glimpse of Cassie's face, but couldn't. Cassie was leaning over obviously concentrating on the knitting, and her shoulder-length dark brown hair fell forward, hiding her face. Kelly stepped closer to the entrance to the main room, and Mimi glanced up and spotted her standing there.

"Why, hello, Kelly!" she said with a bright smile. "Come on in and join us. I'm teaching Pete's niece Cassie how to knit."

Cassie quickly looked up, and Kelly saw that Burt and Jennifer had not exaggerated. Two big blue eyes stared out at her. Kelly saw curiosity and surprise, and maybe a little bit of wariness, looking out.

"Well, hello, Cassie," Kelly greeted, giving her a friendly smile. "I'm a friend of Mimi and Burt and Pete and Jennifer. They told me you were coming."

"Hi," Cassie replied in a soft voice, then glanced back to her knitting needles.

Kelly walked over to the table and sat on the opposite side across from Mimi and Cassie. "Mimi's an excellent teacher. She taught me how to knit when I first came here a few years ago," Kelly said as she reached into her briefcase and brought out the small fabric bag where she kept the baby

151

hat she was knitting.

"That's right, Cassie, and Kelly's an excellent knitter now," Mimi declared, then pointed toward one of Cassie's needles. "That's it, slide the needle to the left of the stitch, dear."

Kelly watched Cassie obediently slide the right needle beneath the stitch on her left needle. Boy, did Kelly remember doing that. Had it really been four years ago when she first came to Lambspun?

"Mimi's being kind, Cassie," Kelly said as she drew the yellow-and-white yarn and partially finished hat from the little taffeta bag Lisa had given her for Christmas. "I was a lousy student. I kept arguing with the yarn."

Cassie looked at Kelly, puzzled. Kelly could tell she didn't know whether Kelly was kidding or not. "How do you argue with yarn?" she asked, a tiny hint of a smile peeking out.

Kelly picked up her stitches where she left off on the small hat. "Ohhhh, I'd get mad when the stitches didn't want to slide off the needle. I'd have to convince them to slide off. Coax them, you know." Kelly smiled at her. "Like, 'You want to leave the needle. You want to go. You want to go. That's it. Slide off, slide off.'"

152

Cassie's hint of a smile grew. "Did it work?"

Kelly shook her head. "Nope. They ignored me. They tightened up and sat there. Drove me crazy." She pointed to the five rows of stitches on Cassie's needle. "Look, your stitches are more obedient than mine. You've got five rows. You're better than I was already."

"Kelly loves to exaggerate," Mimi said with a smile. "I keep telling her how good she is, but she doesn't believe me."

"I suffer from low yarn self-esteem," Kelly said, then gave a dramatic sigh. "Dr. Mimi says it's not fatal, but I do have attacks every now and then."

Cassie gestured to the baby hat. "You must be good. That looks really pretty. Do you have a baby?"

Kelly had to laugh. "No, I don't. I'm knitting this for one of Mimi's charities. Lots of knitters around town knit hats for the babies and young children who have to come to the hospital for cancer treatment. The hats help keep up their body temperature level. We lose most of our body heat through our heads. Did you know that?"

Cassie's big blue eyes widened even more. "Wow, I didn't know that."

"Cassie, you're doing really, really well,"

Mimi said. "You'll have this cute scarf done in no time. And if you'd like, I can show you some of those ribbon yarns that knit up real skinny. You can use them for belts or little scarves."

Cassie looked over Kelly's head into the central yarn room. "You mean like some of those hanging out there?"

"Why, yes!" Mimi chirped, scooting back her chair. "Let me bring some of them over here." She scurried into the adjoining room where several summery scarves hung from the ceiling.

Kelly took that moment to lean over the table and asked, "How's it going, Cassie? You settling in over at Pete and Jennifer's?"

Cassie gave a little shrug. "Yeah, kind of. It's different."

"Feels kind of funny, doesn't it? I moved around a lot as a kid because my dad's job kept assigning him to different states. I remember how funny it felt coming into a new place."

Cassie glanced up. "Yeah, it does. Did you have to go to different schools?"

Kelly nodded. "Lots of them. Sometimes we'd only be in a city two years, then we'd have to move again."

Cassie's eyes widened even more. "Wow. That must have been hard."

Kelly gave a little shrug of her own. "Yeah, it was. I was always having to make new friends." She smiled. "It taught me how to meet new people."

"How'd you do that?"

"Actually, it's easy. You just walk up to them and smile and say 'hi.' That usually worked. And playing sports helped, too. I'd join the school teams, and that way I met a lot of girls my age. I played softball all the way through high school."

"Wow, you must have been good." Cassie had let the knitting drop to her lap.

"I don't know how good I was, but I sure had a lot of fun," Kelly said, smiling. "Have you ever played?"

"Yeah, a few times in school. I was never on a team." Cassie returned her attention to the scarf.

"You know, I'm coaching a bunch of girls your age this summer. Beginners' softball clinic. If you're interested, I'd love to have you join the group. I've got nine girls signed up so far. It's not a team or anything, just real low-key. You know, relaxed, having fun."

Cassie looked over at Kelly with a dubious expression. "I don't know if I'd be any good."

"Hey, it's a beginners' class. You can't be any worse than the others. Nobody is gonna be very good." She gave a good-natured shrug. "You can give it a try and see how you like it."

Mimi bustled back into the room then, four colorful, ribbon-like skinny scarves dangling from her hands. "I found several that you might like, Cassie. Several of my other teenage knitters simply love these new yarns." She spread the four jewel-colored creations across the table in front of Cassie.

"Ooooh, these are so pretty," Cassie said, fingering the ribbony yarns. "Are they hard to make?"

"Not at all, dear," Mimi said, picking up one of the scarves. "See, it's the very same stitch you're doing now. The yarn makes it look different."

Kelly watched Mimi explain, much the same way she had with Kelly four years ago. Calmly reassuring. Just then, the glimpse of a white car slowly passing in the driveway caught Kelly's attention. She turned to get a better look. It wasn't an ordinary white car. This one had blue lettering. FORT COLLINS POLICE.

Curious, Kelly set the baby hat aside and pushed back her chair, noticing that Cassie was engrossed in examining the ribbon scarves. Kelly walked through the central yarn room, past the adjoining room with the Mother Loom, and into the front room where there were more and larger windows. She watched the police car pull into a parking spot along the walkway. Two men in suits exited the car. Detectives, Kelly decided.

"Hey, Kelly," Connie called to her from behind the front counter where she was ringing up a customer's order. "It looks like the cops have come back. Probably want to question the builder guys outside."

"I think you're right, Connie," Kelly replied, her attention focused outside. The two detectives were standing and talking with Hal Nelson. She looked around for Malcolm but didn't see him. *Uh-oh,* she thought, hoping he hadn't taken off for the river trail again.

"Is that the police outside?" the customer asked as she took her package from Connie.

"Afraid so," Connie replied in a matter-of-fact voice. "Did you see those news stories about a dead man who was found in a parked car? Well, that was here. And it turns out the guy was *murdered.*" Connie's voice dropped scary-movie low.

"Ohhhh, my!" the older woman exclaimed, eyes wide as saucers as she stared toward the windows.

Kelly kept her mouth shut, not wanting to

add to local gossip any more than necessary. Thank goodness Mimi wasn't anywhere around to hear Connie's dramatic remarks.

"Hey, Kelly, I betcha the cops have come to question that other builder guy. You know, the one with the beard. The skinny one. He got into a fight with Rizzoli, remember? Right outside in the driveway! You were standing there, too. They were yelling at each other. And that night Rizzoli was killed!" Another dramatic tone.

"Good heavens!" the older woman said, hand to her face now, clearly horrified.

Kelly sighed inside, searching for patience, and found a little. "Yes, I was there," was all she said, not wanting to add to an already blazing imaginary fire.

Meanwhile, she continued watching Hal Nelson and the detectives talking. Nelson pointed toward the remodeled building and walked toward it. A few seconds later, Nelson reappeared with Malcolm by his side. Kelly watched a wide-eyed Malcolm nod and speak to the detectives, who were obviously asking him questions. One detective had his notebook out and was scribbling notes.

Hal Nelson stood right beside Malcolm while the detectives continued to question.

Kelly watched Malcolm glance down at the ground and shift side to side, his hands in his work pants pockets as he spoke. He definitely looked uncomfortable as the detectives kept asking questions. One of them gestured toward the golf course . . . or beyond. She figured they had to ask Malcolm about his Friday night slide away from sobriety. *Oh, brother.*

Kelly couldn't picture Malcolm killing Jared Rizzoli. Stabbing someone in the throat was an act of anger. But, she reminded herself, she had witnessed Malcolm yelling at Rizzoli in anger and helpless fury. Had he been angry enough to kill?

The two detectives stepped away from Malcolm and Hal Nelson. The one taking notes closed his notebook as they walked along the walkway leading to the patio garden. Kelly shifted her position to a tall window on the adjoining wall that looked out into the garden behind the shop. Sure enough, the two detectives walked through the garden flagstone pathway, amid curious stares of the lunchtime customers seated outside.

Burt appeared around the corner behind the front counter. Catching Kelly's eye, he beckoned, as he squeezed behind Connie and into the room. "Hey, Kelly, you should go back to your cottage. The detectives are here questioning everyone who had seen Rizzoli last week. They've just come into the café, so I imagine they'll be knocking on your cottage door soon."

"Thanks for the heads-up, Burt." Kelly started retracing her steps to the main knitting room. "I'll go over right now. Walk with me and let me know what you've learned from these guys."

"I haven't spoken to them yet, but I'll be curious what they ask you. So I'll hang around if you don't mind," Burt said as he followed after Kelly.

Kelly walked to the knitting table and gathered up her knitting project and her briefcase. Cassie was already knitting with the ribbon yarn under Mimi's attentive gaze.

"I have to go back to the cottage and make some business calls," she said as she slipped the briefcase's shoulder strap over her shoulder. "I really enjoyed talking with you, Cassie. Let me know if you want to go to the softball clinic with me tomorrow morning. It's at ten o'clock."

"Okay, sure." Cassie nodded.

"See you later, Kelly." Mimi gave her a smile, then returned her attention to her pupil.

Kelly grinned at Burt as they walked to

the foyer. "Mimi's positively in her element," Kelly said in a lowered voice.

"Ohhhh, yeah," Burt said. "She's been with Cassie all morning. We treated Cassie to breakfast in the café so she could see Pete and Jennifer at work." He chuckled. "She was fascinated. And practically twisted her neck off watching Jennifer and Julie going back and forth serving customers."

Kelly pushed open the front door. "I got to talk with Cassie for a few minutes. Some with Mimi, then alone. She's a really nice kid. I told her about that beginners' softball clinic I'm teaching this summer. I think I told you about it. The kids are Cassie's age group, too. Just two mornings a week, so let me know if she wants to go. It's no problem for me to take her and bring her back to the shop."

"I think it's a great idea, Kelly," Burt said as they went down the steps. "Let's see if Cassie wants to do it."

As Kelly headed across the driveway, Burt beside her, she noticed one of the detectives approach Hal Nelson again. Nelson then pointed toward Kelly, and the detective walked her way.

"Good thing we came outside. I'm betting that detective is looking for you, Kelly."

"Excuse me, ma'am," the middle-aged

man called to her as he approached. "Are you Kelly Flynn?"

"Yes, I am. Are you with the Fort Connor Police? I noticed you asking questions earlier."

"Yes, ma'am. I'm Detective Geller. My partner Detective Lasky and I are investigating the death of Jared Rizzoli over the weekend."

Burt extended his hand. "I'm Burt Parker, formerly with the department. My wife operates the knitting shop here."

"Good to meet you, Mr. Parker. I've heard about you," Geller said with a little smile.

"Something good, I hope," Burt joked.

"Oh, yes." Geller turned to Kelly. "Ms. Flynn, this is your residence, is that correct?"

"Yes, sir, it is. I inherited the cottage when my aunt died a few years ago."

Geller opened his notebook and scribbled for a few seconds. "I'm sure you recall the newspapers' recent stories that Mr. Rizzoli was found in his car early Saturday morning in this parking lot. Right over there beneath those trees."

"Yes, I remember the café staff telling me about it when I came in on Saturday for lunch."

"Well, Detective Lasky is in the café now,

asking the staff what they remember seeing on the day Jared Rizzoli was last seen alive. I believe he was here earlier that Friday afternoon on the day he was killed. And we were told that you had witnessed a confrontation between Mr. Rizzoli and another man that same afternoon. Is that correct?"

"Yes, it is," Kelly answered, noticing Malcolm working outside next to Hal Nelson now. Malcolm glanced her direction more than once. "I was walking over to the shop, and I noticed two men yelling at each other. Since I knew one of the men, I went over to see what was happening."

"And what did you see?"

"Uhhhh, well, they kept yelling at each other." Kelly hesitated to add more.

"Could you hear what they were saying?"

Kelly paused. She did not want to answer, but she had to. "Some of it. Malcolm, one of the workers over there —"

"That would be Malcolm Duprey, who's assisting Mr. Nelson with the remodel?"

She nodded. "Yes. Malcolm said that Rizzoli ruined his life."

Geller scribbled away, and Kelly shot a quick glance to Burt. He nodded, encouraging her. "What else did you hear?"

"Rizzoli called Malcolm a worthless piece of crap. And said that everything that's happened to him was his own fault. Rizzoli said he paid his debt to society."

Geller looked up from his notebook. "Did you see one of the men place his hands on the other?"

Kelly sighed. "Yes. Malcolm jabbed his finger into Rizzoli's chest. Rizzoli slapped his hand away, then he pushed Malcolm back. Hard. So hard, Malcolm fell down backwards to the ground. Hal Nelson came to help him up."

Geller diligently recorded it all in his notebook. "Then what?"

"Rizzoli stomped off to his car, and drove away. Hal Nelson and I helped Malcolm into the café for some coffee and food. He looked pretty shaken up."

"I see." Geller scribbled some more, then flipped his notebook closed. "Thank you, Ms. Flynn. You've been really helpful. If we have any more questions, we'll be in touch."

"I'm glad I was able to help, Detective Lasky," Kelly dutifully answered. But she wasn't telling the truth. She felt awful. Her words made Malcolm out to be a prime suspect in the murder of Jared Rizzoli.

"It was nice meeting you both. Have a good day," Lasky said as he walked back toward the café.

Burt stared after him. "You did the right

thing, Kelly. You know you did."

"Yeah, I know. I just wish I didn't feel so bad."

TEN

Kelly pulled open the front door to the café and stepped inside. She took a deep breath, inhaling the heavenly breakfast aromas filling the air. Crispy bacon, scrambled eggs with cheese, spicy sausage sizzling on the grill, omelets stuffed full of veggies and oozing yummy cheese, rich gravy and biscuits, Pete's special salsa, huevos rancheros, and more bacon.

Breakfast. Kelly's favorite meal. And no one did breakfast like cook Eduardo. Master of the grill. She inhaled another scent. Ooooh, was that cinnamon? Pete had been baking his cinnamon rolls again! Okay, that settled it. She had to have breakfast. Again. Her early yogurt and fruit just didn't cut it when faced with heartier breakfasts. No contest.

She spied a small table along the windows near the grill and headed that way. "Pete's been baking again. I can smell those cinnamon rolls," she called to Jennifer as she dropped her briefcase on the opposite chair and took a seat.

"Ohhhh, yes," Jennifer replied as she walked over, coffeepot in hand. "I take it you'll want one or two?"

"Absolutely. And bring a slice of fresh melon, too. That way I can fool myself into thinking I'm eating healthy."

"Gotcha." Jennifer poured a black stream into Kelly's cup. "Let me refill your mug. It's probably empty." Jennifer reached into Kelly's briefcase and pulled out the over-sized mug, refilled it, then returned it to Kelly. "Oh, Cassie said to tell you she'd like to check out that softball clinic you're teaching. She actually looked kind of interested."

Kelly sniffed the strong aroma. *Ahhhh.* "That's great. Let's see if she likes it." She smiled up at Jennifer. "I got to talk to her a little at the knitting table yesterday. She's a cute kid. She worried that she might not be very good at softball. I told her that nobody was going to be any good because they were all beginners. And they're all her age."

"Thank you for doing that, Kelly. You're a sweetheart. You and Mimi both did a lot to make her feel comfortable yesterday. Of course, Cassie was entranced by the shop and all the yarns. She'd never seen anything like that, she said. And of course, Mother Mimi had her knitting a scarf in no time." She laughed softly.

"Oh, yeah, I saw Mother Mimi in action. She is loving every minute of this." Kelly took a sip. "Burt told me that Mimi had spent all morning with Cassie."

"I know, and you came in. Then Megan dropped by in the afternoon, Mimi said."

"Perfect. Were they at the knitting table?"

"I was at the real estate office, but Pete said Megan was showing Cassie something with the yarn when he came in there."

Kelly caught Jennifer's eye. "Sounds good. Tell me, how's she settling in at the house? It's only been a couple of days."

"Cassie's been doing great. We're all getting used to the house, so we're adjusting together." Jennifer laughed. "This house is even bigger than Ben's in Denver. Cassie's room was tiny there, so she's crazy about this bedroom. Pete promised her they could bring the rest of her books up here. I'm hoping Steve wouldn't mind swinging by Ben's one night and bringing up the bookcase in his truck. Pete could drive down and meet him."

"I'm sure Steve wouldn't mind. He told me he felt bad about not being able to do anything with Cassie because he's working in Denver."

Jennifer gave a dismissive wave. "Don't be silly. Cassie's sleeping on Steve's extra furniture and bed linens. He's done a lot. Tell him I said that, too. I'd better get this to the grill or you won't eat. Are you gonna work here this morning?"

"Just until I have to leave for the softball fields. Tell Cassie I'll come into the shop when it's time to go. What's she up to? Knitting with Mimi again?"

"Actually, Mimi handed her off to Burt this morning. He's showing Cassie the spinning wheel. I'll be back with your cinnamon roll in a minute." Jennifer hurried off toward the grill.

Kelly pulled her laptop out of her briefcase and started it up, waiting for the familiar soft whirring noise. Circuits firing, getting ready. Spreadsheets and expense accounts were easier with a yummy, buttery cinnamon roll. Heck, everything was better with a cinnamon roll.

Kelly looked up from the yellow-and-white yarn on her needles. Several more rows had appeared now. "Why, hello, Madge," Kelly greeted the elderly spinner when she walked into the front room, empty now of customers. "Are you here to help Burt with his spinning class?"

"Hello, there, Kelly." Madge's thin face brightened with a smile. "I'll be teaching Burt's class again. It looks like he's giving a private lesson in the little alcove."

Kelly grinned. "Oh, that's Cassie. She's Pete's niece from Denver. Burt's simply explaining the wheel to her. She'll be living with Pete and Jennifer this summer while her grandfather recovers from heart surgery."

"Ohhhh, yes. I heard about that," Madge said, her expression saddening quickly. "She looks like a sweet girl. She was certainly paying attention. Watching Burt's fingers. Watching the yarn." Madge nodded. "Paying attention is the most important thing."

"She pays attention, all right. I took her to a softball clinic I'm teaching this summer for Parks and Recreation. We had a bunch of twelve-year-old girls. And Cassie really paid attention. I noticed her watching me intently and the other girls. And she did pretty well for a beginner. Her throws got better and better over the hour and a half. And her catches were great." Kelly looked up from the baby hat. "That's where paying attention pays off. You have to watch the ball all the way into the glove, if that makes any sense."

Madge smiled again. "Actually, it does, Kelly. I used to watch my husband play baseball years and years ago. And he played catcher a lot. Keep your eye on the ball, he used to say." She glanced out the window.

Madge's poignant recollection brought back a more recent memory. "How's Barbara doing? I haven't seen her since last week. Is she all right, Madge?"

Madge let out a sigh. "Yes, she's all right. Thank the Lord. And I pray she stays all right. That horrible man upset her so last week. And she was settling down after . . . well, after the weekend."

Kelly read between Madge's words. Clearly, Madge meant after Rizzoli died. "I'm glad to hear Barbara's doing okay."

"She was doing okay until yesterday," Madge said, mouth pinched in a frown. "When those police detectives came to our house asking questions. Arrived right as I was cooking dinner, too."

Uh-oh. Kelly had wondered when the police would question Barbara. Surely they'd had reports of her earlier confrontation with Rizzoli. Malcolm wasn't the only one to have an angry run-in with the swindler. And surely the police had heard from the hotel security guards who escorted Barbara away from Rizzoli's public seminar. Of course detectives showed up at Barbara's door.

"Oh, I'm sorry to hear that, Madge," Kelly tried to console. "I'm sure they were simply following up on reports of Barbara's argument with Rizzoli outside in the garden last week."

Madge's mouth pinched more. "Yes, of course. They asked all sorts of questions about that. And then they asked even more questions about that evening. When Barbara went to that awful man's seminar." She wagged her head. "Why, oh, why, did she do that? That horrible man would never admit to any wrongdoing! Certainly not in public. And now poor Barbara has the police investigating *her.* It's simply too terrible to think about."

Kelly sought something comforting to say, but found nothing. Barbara had done exactly what Madge said. Naturally, the police would be questioning her. Just as they had Malcolm yesterday. But surely Barbara had not gone off on a bender like Malcolm. Not steady, dependable Barbara.

"I'm so sorry, Madge. You're right. It is simply terrible to think about. But surely Barbara could tell police where she was the night Rizzoli was killed. That way she wouldn't be considered a suspect. Not like the poor man who works outside on the remodeling. He had no explanation for his whereabouts that night."

Madge looked over at Kelly. "I hate to say this, Kelly. But my poor Barbara doesn't have a very good explanation for her whereabouts that night, either."

That comment took Kelly by surprise. She stared at Madge. "What do you mean? Did Barbara go out that evening?"

"Yes, I'm afraid she did. And she didn't return until later that evening. I asked her where she'd been, and she said she drove up into the canyon. She needed to think." Madge's worried expression increased.

Kelly couldn't believe what she was hearing. Solid, dependable Barbara had chosen that evening to drive into the canyon to think. The evening that Jared Rizzoli was killed. *What the heck?* "Oh, no! That means she has no alibi, no explanation for her whereabouts when Rizzoli was killed."

Madge sat on the edge of the wooden chair at the winding table and stared at her hands in her lap. "I'm simply heartsick about it, Kelly. Of all the times to drive up into the canyon to think." She wagged her head.

"Did the detectives ask Barbara where she was that evening?"

Madge nodded. "Of course. And naturally, Barbara had to tell them she was driving in the canyon. One detective wrote down everything in his little notebook. The other detective kept staring at Barbara. Poor thing, she started to mix up her words when she tried to explain. I'm so concerned that the police will think Barbara had something to do with that awful man's death."

Kelly reached over and placed her hand on Madge's arm. "I'm so sorry, Madge. I'm sure there will be a way to prove Barbara's innocence." Kelly wasn't at all sure; in fact, she doubted what she was saying. But she had no other comforting words to tell Madge.

Madge looked into Kelly's eyes. "Do you really think so?"

Kelly swallowed. "I — I hope so, Madge," was all she could say. "I really hope so. I cannot see Barbara killing Rizzoli. I just can't."

Barbara gave a firm nod. "Well, I know she didn't do it. I know my daughter."

Spoken like a loyal, devoted mother, Kelly thought. "You're right, Madge."

Rosa walked into the front room then, several skeins of royal blue yarn in her hands. "Hey, Madge, hey, Kelly. How're you doing?" She dumped the skeins on the yarn winding table. "Oh, Madge, a couple of your spinning students arrived early. They're already in the classroom."

Madge glanced at her watch. "Well, now, I should go over then and see if they have any questions before class. They probably will. All beginners do. That's how we learn." She rose from the chair, taking her oversized yarn bag with her. "Take care, Kelly. I'll tell Barbara you asked about her."

"Tell her we've missed seeing her here at the shop. Of course, I know she's busy at the doctor's office."

Kelly watched Madge leave the room, then glanced back at Rosa, who was loosening some of the yarn skeins, then placed the wide loop over the yarn holders on the winding table.

"How I wish Barbara had chosen a private place to have an argument with Jared Rizzoli," Kelly said. "Now police are investigating her like they are poor Malcolm." She pointed outside the window where she saw Hal Nelson and Malcolm lifting another large sheet of fiberboard off the sawhorses.

Rosa turned to Kelly with an astonished expression. "Oh, surely not! How could they possibly think she would kill that swindler?"

"They have to investigate everyone who had a conflict with him, and we all know that Barbara's conflict was very public. Lots of witnesses."

"Well, then they'll have to question all those people who were interviewed in the newspaper this morning. Did you see that article? Several people Rizzoli swindled were interviewed, and they all said they were glad he was dead. Police better check them out, too, if they're going to check out Barbara." She pulled out a long twist of blue yarn and attached it to the spindle of the ball winder on the other end of the table. Then she began slowly turning the handle of the ball winder. Slowly, the yarn began to wind around and around the spindle as the loop yarn holder released more yarn to fill the spindle of the ball winder.

"I hope you're right, Rosa. I certainly don't want Barbara and Malcolm to be the only suspects police have." She noticed a familiar truck come down the driveway. A blond driver. Jayleen. The truck pulled into a space near the remodeled building, and Jayleen stepped out.

"Oh, good, Jayleen's here. I called her this morning to let her know those alpaca fleeces have been spun and dyed and are ready for her to pick up," Rosa said, looking out the window.

Kelly watched Jayleen talk with Nelson

and Malcolm outside. Catching up on what had been happening, no doubt. Kelly wondered whether Jayleen was one of those counselors Nelson mentioned who were called to come to the Mission last Saturday. Kelly thought about how disappointing it must have been for Jayleen and the others when they watched people who had struggled and worked so hard to escape the pull of alcohol dependence . . . only to see them slide back into its grip again.

Jayleen turned away from the two men and started walking toward the shop. Kelly placed her halfway-finished baby hat on the upholstered chair arm and left her cozy knitting spot in the corner, hastening to the front door to meet Jayleen. She wanted to get her reactions to Malcolm's lapse over the weekend.

Kelly pushed open the front door and Jayleen quickly stepped back, out of the way. "Whoa, Kelly-girl, I was just heading inside to meet you."

"I saw you talking with Hal and Malcolm, so I thought I'd meet you here. That way we'll have a little privacy."

"Good idea," Jayleen said, walking over to the recessed seating area located near the front entrance. "Why don't we take advantage of this break in the heat and talk out here." She pulled out a wrought-iron chair next to the patio table.

Kelly followed suit. "Hal told me about what happened to Malcolm over the weekend. He decided to fall off the wagon, right?"

Jayleen nodded her head. "That's about it," she said sadly.

"Apparently some guy found him Saturday morning along the trail, and took him to the Mission. Were you one of the counselors they called?"

"Yes, I was. Jerry and I had counseled Malcolm and sponsored him at AA meetings. So we came in and helped him pick up the pieces. Start all over again." She gave Kelly a rueful smile. "We all fall back or slip up along the journey. But there's help available. We took Malcolm to an AA meeting that afternoon. After we got him all cleaned up and some food inside, he started to come back to himself."

"Wow, Jayleen, you guys really do make a huge difference. Malcolm was lucky to have you."

"It's not us, Kelly. It's AA that makes the difference. We simply show up in these folks' lives to let them know they're not alone. We're walking the same path they are. Every day we don't take a drink is a gift. And we know it. And believe me, it feels good to give back because someone was there to help us when we needed it."

Kelly looked out toward the remodeling project and saw Malcolm carry two lengths of wood from Nelson's truck into the structure. "I was here yesterday when the cops came to talk to Malcolm. Bless Hal Nelson's heart. He stood right next to Malcolm the entire time. I watched as they questioned him. Poor guy. He looked like he wanted to run off to the river trail again. But he didn't. He stood there and answered their questions."

"Good thing. Malcolm knows he made a bad decision the other night. Now he's having to face the consequences. Police consider him a suspect. I already talked to one of the detectives, so I can tell they consider Malcolm a suspect. They'd be crazy not to. He was seen arguing with Rizzoli in front of a whole passel of witnesses. Then he goes off drinking the night Rizzoli is killed. No alibi." Jayleen shook her head. "Bad decisions will get us every time."

Kelly looked at her friend. "Well, Malcolm's not the only one who's gotten on the cops' radar screen. You know Barbara, the one who helps Mimi by teaching knitting classes? She also had a public confrontation with Rizzoli the day before Malcolm did. She was right out here in front of all the lunch-hour customers."

Jayleen screwed up her face. "Are you talking about Big Barb, the nurse over at Doc Garcia's office?"

Big Barb. Kelly laughed at that. "One and the same. She's always been steady and dependable until the other day. Her family lost everything in that Rizzoli swindle. And Barb chose that day to tell Rizzoli off. Not just once, here in the patio, but twice. She also went to his seminar that night and did it again. I was told she was escorted out by security guards."

Jayleen's big blue eyes popped wide. "Lordy, Lordy! What on earth got into Big Barb? Sounds like she kind of lost it."

"You might say that. Her mother, Madge, told me Barb went driving up into the canyon the night Rizzoli was killed. So, just like Malcolm, she has no alibi."

Jayleen let out a low whistle. "What was she thinking? I can't believe it. Both Barb and Malcolm are now suspects. Lord-a-mighty! I'm afraid to ask what else has happened since I drove in from the canyon."

"Well, there is some good news. Pete returned with Cassie on Sunday afternoon. He and Jennifer brought her over to meet

Mimi and Burt and see the shop. Sunday afternoon was a perfect day, because there're no customers or staff around. It was quiet and peaceful. They didn't want to overwhelm Cassie with a lot of strangers all at once."

"That was a good idea. She's just a little kid, who's probably scared about losing her grandpa and now she's having to move to a whole new place."

"Actually, she's not so little. Cassie's going to be twelve in July, and she's tall and skinny. Speaking of a new place, Pete and Jen have moved into one of Steve's three-bedroom houses in Wellesley. They asked if they could rent it even before they knew Cassie would be coming to live with them."

"Well, look at that. Funny how some things just fall into place of their own accord. Pete and Jennifer needed some extra room for themselves and wound up getting a little girl thrown into the mix."

Kelly glanced at her watch. "Do you want to meet Cassie? I think she's still here. She'll go to a summer softball clinic with me twice a week that I'm coaching for girls her age. And Megan can take Cassie to tennis three afternoons a week with her. Lisa can take her to the sports clinic once a week, and Lisa said Cassie absolutely *loved* going with

Greg to his computer lab at the university. Cassie loves everything having to do with computers. So Greg's teaching her how to take them apart. All of us are helping Jen and Pete by filling Cassie's summertime days with supervised activities."

Jayleen's face lit up. "Well, I'll be. Wait'll I tell Curt that all you young folks are taking turns parenting Cassie. He'll bust a gut laughing." Jayleen sprang out of the chair. "Sure, I'd like to meet her. Is she inside the shop or the café?"

"Probably the shop," Kelly said, following after Jayleen, who was halfway up the brick steps. "Mimi keeps giving Cassie little chores around the shop, you know, sorting yarns and filling shelves, stuff like that."

"I think it's a great idea, Kelly-girl, and I'm proud of each and every one of you," Jayleen said as she pulled open the front door.

"Let's try the main room first," Kelly suggested as she walked in after Jayleen. They rounded the corner into the main room, and Kelly spotted Cassie unpacking yet another box of Lambspun yarn.

"What'd I tell you, Jayleen. Mimi's got Cassie working again. Don't tell me that's another box of yarn Mimi ordered?" Kelly teased.

Cassie noticed Jayleen, then gave Kelly a big smile. "These yarns aren't new. I found them in the basement on a back shelf, behind a bag of fleece. Mimi forgot she even had them."

Kelly laughed out loud, and so did Jayleen. "Boy, Cassie, it's a good thing you came along to help out Mimi with her inventory. I'll bet she has more surprise boxes down in that basement." She turned to Jayleen. "I wanted you to meet my friend Jayleen. She has a ranch up in Bellevue Canyon at the northwest end of town, just past Landport. She raises alpacas."

Cassie's eyes widened in curiosity. "Alpacas? Are they like those . . . those animals that climb over mountains and stuff?"

Jayleen smiled at Cassie. "They certainly are, Cassie. Alpacas are smaller cousins of llamas, who're the bigger, curlier-haired animals that you see in movies and on TV. They're the ones carrying packs and all sorts of gear slung over their backs in the mountains."

"Llamas, yeah. That's it. I forgot the name." Cassie nodded. Looking back at Jayleen, she said, "So which one do you raise again?"

Jayleen walked over toward Cassie's end of the table. "I raise alpacas. They're about

183

a hundred pounds lighter than llamas, and people don't usually take them out lugging packs over the mountains. They're raised for their wool. Their blanket is over six inches long when they're shorn every year, and it's softer than any sheep's fleece." She turned to Kelly. "We have to ask Mimi if she has any of my prize-winning fleeces from last year that she can show Cassie."

"We'll find out. But I'll bet Cassie has already spotted several skeins of alpaca yarn around the shop — haven't you?"

Cassie brightened. "Oh, yeah! Now I remember seeing that word on the skein package. So those come from your sheep — uh, alpacas?"

Jayleen gave a good-natured laugh. "Not all of them. Mimi gets yarns from lots of breeders and spinners. But she always makes sure to buy some of my fleeces, and Burt spins them. Especially two of my prize-winning females. They've got gorgeous caramel-colored fleeces."

"Wow, they sound really pretty," Cassie said, clearly interested.

"They sure are. Maybe you'd like to come up to my ranch sometime and see my herd. They've all been shorn, getting ready for the Wool Market in Estes Park weekend after next."

"Jayleen's got a beautiful place up high in Bellevue Canyon. I escape up there whenever I can, simply to relax," Kelly added, noticing Cassie's obvious interest.

"But first, I think you might like to see a working sheep ranch. Kelly's good friend Curt Stackhouse has a spread closer to Fort Connor, near Buckhorn Canyon."

"Boy, there sure are a lot of canyons around here," Cassie observed.

Both Kelly and Jayleen laughed. "You're right about that," Kelly said. "Curt's ranch is on the other side of that big reservoir on the west side of town. And he's got lots of sheep, as well as some cattle, too. You'd like it. We all love going out to Curt's ranch and Jayleen's for cookouts and get-togethers."

"And this Saturday would be a great time for you to come, Cassie. Curt's having his annual summer barbecue for all his grandchildren and nieces and nephews, moms and dads. There'll be a whole passel of kids. And lots of animals, not just sheep and cattle but horses, too."

Cassie's face lit up. "Horses! Wow! I've only seen them up close when our class has gone on some field trip. Or the state fair. Grandpa and I went to the state fair a couple of times. Then it got too hard for him to walk around." She looked away.

Jayleen watched her carefully. "I'd be glad to take you over to Curt's ranch with me this Saturday. I'm bringing over a pot of my famous chili. You can ask Kelly if it's good or not."

Kelly rolled her eyes dramatically. "Good doesn't even come close. It's delicious, Cassie."

Cassie smiled. "Sure, I'd like to try it. And I'd really like to see that ranch. If it's okay with Pete and Jennifer."

"You bet." Jayleen nodded obediently. "I'll go ask Pete right now. If they say it's okay, then I'll pick you up here at the shop on Saturday morning, okay?"

"Boy, that sounds like fun," Kelly said, adopting a disappointed tone. "I wish I could go, but I've gotta go help Megan and Lisa beat Greeley in softball this Saturday."

Just then, the front door's jingle sounded and Megan came racing around the corner into the room. "Sorry I'm late, Cassie. I had a loooong phone call from one of my clients who was having problems. You ready to go whack some balls?"

Cassie gave slightly frazzled Megan a smile. "Sure." Turning back to Kelly and Jayleen, she said, "Can you tell Mimi that I'll finish this up after tennis? And I'd love to go to that ranch this Saturday, if it's okay with Pete. Mrs. . . . uh . . . Miss Jayleen."

"Just call me Jayleen." She smiled broadly. "I'll check with Pete now."

Kelly watched Cassie follow after Megan as they both headed toward the foyer. "See you guys later," Megan called over her shoulder.

"What a cutie," Jayleen said.

Kelly couldn't agree more.

Eleven

Kelly recognized her cell phone's ring as it cut through the noisy conversations of her Denver colleagues around the coffee bar. She took her coffee and stepped away from the crowded area. Donuts and coffee were a necessity to make it through long business meetings.

Burt's number flashed on her screen. "Hey, Burt, what're you up to? You still showing Cassie the spinning wheel?"

Burt's familiar laughter sounded. "No, I didn't want to scare her off. She seems happy with knitting up those little scarves Mimi showed her. She's finished another one already."

"Good for her. I bet she'll be a better student than I was. She doesn't argue with the yarn."

"That's true. Plus, she's got two great teachers with Mimi and Megan. Megan showed up here this morning to see if Cassie wanted to go to another tennis clinic." He chuckled. "I'm surprised how co-operative Cassie is. She's ready to try anything we suggest. She even started drafting some wool with me yesterday when I was spinning with a small class. I'd shown her how to draft when I was demonstrating the wheel the other day, and she got the hang of it pretty quickly. And today, she came into my class and started drafting wool for everybody. She'd sit next to each spinner for a few minutes and draft until they had a big pile in their laps, then she'd move to the next spinner." He laughed again. "I tell you, I'd never seen that before."

"Sounds like Cassie really enjoys learning new things. She's adventurous. That's a good thing."

"I'll bet she's never had the chance to be around so many different activities before. Her grandfather probably couldn't drive her to many places, so she may never have had a chance to participate in lots of different activities. I swear, my daughter is in the car all the time, driving my grandkids to one activity after another. Sports teams, choir practice, music lessons, gymnastics, soccer, Girl Scouts, Boy Scouts. I get exhausted just listening to her tell me."

"You know, I think you're right, Burt. Being around the shop and meeting lots of people are probably entirely new experiences for someone who's been living quietly in a home with an elderly grandparent. Except for friends and activities at school, Cassie probably hasn't had a chance to do as many things as your grandkids, for instance."

"Well, between you and me, I think my grandkids are overscheduled. But with Cassie, her going to the softball sessions with you and the tennis clinic with Megan got her involved with kids her own age. That's good. It's also a great way for her to make friends while she's here in Fort Connor."

"That's for sure. I noticed she fit in well with the girls in my clinic and seemed to really enjoy learning. Oh, that reminds me. Jayleen came in to the shop yesterday and got to meet Cassie. You could tell Jayleen took a shine to her right away. And she invited Cassie to come over to Curt's ranch this Saturday because all his grandkids and nieces and nephews are coming for the first picnic of the summer. Wasn't that nice?"

"It sure was. I'll bet Cassie will have a ball over there at the ranch. Sheep and cattle all around." He laughed. "She'll get to explore even more. Plus, some of those kids are around Cassie's age, so she can be around other kids. That's always good. Keeps them a kid."

Two Warner colleagues passed by, laughing loudly, so Kelly stepped toward the back of the room where it was quieter.

"I can tell I got you when you're in Denver. So, before I forget, let me tell you what I learned from Dan this morning."

Kelly tossed down the rest of the weak coffee. "Oh, yeah. He was going to see what was happening in the investigation of Jared Rizzoli's murder. What'd he find out?"

"Well, a lot of stuff, actually, but it doesn't seem to lead anywhere. They found the knife that was used in the murder. It was on the floor of the car. But they weren't able to get any good fingerprints because the knife was old and the wooden handle was broken and rough. Dan said they couldn't tell if the killer just tossed the knife down or dropped it accidentally, since there was a lot of blood on it."

"Well, stabbing someone in the throat is bound to create a lot of blood, right?"

"Ohhhh, yeah. And the main artery was cut, so it spurted out, I'm sure."

Kelly could picture the gruesome scene. "Yuck. That had to be messy, which means the killer had to have a lot of blood on his . . . or her clothes. That would make them kind of conspicuous, wouldn't it?"

"You're right, Kelly. They've gotten the time of death determined to be between seven and eight in the evening. At this time of year, we still have daylight. So you'd think someone might have seen an altercation around the car at that time of the evening."

"You'd think so. I mean, golfers are still on the course, hitting balls. Of course, the car was parked behind those thick trees."

"Dan says they're still questioning people who were in the area to see if anyone observed someone talking to a man in a car in that driveway. Surely someone drove past, or biked past, or walked. Or even golfed nearby. Who knows? Maybe a golfer lost a ball and went searching for it. Someone must have seen something."

"Well, you'd think they'd definitely notice someone who had a lot of blood on their clothes, that's for sure."

"You'd think. Meanwhile, they're following up on any leads or information that's called in. Something's bound to turn up."

Kelly couldn't resist asking the obvious question, the most important question, to her mind. "Did Dan give any hint as to how the detectives are looking at Malcolm and Barbara? I learned from Madge yesterday that Barbara doesn't have an alibi for that night, either. Can you believe she went driving into the canyon alone?"

Burt's long sigh sounded over the line. "I know, Kelly. I'm as perplexed as you are. Malcolm's lapse is more explainable. Heck, the guy was a recovering alcoholic and he had a traumatic encounter with the man who was responsible for Malcolm's entire life being turned upside down. But Barbara . . ." He paused. "Barbara's unexplained disappearance that night looks more suspicious. It's totally understandable that she'd want some time to think. But to not even remember where she drove for all that time. Well, that's simply out of character for Barbara. She's a take-charge gal who excels at details. What's more troubling, her absence followed not just one but two heated, emotional confrontations with Rizzoli. The last one, she had to be forcibly escorted away by security guards."

Hearing Burt describe Barbara's behavior brought a chill to Kelly's gut. "It does look bad, doesn't it? I swear, Burt, every time I try to explain Barbara's actions, I keep coming back to the question: Where did she go? Madge said she asked Barbara when she came home later that night, and all Barbara said was she was driving in the canyon." Kelly tossed the empty cup into the trash.

193

"That is not good, Burt, and you know it."

"I know, Kelly. I talked to Madge, too. I'm as perplexed as you are. And I tell you, I'm getting concerned because Barbara rarely came into the shop this week. Last time I saw her was the day Rizzoli was killed. She was only here for a little while gathering supplies. She also brought in more of Madge's fleeces. Usually she drops in at least two or three times, but this week, not once. I confess that makes my old detective's sense uneasy. Once again, it's out of character, and, sad to say, it looks suspicious."

Kelly hated that word. It was a good word, except when applied to someone she knew . . . or thought she knew. *But can we ever really know anyone other than ourselves?* she wondered. *None of us can get inside someone else's head or feel what they're feeling.*

"I hate to say it, Burt, but I've had the same thoughts, even though I didn't want to admit it. Old Malcolm may begin looking better when compared to Barbara. What do you think?"

"Boy, that's hard to say, Kelly. Both of them had reasons to kill Rizzoli. He ruined both their lives. But Malcolm could have killed Rizzoli in a drunken rage and not remember it."

"Have the cops found any leads to anyone else? Reading all those stories in the newspaper reminds you that there were a lot of people here in town that did not wish Jared Rizzoli well. And some of them were quite outspoken in their hatred of him."

"Yes, I read those accounts, too. And I asked Dan, but he said that so far no one else has appeared on the detectives' radar. No one else confronted Rizzoli in person like Malcolm and Barbara did. Telling a reporter how much you hate someone in a newspaper or television interview is a far cry from actually confronting someone face-to-face."

"Oh, brother, I was hoping that someone else had aroused police interest in addition to two people we know and care about." She noticed several of her colleagues return to the conference room. "Looks like we're about to reconvene for the rest of this overlong staff meeting."

Burt chuckled. "Seventh-inning stretch, Kelly? Better take more coffee. Are you coming back to Fort Connor or will you and Steve stay in one of those fancy hotels you like?"

"We're thinking of staying over, so we can go to one of our favorite cafés."

"Well, you two enjoy. Oh, hello, Lisa. It's

good to see you. Lisa just walked in, Kelly, so I'll see you tomorrow."

"Say 'hi' to Lisa for me, okay?" Kelly said, walking toward the conference room door-way. "She told me she was coming in to meet Cassie today."

"That makes all four of you girls. Now all we've got left are the guys."

"Yeah, we decided to save the best for last," Kelly said, laughing.

Afternoon, the next day

Kelly walked over to her car in the huge Big Box parking lot. Other stores, large and small, crouched around the brand-name retailer, in hope of attracting some of the customers who clogged Big Box's parking lot. Across the street, the Lambspun knitting and fiber shop hugged the corner, the golf course's greens stretching behind.

Kelly heard the distinctive beep on her smartphone that signaled a text message. *Just saw your message. Our game has been moved to the fields north of town, right?* Steve asked.

She quickly sent her reply: *Yes. I'm about to drive there now. Where are you?*

At a fast food. Tell them I'm on my way.

Kelly unlocked her car door and got in just as her phone sounded with a call this time rather than a text message.

"Hey, Lisa, are you at the fields already?" Kelly asked, noticing her friend's name.

"I sure am, and it's a good thing. The Cheyenne team has brought in a whole bunch of fans, and the bleachers on this side are nearly full. I'm saving a place for you and Megan."

"Good. Steve's on his way. Hopefully traffic will cooperate."

"Let's hope. Pete and Jennifer are coming, and bringing Cassie."

"That's great! Cassie will enjoy it, I bet. She's really doing well at my summer clinic. Most of the girls at that age haven't had a chance to play before, and some are slow to get a feel for it. You know, throwing and catching and stuff."

"Have they started batting yet?"

"They start next week," Kelly said. "That should be fun. I may use the little kids T-ball holder for the first couple of times."

"That's a good idea. Hey, my schedule is a little lighter next week. Why don't I come over and help out and pitch a few times. Real slow."

"That would be great! Thanks, Lisa. You're a sweetie."

"By the way, Greg and I went over to Pete and Jen's last night. I'd had a chance to talk with Cassie yesterday afternoon, so I thought it would be a good time for Greg to come and meet her. He also brought that spare laptop for Cassie to use."

"Wow . . . I bet she was excited when she saw it." Kelly chuckled. "Those big blue eyes must have popped out."

Lisa laughed softly. "I'll say. She was mega excited. She got on it right away. She hadn't had a chance to get on Pete's old laptop, and Jennifer keeps hers at the real estate office. So Greg helped her get all set up and onto a faster e-mail program than her grandpa used. With Pete's permission, of course. Apparently Grandpa Ben monitored Cassie's computer time closely, so Pete said he'd continue that."

"Boy, will they have their hands full. I hear all sorts of horror stories from my Warner colleagues in Denver. Some of their kids spend all their spare time online."

"Oh, yeah, I hear the same at the sports center and at the university. It sounds like some kids never get away from the computer screen. They don't play sports or anything. Call me old-fashioned, but I think kids need to be outside involved in some physical activities after school. Keeps them healthy."

"I agree," Kelly said. "I was in every sport they offered after school whether I was good at it or not. All through junior and senior high school."

"So was I. Let's hope Cassie will stay interested enough to keep playing. Plus, it's a good way for her to make new friends. She'll be starting seventh grade this fall. New school, new people."

That comment surprised Kelly. "Do you think Cassie will still be living with Jennifer and Pete this fall?"

"Actually, I mentioned that to Pete and Jen when we were over there last night. Greg and Cassie were hunched over the laptop. So I asked about Ben and how he was doing. Judging from what the doctors have told Pete, Ben is in for a long recuperation just to be able to move into a wheelchair. Rehab is going to be excruciatingly slow for someone his age and in his weakened condition. I've had some patients like that over the years, and it is a laborious process. Sometimes you'll get a patient who was active before surgery and who was in good physical shape beforehand. But from what I've heard, Ben was neither. So, I had to tell them my professional therapist's opinion was that Ben will not be returning to his home for a year at least, if ever. Most probably, he will transfer from the hospital to a combo hospital–rehab center for the next several months. With luck, he may be able to move into an assisted living facility, but I doubt it. He'll most likely need skilled nursing care."

"Wow . . ." was all Kelly could say, given the enormity of what Lisa told her. "I had no idea."

"Most people don't, Kelly," Lisa said with a sigh. "Only those of us who work in health and rehabilitation know what's happening. How serious it is. So, I advised Pete and Jen to inquire into what was necessary to enroll Cassie in Fort Connor schools. It's already June. Fall will be here before you know it."

"Bite your tongue," Kelly chided. "Summer's my favorite season, so I refuse to even think about its end."

"Okay, okay." Lisa laughed. "Hey, here come Pete and Jen and Cassie. Listen, hurry up and get here."

"I'm on my way," Kelly promised, and clicked off the phone. Tossing it into the adjoining seat, she revved her car's engine and turned onto the street leading to the north part of Fort Connor.

"All right, *Marteeee*!" Megan yelled, jumping up from her bleacher seat to cheer her husband as he ran from home plate toward first base. The grounder he'd hit into left field gave the long-legged redhead time to reach base before the outfielder sent the ball in his direction.

"Way to go, Marty!" Pete yelled. Marty turned and gave a wave to Kelly and friends bunched together on the bleachers.

"He's Megan's husband?" Cassie asked, pointing to the wiry redhead.

"Yes, poor Megan." Pete made a sorrowful face, which caused Cassie to giggle.

"It's a messy job, but somebody has to do it," Kelly added.

"Who's that?" Cassie pointed to home base, where Steve was at bat.

"That's Steve. He's my boyfriend," she added, sensing Cassie was trying to place people in her mind.

"And he's got the big bat," Pete added.

Cassie peered at the field. "His bat doesn't look any bigger than the others," she observed.

Pete grinned. "That means he hits it out of the park a lot. Home runs."

"Ohhhh," Cassie said, nodding.

Kelly watched the opposing team's pitcher send a low pitch over the plate. Steve let it pass. Ball one. The next pitch, however, fell right in the middle. *Oh, boy,* Kelly thought as Steve swung the bat, meeting the ball in the sweet spot. *"Yessss!"* She could tell as soon as she saw Steve's smooth, powerful follow-through. Not surprisingly, the ball sailed up, up, and over the fence.

"What'd I tell you?" Pete laughed. "Yay, Steve!"

"Wow! He's good!" Cassie cried, as they all jumped up and cheered.

"I'd say it's time for popcorn and soda," Pete said, beckoning Cassie from the stands. "You guys want any?"

"Naw, I'm good," Kelly said.

Jennifer moved over on the bleachers closer to Kelly. "While they're gone at the snack stand, I wanted to tell you that those two detectives came into the café yesterday while you were in Denver. They questioned all of us again about the day of Rizzoli's murder. I think they were hoping maybe we'd remember something else."

"Did you guys recall anything more?"

"Heck, no. Eduardo, Julie, and I still don't remember a thing. It was all we could do to keep up with the customers. Of course, the temp help wasn't there yesterday, so the detectives will have to track them down at their other jobs and in between classes at the university. They asked for a copy of their schedules so I gave them the one you made."

"Did they ask anything else? Anything different from the last time?" Kelly probed.

"Matter of fact, yeah. They took me aside and asked if I had any communication with Rizzoli the day he died. I told them I met Rizzoli at the real estate office right after lunch. I needed to give him his copy of the signed contract. He said he'd call me later that weekend and firm up closing details because he planned to leave town the next day. He'd return to Fort Connor for closing.

She leaned closer. "Then the cops told me they found a text message on Rizzoli's phone sent from *my* phone Friday afternoon of the day he died! The message said I wanted him to meet me in Lambspun parking lot at seven p.m. *Can you believe that?* That's the day my phone went missing!"

Kelly stared at Jennifer. "Good Lord! That can't be an accident, Jen. That's the day Rizzoli was killed. That means the murderer stole your phone and used it to set up Rizzoli!"

Immediately, images of Barbara and Malcolm started dancing through Kelly's head. Both of them had been in Lambspun on the day of Rizzoli's murder.

Jennifer's expression saddened. "I know what you're thinking, because I'm thinking the same thing."

"Barbara and Malcolm. They were both

in the shop that day. So, both of them would have had the opportunity to take your cell phone."

"Aside from you and the Lambspun and café staff, the only people who knew I was doing a real estate deal with Rizzoli were Barbara and Malcolm. They'd both seen me with Rizzoli outside."

"So it would be natural for you and Rizzoli to exchange phone calls and text messages," Kelly continued, sorting through the images in her head.

"That's right," Jennifer said, nodding.

"And Barbara and Malcolm are the only ones who threatened Rizzoli in public." Kelly released an exasperated sigh. "And to make matters even worse, neither Barbara nor Malcolm can explain their whereabouts the evening of Rizzoli's murder."

"Oh, brother," Jennifer said, shaking her head.

Kelly stared off into the trees surrounding the ball fields. "After I found your phone Saturday, did you check the messages?"

"Of course, but not right away. As you know, we were swamped Saturday even with Doreen and Bridget. So I never even had time to check for messages until it had slowed down a little after lunch. I didn't know there was a message sent from my phone, so all I saw was Rizzoli's message to me. By then, we all knew that it was Rizzoli who was dead in his car outside. So when I saw a message from Rizzoli confirming that he would meet me outside Lambspun at seven p.m., it freaked me out. You know, like he wanted me to find him in his car dead or something. *Yuck!*" She gave a dramatic shudder. "Naturally, I didn't mention it to anyone."

"You told the cops all this, right?"

"Of course. They looked really interested and wrote down every word I said. They showed me the message on Rizzoli's phone and I found it in my 'Sent' file. It was real short. *Meet me in Lambspun parking lot at seven p.m.* That's all."

"What else did the detectives ask you?"

"They also wanted me to tell them exactly where I went that Friday after I left Lambspun. And they said they needed to confirm my whereabouts that evening. I told them I did errands at a couple of stores, then went to see you guys." She sighed. "Thank goodness, that seemed to satisfy them."

"Don't worry, Jen. We'll vouch for you," Kelly said with a smile, patting her friend on the back. "I'll tell Burt you were questioned. Meanwhile, see if you still have any of those receipts from shopping Friday afternoon and early evening. They'll have date and time and location on them. Proof positive that you were in another location entirely. And we can verify when you arrived at Megan and Marty's."

"Proof positive, huh?" Jennifer said, her smile relaxing a bit. "I like the sound of that."

TWELVE

"Hey, Kelly," Connie greeted her as she stepped into the foyer of Lambspun. "Where were you the last two days?"

"Day before yesterday I was in Denver all day and overnight, and yesterday I was huddled with my other client, the real estate investor here in Fort Connor." Kelly fingered some of the fuzzy balls of synthetic fiber Connie was stacking in a pile.

"Well, you missed the excitement. Those police detectives came to question all of us again. They wanted to see if we remembered anything else about the day Rizzoli was killed."

Kelly kept from smiling at Connie's dramatic description. "Yes, I saw Jennifer at the guys' baseball game last night, and she told me the police questioned everyone in the café again. So, they came in here, too, huh?"

"You bet they did!" Connie said emphatically. "That's three times we've been questioned. I'll bet it's because *we've* got these big windows, and we can see everything that's going on outside!"

Kelly couldn't keep her grin hidden. "Well, you're right about that. When I stopped in the café that Saturday, I had to come over here to get a look at what the cops were doing outside. That's when I spotted Rizzoli's car being towed away, remember?"

Connie's index finger jabbed the air. "You're right! That's when I recognized it as Rizzoli's, too."

"Did the cops question Hal Nelson and Malcolm again? Or did you notice?"

Connie nodded vigorously. "Oh, yeah. You betcha! They questioned both of them again. And they also questioned Madge, too." Connie's expression changed. "Poor Madge. I felt sorry for her. Having to answer questions about her daughter like that."

Concerned about Barbara, Kelly picked up on Connie's comment. "Has Barbara been in this week? I haven't seen her since right before Rizzoli was killed. Have you?"

Connie shook her head, her expression conveying her obvious concern. "No, Kelly. And I'm worried. I've asked Madge about her, and all she says is Barbara feels really guilty about how she acted with Rizzoli before he . . . uh, he was killed, you know. You know, she's yelling at him and accusing him of all those terrible things, then someone goes out and kills him!" Connie's voice dropped into conspiratorial range again.

"Did Madge mention if police have questioned Barbara again or not?" Kelly asked, worried now.

"Yes, they went to see Barbara that night. Madge told me when she came in yesterday to teach the spinning class."

"Did Madge give any idea how it went? Anything at all?"

Connie's expression saddened. "Madge is really worried. She said she could tell from the detectives' tones of voice that they were suspicious of Barbara's whereabouts the night Rizzoli was killed."

Kelly was about to ask Connie more, but a customer suddenly walked up with yarn skeins in hand. So Kelly retreated to the corner armchair. Clearly, the police had drawn the same conclusions that she and Jennifer had. And now they were zeroing in on Barbara and Malcolm.

Kelly looked up from her laptop screen and noticed Hal Nelson climbing the back steps into the café. She rose from the chair near the back and stepped over to open the door for him. "Hi, Hal. How're you guys doing out there?"

"Thanks, Kelly," Hal said as he entered, well-worn coffee mug in hand. "We're doing pretty well, considering we've had some interruptions." He gave her a wry smile.

"Yes, I heard the police returned to question you and Malcolm again," she said, walking with him toward the waitress station.

"I bet you want a refill," Julie said, walking up to Hal. "You need any more, Kelly?"

"No, thanks, I'm good." Kelly held up her hand. She waited until Julie returned Hal's full mug to him and they had stepped away before she continued her questions. "Tell me, Hal. How did Malcolm hold up under police questioning this time? They were bound to be more intensive than the first time."

Hal nodded. "Malcolm held up okay, I guess. They asked about that evening, and Malcolm admitted a few things, but not a lot. He remembered I dropped him off in Old Town, where he went to a liquor store and bought a bottle of whiskey. Then he walked down to the river trail and sat under a tree in one of his old hiding places near the bridge over the Poudre River. Then he said he sat there and drank. Unfortunately, he doesn't remember anything after that."

Kelly met Hal's sad gaze. "Oh, no. I remember Jayleen and Jerry telling me about a place where Malcolm and some others liked to roll up in their bedrolls and sleep in the leaves not far from the bridge crossing. That's right down the street from Lambspun and the golf course."

"I know, Kelly. That puts Malcolm right over here in the vicinity of where Jared Rizzoli showed up in his car that evening."

Both Kelly and Hal stared at each other, and Kelly could read her own thoughts in Hal's eyes. *Not good. Not good at all.*

"Hey, Kelly, good to see you," Megan said as she walked toward Kelly's table by the window. "I didn't see you at the table working, so I thought you were still at the cottage."

"I was for morning phone calls, but I left to work outside. However, this heat is getting so bad, I had to escape into the air-conditioning."

Megan sipped from her coffee cup. "I know what you mean. I've switched over to iced coffee. You should, too. I don't know how you take that hot, hot coffee in this weather."

"I'm thinking about it, believe me. It's gotta be ninety-eight degrees outside, and it's early June. This is crazy." Kelly leaned back in her chair. "Aren't you going to tennis with Cassie?"

"Yeah, she was finishing up a project with Mimi, so I decided to get a refill."

"How's she doing? She's really learning a lot at my softball clinic."

Megan's eyes went wide. "Oh, yeah. She's picking up tennis quickly, too. She's hitting the ball squarely, and her swing is nice and natural. I think we've got a budding athlete here."

Kelly grinned. "Excellent. Is she meeting kids over there? That's what's so good about the clinic. There are several girls her age."

"Oh, yeah. There are at least three other seventh-grade girls taking classes. All good. And tomorrow Cassie will get to meet all of Curt's family. Lots of kids in that bunch. Marty and I will be over at the Stackhouse spread the entire day, helping ride herd over them. Jayleen told me she's bringing Cassie with her. And the chili." She winked at Kelly.

"Is Marty gonna bring Spot the Wonder Dog along? To entertain the kids, I mean?"

Megan rolled her eyes. "Please, don't

remind me. He probably will." She drained the cup and tossed it into the trash. "Listen, you guys beat that team tomorrow, you hear? Or I'll be all over you next week. Got it?"

Kelly whipped out her version of a Star Trooper salute. "Heard and obeyed, Commander!"

Megan gave a dismissive wave, ignoring Kelly's laughter on her way out. Kelly settled back at her laptop once again, ready to return to her clients' accounts, when Julie stepped over to her table.

"Did you see that article in the paper this morning?" Julie asked, leaning closer to Kelly.

"Probably not. I only had time to glance at the paper before I jumped in the shower. I had early client calls. What was it?"

"I didn't, either, but Rosa says there was a short article about car thefts and robberies in this part of town recently. And it said there was a gang of four guys who stole some woman's SUV from the Big Box parking lot late one night last week. And there have been other car thefts in the Big Box lot the week before. Rosa thinks they might be involved in Rizzoli's *murder.*" Julie emphasized the last word in a dramatic whisper.

"Wow, I hadn't heard that."

"I mean, maybe they tried to steal his fancy car and Rizzoli fought back? Maybe they killed him out of panic."

Kelly had to give Julie credit. She'd certainly created a credible scenario. "Who knows, Julie? That could be possible."

"I'm hoping the cops start looking for those guys and leave Barbara and that poor man Malcolm alone," Julie added as she wiped a nearby tabletop.

"I hope you're right, Julie," Kelly agreed in an encouraging voice, wishing that could be true. Unfortunately, even if the gang of car thieves were experienced criminals, they still wouldn't have been able to swipe Jennifer's cell phone and send a secret text to her real estate client. Alas, that act was done by someone far more familiar to the Lambspun staff and the people who frequented the shop.

Thirteen

Kelly hurried up the steps to Pete's café's back door. The caffeine lobe of her brain had been throbbing throughout the phone call from one of her Warner Associates colleagues. Kelly thought she'd remembered to buy coffee when at the store. Alas, she had not. The canister was as empty as the proverbial gourd when Kelly opened it this morning. Steve gave her a quick kiss and raced over to the fast-food outlet in the Big Box shopping center across the street to grab some coffee and a bagel before attacking the interstate to Denver. Only an intense two-mile run and a hot shower helped Kelly drive from the house to the knit shop and café. Her colleague caught her mid-drive. It was all she could do to keep a civil tongue.

Kelly charged through the door and headed straight for the grill, both arms outstretched and stiff, TV-zombie style. *"Cof-*

fee! Coffee!" she croaked in guttural zombie-speak.

Julie hooted with laughter as Kelly lurched toward the grill. Eduardo simply grinned, gold tooth showing. He'd met Zombie Kelly many times before.

"Oh, look, everyone! It's the Walking Caffeine-Deprived!" Jennifer teased, pointing to Kelly. She snatched the mug dangling from Kelly's hand.

"Fill it quick!" Kelly instructed as she leaned her arms on the counter above the grill where Eduardo was turning bacon strips. Their sizzle sent an unbelievably tempting aroma into the air. Kelly inhaled the luscious scent and her stomach growled. "I forgot to buy coffee last night and had to do a two-mile run, shower, and drive here with no sustenance."

"Didn't you eat?" Jennifer asked as she poured the divine black stream into Kelly's mug.

"I forgot that, too." Kelly gave her a sheepish look. "I was counting on the run and hot shower to help me make it here. Unfortunately, one of my Warner colleagues made the mistake of calling while I was midway through my hunger drive."

"I pity that guy," Julie said, as she lifted a basket of breakfast breads — cinnamon toast, bran muffins, hot biscuit — to her tray.

"You'd have been proud of me. I didn't take his head off. And I was able to control the Hunger Beast during the entire call." Noticing two crumbs of muffins that dropped to the counter, Kelly licked her finger and captured them.

"Did you see that, Eduardo?" Jennifer said. "We need to feed her fast."

"I've got just what you need, Kelly," Eduardo said as he placed a crisp bacon slice on a small plate in front of her. "That ought to keep starvation away until you order."

"Ooooh, bacon!" Kelly's eyes lit up. A childhood and into-adulthood favorite. "Thanks, Eduardo." She popped the slice into her mouth and savored the luscious, familiar flavors. *Mmmm.*

"It's the fat. Works every time," Jennifer said, giving a sage nod. "She's coming around. Saved from zombie-hood in the nick of time. Why don't you sit over there at the smaller table and have breakfast."

"Wait, I'm communing with the caffeine gods." Kelly inhaled the aroma drifting up from her mug. Then she took a deep drink. "Ahhhh, now I'm saved." She dropped her briefcase on the chair. "But starvation is about to set in. Why don't I continue down that fattening road Eduardo started me on and have an order of biscuits and gravy. Add a little sausage to the bacon."

"Why not?" Jennifer scribbled on her pad and placed the order on the counter. "She's staying on the Fat Road, Eduardo. Biscuits and gravy."

"You girls make me laugh." He grinned. "Always worrying about your weight. A little bacon is good for you," he decreed as he flipped over two spicy homemade sausages.

"I thought you always said it 'never hurt anybody.' Don't confuse me, Eduardo." Kelly settled into the chair beside the window looking into the garden and tables outside. She spotted Hal Nelson and Malcolm carrying two large paint cans into the remodel.

"Rosa swears by it," Jennifer said. "Ask her. She says it's good for your skin."

Now Kelly was really confused. "Your *skin*? What do you do, smear bacon grease on your face?"

This time Eduardo cackled out loud, joined by Julie, who was loading two breakfast platters onto her tray. "Crazy Kelly." He shook his head as he cracked two eggs at a time into his mixing bowl.

"No, silly, you eat it," Jennifer said, laughing softly. "You accountants are too literal."

"Hey, we can't help it. The numbers make us that way." She took another deep drink and savored.

"You guys were gone for that tournament in Denver this weekend, right? I know you'd mentioned it."

"All of us except Megan and Marty. Curt was having a family gathering at his ranch Saturday afternoon, so they opted out. Say, didn't Cassie go to that? I was here when Jayleen asked her last week."

Jennifer wiped off an empty table, pocketing the tip and check. "She had a blast. Jayleen actually took the time to drive over and pick up Cassie and take her to Curt's. She called around dinnertime and said the kids were still playing and having a great time and wanted to know if Cassie could stay for more burgers and chili."

"It sounds like Cassie was enjoying herself. That's great."

Jennifer looked over at Kelly. "Cassie loved Curt's ranch. Jayleen told me she was captivated by the sheep and the cattle. And the horses. Oh, boy. She just loved them. Curt and Jayleen took all the kids for horseback rides. Just around the property. Cassie had never been on a horse before."

Kelly smiled, watching her friend's face

light up as she related Cassie's adventures. "Oh, I'm so glad Cassie had a good time, Jen. I know you and Pete were worried about her making friends. I keep forgetting how old Curt's grandkids are."

"They're all ages, and Curt has a bunch of nieces and nephews and grandnieces and -nephews." She looked out the window. "And there are two or three Cassie's age. Jayleen said Cassie fit right in."

"I can picture Jayleen watching over Cassie like a mother hen, can't you?" Kelly said from behind her mug.

"Ohhhh, yeah," Jennifer said, catching Kelly's gaze. "I can't tell you how grateful Pete and I are that Jayleen and Curt have been so welcoming. Jayleen even invited Cassie to her ranch this week. Wasn't that sweet?"

Kelly nodded. "It sure was. That sounds just like them. Well, if Cassie liked Curt's ranch in the foothills, she's going to love Jayleen's spread up in the mountains."

"That's for sure."

"You know, I watched Jayleen the first time she met Cassie, and you could tell she really took to her. That's not surprising. Remember, Jayleen doesn't get to see her kids or grandchildren down in Colorado Springs. So, she's a grandmother without grandchildren. Don't be surprised if she adopts Cassie."

"Just like Mimi. Mimi doesn't have grand-kids, either. We predicted that Mimi would take to Cassie like a cat to cream. And we were right."

Kelly laughed softly. "Cat to cream, huh? We're really going with the food analogies today."

"Hey, I can't help it. I work in a restaurant. And I'm not surprised. In fact, Mimi and Burt invited Cassie to their place Sunday morning and afternoon while Pete and I were working. They gave her a tour of Old Town."

"Perfect." Kelly took another deep drink. Nerve cells had fully awakened now, synapses snapping. "You know, it looks like Pete's grandfather's heart attack is turning into a good thing for Cassie. She's come up here to Fort Connor and she's finding all sorts of things to do and people to meet. I can't help thinking that she might never have had those same opportunities living down in Denver with Ben. No disrespect intended, you understand."

Jennifer leaned against a café table. "No, I understand what you mean. And you're probably right."

Julie walked up then, Kelly's breakfast

platter in her hand. "I didn't want this to get cold sitting on the counter. Eduardo would be insulted," she said, placing the platter in front of Kelly.

"Oh, boy . . . biscuits and gravy," Kelly said, sniffing the scrumptious flavors drifting from the plate to her nose. "Good thing I ran this morning. My arteries won't like this."

"You'll run it off," Julie said with a dismissive wave of her hand as she headed to the grill.

"Well, I'd best return to the rest of my customers. I'll leave you to commune with the Fat Gods."

"Go ahead, rub it in," Kelly retorted, sinking her fork into a thick piece of biscuit and swishing it through the thick gravy, then popping it in her mouth. Heaven. Yummy and fattening and altogether delicious. Why was everything delicious also fattening? She'd have to ponder that another time. Right now, the biscuits and gravy claimed her full attention.

Glancing through the window, Kelly watched both Jennifer and Julie move back and forth, back and forth, between the grill and the garden, taking orders, carrying trays, serving every type of breakfast from the high-calorie treat Kelly was indulging in to fiber-filled bowls of granola and fresh fruit.

Morning sun streaked across the golf course, highlighting the clusters of golfers making their way methodically around the course. Some lingered, talking, while others moved as if on a tight schedule. No doubt they were — fitting in a fast round or even a few holes in between customer or client or patient appointments.

The thick screen of cottonwood trees that lined most of the driveway provided ample shade for the café garden as well as Kelly's cottage. And the former garage was looking ever so much better now that Hal and Malcolm had remodeled it. There was even a new coat of adobe mixture applied over the outside walls, and the red-tile roof had some tiles repaired. She swirled the last of the biscuits through the last of the gravy while she watched Malcolm carrying what looked like a drop cloth from the truck into the storage building.

"Hey, there, Kelly." Burt's voice came from behind her right as she swallowed.

She turned to him and waved, then pointed to her mouth. Speech was still impossible with a mouth full of breakfast delight. She did manage "Umphhh," as she pointed to the chair.

Burt chuckled as he sat. "Caught you with your mouth full, huh? Well, I won't tease you. I already had some of Pete's delicious gravy this morning. Half a portion, so I'm feeling really virtuous."

Kelly swallowed, then chased it with a big sip of coffee. "I succumbed, too. Couldn't help myself. I'm still adjusting to that longer drive from the housing development in Wellesley to here. I'm used to simply walking across the driveway."

"You're tough. You can last."

She gestured toward the remodeled garage with her mug. "Hal Nelson and Malcolm have done a good job, Burt. It looks like they're painting inside today."

Burt's smile faded. "Yep, they're finishing up. They should be done this week." He stared off toward the building.

Picking up on his swift change of mood, Kelly asked, "Something on your mind, Burt?"

Burt looked back at her, and one side of his mouth curved up. "Yeah, I'm afraid there is. I heard from Dan early this morning. Apparently someone called into the department and said they had been playing golf that same evening of Rizzoli's murder. The golfer said he remembers seeing a disheveled man wandering around the edge of the course that borders Lambspun and the driveway. Of course, Dan and the guys asked the man to come in and maybe he could take a look at some photos or maybe have an artist draw a description."

Kelly felt a cold spot appear in her gut, despite the warm breakfast. "Oh, brother. Do you think it was Malcolm?"

Burt looked at her sadly. "It could be, Kelly. Dan said the golfer came and gave a description to the police artist, and she sketched a figure that could very well be Malcolm. I even went over to take a look, and it definitely resembles him. Even if from a distance."

Kelly made a face. "Damn. That would put Malcolm right here in the same vicinity where Rizzoli was killed. What time was it? Did the golfer remember?"

"Yes, he recalls it was close to seven."

This time Kelly rolled her eyes. "Oh, man, it keeps looking worse. That's right at the same window the medical examiner gave for time of death."

"I know. Definitely not good news for Malcolm."

"Do you think they'll come and question him again?"

Burt shrugged. "I don't know if it would do any good, Kelly. Malcolm admits he was drunk at the time and can't remember a thing. That's what makes this witness's testimony so damning. Malcolm can be shown to be at the place where Rizzoli was killed at the approximate time Rizzoli was killed. But Malcolm doesn't remember a thing. So . . . as far as police are concerned, he's the prime suspect right now."

"How about Barbara?"

"I wish I could say Barbara is no longer being considered, but Dan confirmed that she's still very much on the suspect list. And from the way he was talking, she's just a notch below Malcolm."

"But there's no proof Barbara was any-where close to here that evening. She was in the canyon driving." Kelly glanced out the window into the flowering bushes outside. "Or so she says."

"That's right, Kelly. Barbara can't prove she didn't drive here that evening. She definitely had even more motive than Malcolm. Because she had two public confrontations with Rizzoli. She definitely demonstrated she had enough hatred of Rizzoli to want him dead. Plus, she was here in the shop the day Jennifer's cell phone went missing." He shook his head. "Hell, even Malcolm came into the shop to use the rest-room."

"I figured the cops must have asked Malcolm that question. I remember seeing him leave the bathroom corridor one time myself. But he usually came in the back way through the café. I saw him enter and leave that way once when I was working in the café."

"So, you can see why both of them are front and center on police radar. Malcolm had a public confrontation with Rizzoli and got drunk that night so he doesn't remember what he did. Meanwhile, a witness now stated that a man matching Malcolm's description was seen in the vicinity at the time of Rizzoli's death." Burt sank back into his chair. "Malcolm also had access to the shop and could have taken the phone. Now, Barbara had two public confrontations with Rizzoli and has no explanation for her whereabouts the evening he was killed. And she, too, was in the shop the same time Jennifer's phone disappeared. So, both of them are squarely in police crosshairs."

Kelly pondered what Burt said for a minute. "You know, there's one thing about that Malcolm litany that doesn't make sense. If Malcolm took the phone, that means he would be planning to kill Rizzoli. If so, then why would he get drunk before doing it? Wouldn't he want to be thinking clearly if he was going to commit such a crime?"

Burt gave her a crooked smile. "Right as always, Sherlock. That's exactly what Dan and I discussed. It wouldn't make sense in the Malcolm-did-it-while-drunk scenario. But taking the phone would definitely make sense in the Barbara-did-it-for-revenge scenario."

Kelly stared back at him. "Either way, someone we care about would be guilty. Damn!" Her cell phone's ring sounded then, reminding Kelly that client work was waiting.

"Work calls, right?" Burt teased as he pushed back his chair. "Why don't you work right here? That way you'll be close to Eduardo's grill if the biscuits and gravy urge comes over you again."

"Don't tempt me, Burt," Kelly said as she clicked on her phone.

Kelly rounded the corner from the central yarn room into the main room. Cassie stood at the end of the long library table, with several skeins of yarn piled on the table in front of her. "Hey, there, Cassie. What are you up to? Picking out a new yarn?"

Cassie turned quickly and gave her a big smile. "Hi, Kelly. Mimi gave me another

228

job. I've got to switch all the yarns in the middle bins in these shelves" — she gestured behind her — "and move them to the lower shelves. And all the yarns on the lower shelves have to go into storage in the basement." She took in a breath. "And then I have to fill the upper shelves with the new yarns Mimi has in boxes over there."

Kelly dumped her briefcase at the other end of the library table. "Wow, so that's how all those yarns get switched. I thought it was elves. Lambspun elves. But I could never catch them in the act."

Cassie laughed as she moved a pile of pale blue yarns across the table. Then she started removing a bin filled with light pink yarns and placing them all on the table beside the blue ones.

Kelly watched Cassie move through her task. Clearly, she had established a routine already. "Boy, I'm glad you're doing that. I'd probably drop all the yarns and get the pinks mixed up with the blues and mess it all up."

Cassie giggled this time. "No, you wouldn't, Kelly. You never drop balls. At least I haven't seen any."

"Ahhhh, that's because it's a ball. Not a ball of yarn. Anything having to do with sports, I'm okay. But I always make mistakes with yarn. Hey, I heard from Lisa that you've gone over to Greg's computer lab at the university several times and you really liked it."

Cassie's face lit up. "Oh, it's *awesome*! They've got all sorts of computer stuff over there. Greg showed me how to take apart a computer and how everything works inside. Then he showed me how to build a circuit board and wire it so a bell would ring. That was so fun! And all the guys there in the lab are real nice and they showed me stuff, too. Greg calls them all the Geeks." She giggled. "Greg's funny. And so are the guys. The Geeks. Greg showed me some amazing things on this superfast computer he's got there. It's *awesome*!"

Kelly started to laugh, listening to Cassie's description of Greg and the Geeks. "Didn't Greg bring you one of his older laptop computers?"

Cassie's blue eyes popped wide. "Yes! But it's *new*! Well, practically new. I mean . . . it's only a couple of years old. That's just like new. Grandpa's computer was *ancient*! It was *so* slow! It took forever to look at stuff on the Web. And this one is so fast! It's totally *awesome*!"

"Tell me, what are some of your favorite websites?" Kelly asked as she pulled the yellow-and-white baby hat from her brief-case, then sat there and knitted while Cassie described all the websites she'd visited with her new superfast, just-like-new, totally *awesome* computer.

FOURTEEN

Kelly stepped onto her backyard patio and sipped her coffee. Carl was snuffling around the edges of the fence, right side, then back. Scenting squirrel tracks, no doubt. Tiny squirrel feet in the grass.

"He's long gone, Carl. You were asleep on the grass while the squirrels were running around the yard."

Carl's head popped up at the mention of *squirrels.* He stared at Kelly in disbelief. *More than one? Oh, no! How could I have missed it!*

"They're back in the trees now." Kelly pointed up into the cottonwood trees spreading their branches and the welcoming shade. She spotted two smaller squirrels skittering across the branches while one larger squirrel — Brazen Squirrel himself. The Ringleader. El Jefe of Squirrels — sat on a branch nibbling succulent young seed-pods.

Carl looked over his shoulder, as if heeding Kelly's instructions, and must have spied his Nemesis, El Jefe, Brazen, in the branches above because Carl gave a small "woof." Just one.

Brazen didn't even move. He sat right where he was on the branch, nibbling away, unperturbed by Big Dog's bark. Barks couldn't hurt him.

Carl trotted over to where Kelly stood on the patio. He shoved his big head against her hand. Kelly stroked his silky-smooth black head. "It's frustrating, isn't it, Carl? The squirrels have your nap schedule memorized. So they wait for you to fall asleep before they race around and cavort about your yard. Without your permission!"

Carl frowned in that Rottweiler way, knotting his eyebrows together in a worried/puzzled expression. *Not fair! Not fair! I want to chase them!*

"I know," she soothed as she continued to stroke silky ears now. "Big dogs have to have their morning naps. It's necessary. Just like squirrels have to watch and wait so they can scurry about your yard and find good things to eat. The little guys need an advantage. Big dogs can be scary."

Almost as if he were agreeing with her, Brazen chattered loudly from the branches above the back fence. Of course, that totally distracted Carl from his head rub and he raced toward the back fence, barking his displeasure.

Kelly went back inside her cottage office and slid the screen door shut. Carl was happily barking at Brazen, and Brazen was just as content to chatter from above, fussing at Carl in squirrel-speak. *All is well.*

Kelly slid her laptop into her briefcase and shoved in a client file for good measure. Maybe she'd finish Arthur Housemann's rental real estate spreadsheets outside in the garden once the lunch crowd left. Grabbing her briefcase and half-filled coffee mug, Kelly headed out of the cottage and across the driveway. Glancing toward the nearly completed remodeled storage building, she didn't see either Hal or Malcolm, so she figured they were still inside the building painting. Hal Nelson's truck was still parked along the driveway.

Kelly saw Jennifer moving about the tables in the shady garden, now crowded with customers. Every table was full. Speeding up the brick steps to Lambspun's front entry, Kelly made herself pause, then slowly opened the door. She'd learned to slow down after several near collisions occurred. Entering the foyer, Kelly trailed her fingers across a soft rose red mohair yarn, its color deepening into scarlet.

"Hello, Kelly," Mimi said as she walked into the central yarn room. "Are you going to work here in the shop?"

"For a little while, until the lunch crowd diminishes. Then I'm going to settle into the garden before it's too hot." Walking over to the library table, she dropped her briefcase onto a nearby chair. "Let's see, it's Tuesday afternoon, so that means Cassie is visiting Lisa at the sports center, right?"

Mimi smiled. "Yes, she is. Lisa came by about an hour ago. By the way, Cassie told me she really enjoyed your softball clinic this morning. It sounds like she's made some new friends, too."

"She's doing great, actually," Kelly said as she settled into the chair. "She's moving well on the field, and her throwing has improved, too. And the girls all seem to get along well together. So I've noticed some teamwork happening. Always a good thing." She gave Mimi a wink.

Mimi started straightening the items scattered about the middle of the long table. A bunch of miscellany like scissors, crochet hooks, and stitch holders were spread on a tray in a small pile, next to the teapot and cups. "Did Lisa get to help with the batting practice? I know she wanted to."

"Yes, bless her heart," Kelly said as she slid her laptop from her briefcase. "With the two of us coaching them, the girls have *really* improved. I have no doubt they'll all be chosen for the softball team wherever they're going to middle school this fall."

"I agree with Lisa. I don't think Pete's grandfather will be able to return to parenting Cassie anytime soon. If ever. So, that means she'd be going to middle school here in Fort Connor."

Kelly nodded. "Lisa told me she'd talked to Pete and Jennifer about it. So they'd start looking into getting whatever documents they'd need to enroll Cassie."

Mimi straightened and stared off toward the windows with a pensive expression. "My goodness . . . think of all the changes that are happening all around us. Look at Pete and Jennifer, suddenly having to become parents of a preteen. And they're doing such a great job, too. Cassie seems very happy with them." Mimi's smile returned. "It sounds like they've all finally gotten used to the new house and where to find things. I'm so happy Steve had a house available for them to rent."

"Well, everything just sort of fell into place. I've noticed when that happens, it's a good sign."

Mimi's expression sobered once again. "Yes, that is a good sign. And we need those. Goodness knows, we do. There are other things happening all around us that aren't good at all."

Kelly leaned back into her chair and picked up her mug. She could tell Mimi was worrying about something, and Kelly had a good guess about what. "You're worried about the Rizzoli investigation, aren't you? Burt told me yesterday that someone saw a man who looked like Malcolm around the driveway the same night Rizzoli was killed."

Mimi walked around the table and pulled out a chair near Kelly. She glanced over her shoulder toward the browsing customers in the central yarn room. "I know, and I feel sorry for that poor man," she said in a lowered voice. "But this morning, I heard something worse. One of the detectives returned to ask Rosa and Connie more questions. He wanted to know if they'd seen anything unusual on the days before the murder, either inside the shop or outside. And he mentioned both Malcolm and Barbara in particular."

Kelly leaned closer. "They're probably making sure both Barbara and Malcolm had access to the shop. That's the only way either of them could have taken Jennifer's phone."

Mimi's face screwed up in vexation. "I know, but it sounds so horrible to even talk about it. It sounds like we think both of them are capable of murder!" She rasped the last word softly.

"I know how you feel, Mimi. I feel the same way. It's disloyal to talk about people we know and care about that way. But the police have to ask those questions." She peered at Mimi. "Did they learn anything new? You were there when they questioned Connie and Rosa. Did you hear anything that surprised you?"

Mimi chewed the inside of her bottom lip, and worry lines furrowed her face. Not a good sign, Kelly had learned. Mimi definitely heard something she didn't like. "Unfortunately, yes. Connie simply repeated everything she'd said before. But Rosa said she had noticed something outside. One afternoon, she said she saw Barbara and her mom having lunch in the garden patio. Then, when she noticed them a little later, Barbara was talking with Hal Nelson, and he was showing her some of the tools in his toolbox. Barb's mom was pulling dead leaves off plants in the garden."

Kelly looked back into Mimi's worried

gaze. "Oh, brother. That means Barbara saw the knife. I've seen Hal Nelson's toolbox. It's filled to the top with all kinds of screwdrivers, wrenches, wire cutters, knives, all sorts of stuff. Just like Steve's toolbox in the back of his truck." She shook her head sadly. "That means Barbara knew where to find a knife. Not good, Mimi. Not good at all."

"I know, I know, I know," Mimi chanted. "And I've been worrying about it ever since. I called Burt while he was out doing errands this morning, and he said exactly the same thing you did. Not good." Mimi glanced over her shoulder again at the central yarn room, empty of customers now. "I simply cannot picture Barbara killing that . . . that Rizzoli. I simply can't. Barbara's a nurse, for heaven's sake! She takes care of people."

Kelly gave Mimi a little smile. "Yes, she does, Mimi. But you weren't here to see Barbara confront Rizzoli outside at the edge of the garden. She was white with rage. Pure rage. It blazed out of her. She was shaking. It was scary to watch. I was scared for her . . . and scared what she might do. I was inside with her when Barbara spotted Rizzoli outside with Jennifer. She jumped up and yelled, 'Bastard!' then ran outside. I ran after her because, frankly, I wasn't sure what she would do once she confronted Riz-zoli."

"Oh, no . . ." Mimi's concerned expression deepened.

"It was frightening to watch, Mimi. Rizzoli exploded, of course. He told Barbara she needed therapy or something. He'd paid his debt to society. Instead of being cowed, Barbara accused him again. Saying he'd only served his shorter term at a minimum-security prison. He didn't deserve an early release because he'd destroyed too many people's lives."

Mimi stared into her lap. "Oh, my, oh, my. I'm glad I wasn't here to witness that. It sounds awful."

"It was, believe me. When Rizzoli stalked off, Jennifer took Barbara into the café to calm down. Madge came running out, too. Poor woman. I'm sorry she was here to witness it." Kelly took a deep drink of coffee, memories of those volatile scenes dancing through her head. "Of course, I watched Malcolm do the same thing the next day. Of course, Malcolm was more easily cowed by Rizzoli. Once Rizzoli pushed him to the ground, Malcolm just stayed there, staring at Rizzoli when he cursed him. That's when Hal Nelson came over to Malcolm to help him up. Poor thing. Malcolm looked like a limp balloon with all the air let out of it."

"Hal Nelson is a good man." Mimi nodded. "And Malcolm seems like he's really turned his life around . . . until Rizzoli showed up. Why, oh, why did that awful man have to come to Lambspun? None of this would have happened if he'd stayed away!"

"We don't know that, Mimi. Remember, Barbara went to Rizzoli's seminar the next night and confronted him there. Whatever was brewing inside her was going to come out, whether it was here or somewhere else."

Rosa appeared in the archway leading from the central yarn room to the main room. "Mimi, that Wisconsin vendor is on the phone."

"Oh, yes, I definitely want to talk to him." Mimi fairly jumped up from her chair. "I've heard enough sad news. I can't listen to any more. We'll talk later, Kelly." She hastened toward the front of the shop.

Rosa lingered in the archway, straightening one of the yarn displays. "Poor Mimi, she can't stop worrying about that Rizzoli murder. I don't blame her. It's awful to think we've got people here at Lambspun who're suspected of murder." Rosa's voice was softer than usual.

Kelly drained her coffee mug and used

that as an excuse to walk toward the front with Rosa. "You know Mother Mimi. She can't bear to think ill of any of her 'people.'"

"I know. I felt so guilty when I saw Barbara this morning. The detective had just come to question Connie and me again." Rosa looked over at Kelly as they passed between yarn displays. Her dark brown eyes shone with obvious concern. "And then Barbara and her mom came in right afterwards to teach spinning classes."

Kelly trailed her finger across the balls of silk and cotton yarns as she walked past. "Mimi told me you'd seen Barbara talking with Hal about his tools."

Rosa released a sigh. "What could I do, Kelly? I had to tell the detective what I saw. I had to tell the truth!" She paused at the two steps leading down into the front of the shop. Customers were already lined up at the counter. Mimi was handling their requests, phone still pressed to one ear.

Kelly reached out and gave Rosa's arm a squeeze. "You did exactly the right thing, Rosa. You had to tell the truth. I would have done the same thing, no matter who was affected."

"Thanks, Kelly, I needed to hear that," Rosa said. "I'd better go help Mimi." She skipped down the small steps and sped toward the front counter.

Kelly backtracked through the loom room and into the hallway leading to the café. Spying Jennifer near the grill, Kelly walked over to her, mug outstretched. "May I have a refill, please, ma'am?"

"Sure, you can. No lunch?" Jennifer poured a hot black ribbon into the mug. "You working in the café or in the shop today?"

"Actually, I want to hunker down in the shade outside once the lunch crunch eases up. Until it's too hot, that is."

"Good idea."

Kelly took a quick sip of the hot brew. Scalding hot. It was a wonder she still had taste buds on her tongue. "Mimi told me the cops came in this morning to question Connie and Rosa again."

"Yeah, I know. The detective stopped in here and said he'd been able to meet our temp worker Doreen. But he hadn't been able to meet with the other temp worker, Bridget, yet because of her schedule. I explained to him that she's wicked busy. She's juggling three classes a semester plus part-time waitressing jobs to pay for it all. Oh, and in the summer, she takes three intensive classes."

"Wow, I'm surprised she finds time to sleep. By the way, Rosa told police she saw Barbara talking to Hal Nelson before Rizzoli's murder, and he was showing her some of his work tools. That means Barbara had to see the work knives Hal keeps in his toolbox. I've seen them."

Jennifer looked at her, clearly surprised. "You're kidding!"

Kelly shook her head. "Nope. Rosa repeated it to me a few minutes ago. I'm sure the cops found that interesting. Apparently, Barbara's just a notch below Malcolm in the cops' suspect list."

"Oh, brother. And today of all days, Barbara accompanied Madge to the shop for the spinning lessons. I surely hope she didn't see that detective questioning Connie and Rosa." Jennifer lifted two platters of pancakes, bacon, and fried eggs to her tray. "Barbara and Madge are around the corner having lunch if you want to say hello."

"Thanks, Jen, I will. I've missed seeing Big Barb, as Jayleen calls her."

Jennifer grinned as she lifted the tray to her shoulder. "Big Barb. I gotta remember that. Talk to you later." She walked toward the main section of the café.

Kelly followed after her until she rounded the corner and spotted Barbara and Madge hunched over a small table in the alcove. Plates were empty, and they were sipping their coffees.

"Hello, there, you two," Kelly greeted them in a cheerful voice. "You're teaching some spinning classes today, I'll bet."

"Why, hello, Kelly," Madge said, her lined face crinkling into a smile.

"It's so good to see you, Barbara," Kelly said, looking into Barbara's eyes in an attempt to convey her sincerity. "I've missed seeing you here at the shop these last few days."

Barbara glanced down at her plate, almost as if she was embarrassed. "That's kind of you to say, Kelly. I haven't come in as often since, uh . . . after recent events. It's nice to know I've been missed."

For the second time that day, Kelly reached over and gave another Lambspun regular a reassuring squeeze on the arm. She had no idea whether it helped the person or not. But Mother Mimi did it all the time, so Kelly figured it must convey things that words could not.

"I completely understand, Barbara," she said, giving Barbara's arm a final pat. "But I wanted you to know that we're all your friends here, and we only want the best for you."

Barbara met Kelly's gaze this time, and Kelly saw the gratitude there. "Thank you, Kelly. Thank you very much," she said in an uncharacteristically soft voice.

"Why don't you sit in on our second class, Kelly?" Madge asked, as she placed a twenty-dollar bill on the table beside the check. "We've got the next class in half an hour."

"I think I'll do that. Watching you spinners always relaxes me," Kelly said, quickly reorganizing her work schedule in her head. Hopefully, that shady table in the café garden would still be available after the class.

Kelly slid her right needle into the left side of a stitch on her left needle. Wrapping the yarn around the needle, she smoothly slid the stitch from the left needle onto the right in the familiar movement. *Slip, wrap, slide. Slip, wrap, slide.* More rows appeared on the circular needle. The yellow-and-white baby hat was three-quarters done. A few more rows, and she could start the crown of the hat. Narrowing toward the center point.

"Well, I'm surprised the police haven't found out who the killer is yet," a middle-aged blond woman commented, breaking the last few minutes of tranquil silence. Her wheel turned slowly as she allowed the rose-colored yarn in her lap to move in the gap between her fingers and join the yarn twist on the wheel.

"I imagine there are a lot of people they have to interview," a gray-haired older woman answered. The pale blue yarn in her lap slid smoothly between her fingers and onto the wheel.

Kelly glanced surreptitiously at Barbara, who sat mute as she drafted a pile of moss green yarn into batten for a younger brunette woman beside her. This woman's wheel was still and only moved in fits and starts, Kelly had noticed. Still a beginner, the woman had not yet mastered the coordination of feet moving the treadles and yarn sliding between fingers and onto the turning wheel. A tricky maneuver, Kelly had observed. That was another reason Kelly admired spinners. There was no way she could possibly coordinate those treadle movements with her feet and the yarn movements with her fingers. Athletic as she was, Kelly gladly left the spinning to those gifted with that talent. She still had trouble knitting, for Pete's sake!

"Well, I certainly hope that the police questioned all those people who spoke out in the newspaper about how much harm

Jared Rizzoli caused them. I mean, if police questioned Barbara, they certainly should be questioning those people!" the gray-haired woman said adamantly.

"I agree, Ruth," the blonde added. "I've heard countless stories over the years about that man, and all the financial disaster he caused. So, I wouldn't be the least bit surprised if police are questioning all of the people interviewed by the newspaper."

"That's probably why it's taking so long," the brunette said as she allowed the moss green batten to slide slowly between her fingers and onto the wheel. Her feet moved the treadles back and forth.

"That's it, Karen. Nice and easy does it," Madge encouraged the younger woman, carefully watching her movements. "If you ask me, I think police should put more effort into finding that bunch of young thieves who've been attacking people in the shopping centers at night. Personally, I think they're far more likely to commit violence than any of the other Fort Connor citizens who were victimized by the awful man."

Kelly recalled Mimi using a similar phrase to describe the late, departed Jared Rizzoli. Clearly, the former swindler would not be mourned in this city. But Kelly also recognized Madge's subtle attempt to shift conversation away from getting too close to her daughter.

"I agree, Madge," another spinner spoke up. "I read that they attacked others in Fort Connor recently. One man reported that he'd been struck in his head and dragged from his late-model car so the thieves could steal it."

"I think it's entirely possible those guys could be responsible for Rizzoli's murder," the brunette said. "I'd heard that they had assaulted a man and stole a car in the Big Box parking lot that very night. I'm hoping police find those guys soon and question them."

Kelly glanced at Barbara, who was focusing her attention on stretching the green yarn once more, turning it into batten or roving.

Madge, however, looked over at Kelly and smiled. "Well, now. Mimi tells me that Kelly is Lambspun's resident sleuth. So, I'm wondering what she thinks. Are you suspicious of those thieves, dear?"

Taken by surprise at Madge's comment, Kelly simply returned her focus to the baby hat, while she thought of something she could say to the spinners — without getting anyone into trouble. Including her.

FIFTEEN

"Hi, Cassie. I see Mimi's put you to work again," Kelly said as she rounded the corner into the main room of the knitting shop.

Cassie looked up from the large cardboard box she was bent over. "Hi, Kelly. I saw these boxes stacked up in the other room and offered to unpack them. Mimi and Rosa are way too busy with customers."

Kelly noticed the two additional sealed boxes stacked on the floor beside Cassie's chair. Setting her briefcase and coffee mug on the library table, Kelly watched Cassie remove several skeins of coral pink and lemon yellow yarns. "More yarn? Where in the world are you going to put them? The shelves are full in here now."

"I know, I filled them the other day," Cassie said with a grin. "Mimi told me to make little stacks wherever I could find space. Then put the other two boxes in the basement."

"Mimi probably found a great sale some-where and ordered ahead. What's amazing is that all of that yarn will probably be sold in a year." Kelly dug into her briefcase and removed the plastic bag containing the baby hat project.

Cassie looked around the room, shelves stacked with yarns. "All this yarn will be sold? Wow!"

"Well . . . not all of the yarns, but enough of them will sell so that there's a regular turnover. I've watched Mimi's schedule for a few years now. She changes the whole shop at least four times a year. For each new season. And then she'll also bring in special yarns to spotlight, as she calls it." Kelly leaned back in the wooden chair and sipped her coffee.

"You've really been paying attention," Cassie said, observing Kelly.

Kelly smiled. "It's the accountant in me. I can't help it. By the way, Jennifer said you had a good time at Curt Stackhouse's ranch last Saturday. Did all his grandkids and grandnieces and -nephews come, too? Jay-leen says there a bunch of them."

Cassie's face lit up. "Wow, there was a whole lot of kids there, that's for sure. It was a *blast*! His ranch is huge!" Her hands spread wide. "But Curt let us go all over.

The cattle were out in the pasture, so we stayed out of there. But he let some of us who were older go into the sheep pasture and pat the baby lambs that were born this spring. They're so cute and fuzzy. I can't believe we get all this yarn from those little guys. And then we went to the stables and saw the horses, and we even got to ride them! Curt and Jayleen took us out in little groups riding around the ranch. It was *so* much fun!"

Kelly couldn't help catching Cassie's excitement. It was contagious. "I love Curt's ranch. It's so relaxing to go out there and just stare into the distance, open space on one side and the foothills on the other. It's great. I'm so glad you got to go. Were any of the kids there your age?"

"Oh, yeah. Curt's grandson Eric is my age. He turned twelve in May and is going into seventh grade like me."

"What?" Kelly said, surprised. "I thought his daughter's kids were all little."

Cassie shook her head. "Robbie, the youngest is five, but Tina is ten, and Eric's twelve."

"Wow, that's hard to believe. The last time I saw them was at a Christmas-tree decorating party at Curt's farmhouse. His grandkids were there. Jayleen was there, and Mimi and Burt, and Lisa and Greg, Steve and me, and Megan. And . . ." Kelly stopped abruptly, her eyes popping wide as she remembered when that was. "Oh, my gosh! That was three and a half years ago! I can't believe it. No wonder I thought the kids were still little." Memories flooded her mind then. "Wow, that's the first time we met Marty. And got to see Spot the Wonder Dog in action." She laughed softly.

"You're kidding!" Cassie exclaimed. "Marty showed us Spot last weekend. He's *hilarious*!" She giggled even louder.

"Oh, yeah. We nearly killed ourselves laughing. All of us except Megan. She was furious at Marty because he was such a klutz he broke half of Curt's glass Christmas tree ornaments." Kelly laughed again. "Old Marty fell for Megan right away, but she couldn't stand him. We were afraid Megan was gonna punch him, so Steve and Greg took Marty into the other room to play Spot with the kids."

Cassie fell back into her chair, laughing. "That is hilarious!" she said when she could catch her breath.

"Yeah, it kind of was," Kelly admitted, reminiscing. "It was fun watching Marty slowly work his way into Megan's good graces."

"He was in love with her already? Like love at first sight or something?" Cassie asked, clearly fascinated by this courtship tale.

"Oh, yeah. especially after he tasted her blueberry pie. That sealed the deal for old Spot."

Cassie fell into another fit of laughter as Kelly sipped her coffee and let more memories dance through her head.

Kelly cruised slowly through the crowded parking lot at the business complex where client Arthur Housemann's office was located. Seeing an empty parking space at last, she nosed her car into the spot. Her cell phone jangled as she turned off the engine.

Burt's name and number flashed on the phone's screen. "Hey, Burt, how're you doing? I've missed you the past couple of mornings when I've been at the shop."

"I've been swamped with errands, Kelly. Whoever said retirement meant relaxation was crazy. Either that, or they'd never been around a shop like Lambspun." Burt's chuckle sounded over the phone.

"That's the world of small businesses, Burt. I remember doing the accounting when I was interning with a small business during the summers at college. The guy operated three automobile service centers in northern Virginia, and he was running around nonstop all day."

"I feel his pain," Burt joked. "Did I catch you mid-errands?"

"Nope. I'm going to see Arthur Housemann and go over those May financial statements. He wants to run some project ideas past me so I can work up an analysis on each one."

"Whoa, analyze a project rather than just jumping feet-first into it. What a concept."

"Arthur is a man after my own heart." Kelly turned the car's power back on and sent the driver's window down with a soft *whirrrrr* sound. "Jennifer told me you and Mimi took Cassie to Old Town on Sunday. I'll bet you all had fun. Where'd you take her? Did you stop at Walrus for ice cream?"

"You betcha. Mimi and I had a great time showing Cassie the sights, so to speak. Fort Connor may be a small town compared to Denver, but it's certainly got its own charm. And it's certainly easier to get around."

"I'm sure she enjoyed roaming around with you two. Since it looks like she will be living with Pete and Jennifer for the near future, this will become *her* town. And for all we know, maybe her grandfather didn't take her sightseeing. Has she ever been into the mountains?"

"You know, I asked her that, and Cassie said she's never been. Now, that's a shame. I can understand, because Ben apparently wasn't in good shape, but to live in Colorado and not get into the mountains . . . That's just sad. Mimi and I will definitely take her into the mountains, you can bet on it. That's if Jennifer and Pete don't mind."

Kelly settled back into her car seat, relaxing. She could tell experienced grandfather Burt would be eager to join grandmotherly Mimi in "grandparenting" Cassie. "I'm certain they will be happy to let Cassie take mountain trips with you two. In fact, Jen told me yesterday that she and Pete were so grateful that you and Mimi and Curt and Jayleen had been so gracious about spending time with Cassie. They appreciate it, believe me."

"Well, the pleasure is entirely ours, Kelly. And I mean that sincerely. Cassie is a sweet, smart, good-natured girl who's interested in everything. So she's great fun to take around. Clearly, she'd never been taken outside of Denver. She's been all around the state capitol buildings and has been to all the city parks and lakes with her grandfather. Oh, and the aquarium and the planetarium and the amusement parks. So, she has seen those. Plus, I quizzed her on Colorado history and she's got that down pat. In fact, she's got a real interest in history. Ben apparently took her to all the history museums in Denver. Including Molly Brown. Cassie was fascinated with all the photos of the *Titanic* and Molly and her husband. So, we may take a little trip this summer down to Leadville and some of the other mining towns. She's got a few gaps in American history, but she loves to read. So I gave her one of the books that I started my daughter with when she was in elementary school. It's a little young for Cassie, but the author does a great job of covering every part of American history from the earliest beginnings to present day. Or, rather, a couple of decades ago."

Kelly smiled as she sat, listening to Burt ramble on about Cassie and history and museums and sightseeing trips. What a great grandfather he was. Burt sounded like the ideal grandfather to Kelly's way of thinking. He was genuinely interested in Cassie, even her education. Jennifer and Pete didn't know how lucky they were. Or . . . maybe they did.

"Boy, Burt, Cassie is going to be one lucky kid to have you as a history teacher. I can sit and listen to you talk about history for hours. Whenever Steve and I come over for dinner, we love to hear you talk about the books you've read."

"That's sweet of you to say, Kelly. And I confess, it is a joy to be able to talk about history to someone who's interested in learning. That's what I see in Cassie. That eagerness to learn. It's wonderful."

"I wish some of my history teachers in high school had been as interesting as you, Burt. It was all I could do to stay awake in some of those classes." Kelly made a snoring sound.

Burt chuckled. "Listen, Kelly, I called to let you know what's been happening in the investigation into Jared Rizzoli's murder."

Kelly snapped out of relaxation mode. "Good. I heard yesterday that one of the detectives returned to ask more questions of Connie and Rosa. And Mimi told me what Rosa said. That was sad to hear."

"I know, Kelly. Barbara has moved closer behind Malcolm, from what I can tell. I saw her at the shop yesterday, and I swear, Barb is just a shadow of her former self. She's quiet as a mouse now, and you know . . . Barb never was one to keep quiet before. I don't know how to interpret her change in behavior. She acts ashamed. And that could mean many things." Burt paused. "She may indeed have committed the murder. If so, it was in another moment of rage, no doubt."

Kelly still could not bring that picture into focus in her mind. "Still, Burt, no one saw Barbara anywhere near the shop or driveway the evening of the murder. I know it looks bad because she saw Hal Nelson's toolbox and had to see the work knives. But there's no proof she came back to Lambspun or spoke to Rizzoli again. And you said police couldn't get any good prints off that old knife that was used."

"That's true, Kelly. So far, the only person who's been placed in the vicinity at the time of the murder is a disheveled man resembling Malcolm. But we may learn more today. Dan called me last night and told me that one of the temporary waitresses who worked in the café while Pete was gone gave police a lead. Doreen is her name, and she said that the same temp cook who filled in for Pete at the café works occasionally on Friday and Saturday nights at the brewery café across the street from the golf course and Lambspun. That café is also right across from the entrance to the driveway, so maybe this cook saw someone here that night. Dan said the detective would be going over to the brewery tonight before the guy's shift starts."

Kelly brightened. "Excellent! Let's hope Frank the cook saw something no one else did. I remember he seemed real interested in what the cops were doing that Saturday in the driveway and parking lot. He said he'd been keeping track of them out the window. Watching them. So, maybe he kept looking that night when he was working at the brewery."

"Maybe so, Kelly. And let's hope Frank the cook saw someone else in that driveway with Jared Rizzoli. Someone other than Malcolm or Barbara."

"I'll keep my fingers crossed, Burt. Rizzoli's car was parked right there in that section of the driveway, close to the entrance. It couldn't be seen from the golf course, but I'll bet the brewery café across the street had a good view."

"Let's hope so, Kelly. Well, I'm at the Big Box, so I'd better hang up."

Kelly reached for her briefcase and opened her car door to exit. Time to return to business. "Keep me posted, Burt."

"Always."

"Do you want any more iced coffee, Kelly?" Julie asked as she wiped off the patio café table.

"I'd love some, Julie. Thanks." Kelly looked up from her spreadsheets on the laptop computer screen.

"We're going to be closing soon, so I could fill a small pitcher with iced coffee for you if you're going to be working out here for a while."

"Oh, what a doll you are." Kelly smiled. "And put a double tip on my bill, okay? Don't argue with me."

Julie's face spread with a grin. "Kelly, we all know better than to argue with you. I'll be back in a minute."

Huge cottonwood trees shading the back stucco wall and the entire section of the garden kept the afternoon heat down.

"Well, well, Kelly-girl! I'm glad I ran into you." Curt's voice came from the side. She looked up to see the tall, broad-shouldered, silver-haired Colorado rancher stride along the flagstone pathway toward her.

"Hey, there, Curt," she greeted her mentor and advisor on all things ranching-related. "I haven't seen you for a while. Have a seat and join me in a glass of iced coffee."

"Don't mind if I do," he said as he pulled out the wrought-iron café chair across the round table from Kelly. "I've been busier than usual taking some visitors out to check

261

property northeast of here. They're looking to buy some land."

Kelly looked out toward the golf course, golfers enjoying the sunny June afternoon. "That reminds me. I was thinking I might take a daytrip up to Wyoming and check out the properties. I haven't been in six months."

"It's been seven months, Kelly-girl. I keep track." He gave her a fatherly smile as he placed his Stetson on his knee.

"I should have known you'd be keeping track, Curt. I was hoping you'd accompany me. That way we can go out and look at the sheep and take a look at the gas wells. They've added more, you know. I sent you a copy of the drilling company's report."

"I was thinking you might like to take a little ride around up there. Chet Brewster is still taking care of things for you, right?"

"Yes, he is, and he's getting married this month." Kelly smiled. "He's always looked so young to me. I wonder if he's going to want to continue supervising the ranch. He may want to start building his own."

Curt gave her a look. "Chet Brewster may want to start building a place of his own, Kelly, but you know young folks nowadays can't qualify for mortgage loans. Certainly not someone like Chet, who works part-time as a rancher and part-time for the building supply store in Cheyenne." He shook his head. "It's a damn shame. Youngsters like Chet who want to go into ranching won't be able to buy any land of their own to start a spread for several years. Who knows how long it'll take for banks to get back to business as usual lending money."

Kelly pondered what Curt had said. "I wish there was a way to help. Chet's a good man and a good ranch supervisor." She looked out over the golf course again. "There's a lot of unused space on that property."

Curt peered at her. "I can see your mind working, Kelly. You'd like to provide housing for Chet and his new bride. But you've got the charity school for girls in your cousin Martha's ranch house. That only leaves the barns and the outbuildings, but they're taken up with feed storage and the animals. There's no other space, unless Chet wants to bring in a mobile home."

"Hmmmm, that's a possibility," Kelly said with a smile.

Curt looked at Kelly for a long minute. She knew him well enough to know Curt was considering what she'd said.

SIXTEEN

Kelly pushed open the café front door and hurried inside. Determined to resist the tempting breakfast aromas wafting through the air this time, she walked around the corner leading to the back of the café and the grill. Then she spotted Cassie sitting alone at a small side table in the alcove, knitting.

"Hey, Cassie, is that a new scarf you're making? I love that cherry red with green running through it."

Cassie looked up from her needles and smiled brightly. "Hi, Kelly. I'm waiting for Lisa to pick me up, so I thought I'd finish this scarf while I wait."

Julie snatched Kelly's dangling coffee mug as she passed by. "Looks like you could use a fill-up."

"Mind reader," Kelly teased as Julie headed to the grill. "Boy, I'm impressed, Cassie. You finish scarves way faster than I ever did," she said as she walked over to Cassie's table. Leaning over, she fingered the long, dangling end of soft mohair and wool combination. "Your stitches are better, too."

"You're always saying you can't knit stuff, Kelly. Then I see what you've done, and it looks great to me."

Kelly dumped her briefcase on an adjacent chair and sat across from Cassie. "Great is stretching it. On my best day, I'm good. Or, halfway good. Or . . . partially good." She gave a dismissive wave. "But I never got close to great. Now, Jennifer is great. So is Megan. And Lisa, too."

"And Mimi," Cassie added, her fingers working the needles. Stitches appearing neat and orderly, filling the row.

"Mimi? Oh, she's in another dimension. Sometimes I don't think she's human. Maybe she's an alien, that's why she's so super good. She's from outer space, a planet of advanced beings." Kelly let her voice drop into a melodramatic tone.

Cassie broke into a giggle as Julie appeared with Kelly's refilled mug. "You're so funny, Kelly," Cassie said when she caught her breath.

"Only my friends think I'm funny," Kelly teased. "Say, what do you think about the

Health Rehab Center? I've been there when I was rehabbing a broken ankle a couple of years ago."

Cassie's eyes lit up. "It's amazing! There's all kinds of machines and equipment and stuff. And all these people are coming in on crutches or with their arms or legs in a sling, and they're actually *exercising*! And the PTs like Lisa — oh, wow, they must have magic hands or something, because the patients lying down on the tables in therapy rooms, you know, well, they're always saying 'ohhhh' or 'ahhhh' and stuff like that. Of course, some of them say 'ouch' or 'No, that hurts.' But the PTs still keep working on them."

Now it was Kelly's turn to laugh. "That's funny. And very accurate, too. I remember what it was like rehabbing my broken ankle. Of course, I also got to go in the therapy swim pool and practice walking. Now, that felt good! And it really helped speed up recovery."

"Oh, yeah, I've seen people in that pool. And they look kind of happy." She grinned.

"Jayleen told me you were going to her ranch. Yesterday, right? How'd you like it?"

Cassie dropped the yarn and sat up straighter. "It was *awesome! Totally!*" Her blue eyes grew huge. "It's *so* pretty up

266

there! I've never seen anything like it. And the alpacas are amazing. They are *so* sweet and gentle. And their big brown eyes are *enormous*! Jayleen introduced me to them inside their corral, and we walked around with them. They'd come up and gather around me and sniff. Kinda like doggies do when they see you the first time. They sniff you."

Kelly grinned, thoroughly enjoying Cassie's descriptions. "I call that an ID check. That's how dogs figure out what you are. They sniff you, then decide if you're okay or not."

"Yeah, kind of like that. Of course, alpacas are bigger and furrier than dogs. Except they've all just had their fleeces shorn, so they look a *lot* happier. Not so hot. Jayleen's taking all the fleeces, or blankets, she calls them, to the Estes Park Wool Market this weekend. Mimi's going to the market, too. Pete said I could go with them. It sounds like fun. Burt says there are lots and lots of animals there."

Kelly nodded. "There sure are. Even llamas are there. And they have demonstrations, too. Sheep are exhibited as well. They've even got sheep shearings and sheepdog-herding demonstrations."

"Oh, wow! That sounds awesome!" Eyes

popped wide again.

"I figured you'd like Jayleen's ranch. It's beautiful, and it's cooler up there, too. Her place is pretty high up in the canyon."

"I know . . . It's so pretty. And I love her ranch house. You can see the mountains from every window." Cassie gazed off through the window looking out onto the driveway.

Kelly recognized that "mountain look" in Cassie's eyes. She had it herself. Or she did once. Talking with Cassie brought back some of those old feelings. A "mountain home." Would she ever have one? Who knew? Steve was an architect. And she knew him well enough to know that the urge to get his hands dirty once again and build houses had never left. Even though Steve had become a partner in Sam Kaufman's company, Sam was already talking about retiring "one of these days." Steve would take over a very successful medium-sized Denver area construction firm. Would he ever build something in northern Colorado again? Kelly figured it was just a matter of time. Fort Connor and the canyons surrounding them were Steve's home turf. It was just a matter of time.

A slight breeze lifted the cover of a file

folder and ruffled the papers inside. Kelly put her cell phone on top of the folder, holding it in place. Hazards of working outside in nature, but the benefits far outweighed the disruptions.

The café patio garden was empty of customers now in this early June afternoon, and the café was now closed until tomorrow morning. Jennifer was at her real estate office, and Pete and Cassie had gone to Denver to visit Grandpa Ben in the hospital rehab center. The garden had settled into a peaceful, quiet, green retreat. Kelly's favorite place to work. Even accounting spreadsheets were enjoyable when done in such a setting. The intense summer heat had dropped due to the clouds darkening the skies now. Maybe they would have rain at last. If they were lucky. The last few times it had clouded up and thundered, there had been lightning strikes, but only a token sprinkle. Kelly could swear she could count the raindrops.

A musical tinkling sound drifted on the breeze from the wind chime that Julie had hung in the huge cottonwood tree near the front entrance steps to the café. The soft metallic sounds blended together pleasantly as they floated by. Kelly tabbed through one of client Don Warner's accounts, entering numbers, calculating, as the soft tinkling drifted on the light breeze.

Suddenly Burt's voice sounded over the wind chimes. "Hey, there, Kelly." She turned to see Burt walking along the flagstone pathway through the garden, coffee shop takeout cup in hand.

"Hey, Burt," she called as he approached. "What are you up to this afternoon?"

"I've finished all the errands and am going to teach a spinning clinic. How to fix your mistakes." Burt pulled out the chair across the patio table. "But I wanted to update you first on what I learned this morning."

That got Kelly out of her spreadsheet focus quickly. She saved the spreadsheet, and pushed her laptop to the side. "What did you hear, Burt? Did the cops get to interview temporary cook Frank?"

Burt nodded. "Yes, they did. Apparently Frank worked both Friday and Saturday nights at the brewery café across the street from Lambspun. When the detectives questioned Frank the first time, it was the Saturday after Rizzoli was found dead in his car in the parking lot. All the café staff were asked if they'd seen anything unusual or noticed anyone walking around the car. No surprise that none of the café workers saw anything because they were too busy cooking and serving customers. But this time, the detective asked Frank if he'd seen anyone around the driveway leading into Lambspun that Friday night. After all, the brewery's grill is at the end of the café next to a large window looking out on the street and right into the driveway. Frank told the detective that he remembers seeing an expensive car in the Lambspun driveway that evening. He'd paid attention because he loves European sports cars. Frank also said he saw someone standing beside the car, talking to the driver. He said when he saw the car being towed away on Saturday and noticed the license plate, he realized it was the same car. So, Frank sounds like a pretty reliable witness to me." Burt took a deep drink of his take-out coffee, the familiar green logo on the cup.

Kelly watched Burt closely. She'd learned to read his body language over the last few years, just as she knew he'd learned to read her signs. Burt had learned something else. Something he didn't like. She leaned back into the wrought-iron café chair and sipped her coffee. "That sounds like great news, Burt. But you don't look too happy. Don't tell me he saw Malcolm."

Burt gave her a crooked little smile. "No,

it wasn't Malcolm."

Kelly exhaled in relief. "Whew. I was afraid you'd say it was. Thank goodness. So, did Frank describe the man he saw? Is there enough for police to investigate?"

"Frank didn't have to describe him. He recognized the man. He said it was Hal Nelson who was standing beside Rizzoli's car, talking."

Kelly stared back at Burt, not believing what she'd heard. But the sad expression in Burt's eyes told her she'd heard correctly. *Hal Nelson?* She couldn't believe it. What was he doing there in Lambspun's driveway Friday evening? Surely, Hal Nelson couldn't be Rizzoli's killer . . . could he?

"Oh, no! I don't believe it! Is Frank sure it was Hal?"

Burt nodded sadly. "Dan said Frank was positive. He'd been working at the café for nearly a week, and he'd seen Hal and Malcolm outside and in the café every day. Frank even described Hal's jacket. It sounds exactly like the jacket I've seen Hal wear many times."

Kelly closed her eyes, not wanting to picture the blue sports jacket with the logo she'd seen him wear. Not wanting to believe that good, kind Hal Nelson could be involved in Jared Rizzoli's murder. That "awful man," both Mimi and Madge called him. "This is awful, Burt. Surely police can't suspect Hal Nelson of killing Rizzoli, can they?"

Burt leaned both arms on the table. "I'm afraid they do, Kelly. Dan said he checked into Hal Nelson's background after he spoke to Frank. Nelson does have a link to Rizzoli, unfortunately. Hal's mother lost all her life savings in Rizzoli's Ponzi scheme. And she was recovering from breast cancer surgery when she learned that her savings were wiped out." Burt shook his head. "Dan said he spoke to one of the attorneys who prosecuted Rizzoli years ago, and they had written depositions from all the Fort Connor residents who accused Rizzoli. One of the depositions was from Hal Nelson. In it, Hal said that his mother's despair at suddenly finding herself bereft of the funds she'd saved her entire life and counted on to pay her doctor and hospital bills caused her cancer to return. Tragically, she died a year and a half later."

The images from the newspaper stories relating accounts of Fort Connor residents who'd lost money in Rizzoli's swindle — sad stories, angry stories, tragic stories — appeared before Kelly's eyes. Barbara's father took his own life because of Rizzoli's scheme. Malcolm lost his wife and his career because of Rizzoli. And Hal Nelson's mother's life ebbed away with despair. All because of that "awful man." Rizzoli.

"This makes me sick, Burt. More people we know keep getting entangled in this Rizzoli murder."

Burt let out a long sigh. "I know how you feel, Kelly. It makes me sick, too, just thinking about any of the three we know being involved in this." He wagged his head in the way Kelly had seen him do since she first came to Lambspun. A lifetime of watching and investigating people committing crimes against one another.

"I would never have expected Hal Nelson. No one would have if not for Frank."

"You're right, Kelly. And Hal also was in the shop and café when Jennifer's phone went missing."

Without even thinking, Kelly found herself wagging her head in imitation of Burt. Three people she cared about were now suspects. This Rizzoli murder web was widening, stickier than any spider's web. She looked up at the gray clouds, darkening. A thunderstorm was definitely coming. Kelly could feel it.

Kelly shoved her laptop into her briefcase

and gathered her client account folders that were spread over the outside café table. The wind gusts were picking up as the sky darkened even more. Threatening. Rumbles of thunder and more lightning strikes. Still, not a drop of rain fell.

She'd decided to do a few errands before driving back to the Wellesley house, and was about to pour the last of the iced coffee from the carafe into her mug when she heard the sound of a truck engine coming down the knitting shop driveway. Kelly looked up to see Jayleen pull into a parking space outside the patio garden fence. She waved as her alpaca rancher friend stepped down from the truck.

"Hey, Jayleen. Come on over. I've got some iced coffee left if you want it."

"Hi, there, Kelly-girl. Looks like you'd better move inside," Jayleen said as she approached, walking through the garden. "We may finally get ourselves a rainstorm."

"I sure hope so. I was just getting ready to do some errands. What brings you here this afternoon?"

Jayleen pulled out a black wrought-iron chair across the table from Kelly. "I brought my champion gray's fleece to show her. It'll be in the Estes Park Wool Market this weekend."

"Ooooh, is it in your truck? I definitely want to sink my hands into that gorgeous gray."

"Treat yourself, Kelly," Jayleen grinned. "Or you can wait until the Wool Market. Why don't you and Steve drive up this Saturday. It's been a while since Steve's been there. He'd enjoy it."

"That's a good idea. I'll mention it. By the way, Cassie told me all about her visit to your ranch this morning when I dropped by the shop. She was beyond excited."

Jayleen beamed. "She sure was. Bless her heart. She had such a good time at Curt's place last weekend, I figured she'd enjoy seeing my place. What with the alpacas and all. And, boy, did she ever! She just loved those critters exactly like I thought she would. She wanted to wander all around the place. And she sure enough fell in love with those mountain views, yessiree." Jayleen gave Kelly a sly smile. "Just like someone else I know."

"I got a big kick out of listening to her describe everything. *Awesome* was her favorite word." Kelly grinned.

"She's such a cutie. And sharp as a tack, too. She was full of questions the whole time she was over at Curt's and at my place. Wanted to know where the animals ate and slept and what we fed them and how often they had babies." Jayleen laughed softly. "And of course she fell in love with Curt's horses last weekend. I expect he and I will be taking lots of trail rides this summer with the young'uns. Eric loves to ride. He's pretty good, too. Cassie will be a fast learner. I can tell by how she handled herself last weekend."

"I kind of figured she'd fall in love with your ranch. And the alpacas."

Jayleen leaned back in the chair. "Yeah, she took to those critters like a duck to water." She glanced around the garden and toward the remodeled garage. "Have Hal and Malcolm finished up? I don't see Hal's truck."

"I think they have. They were painting inside the last time I saw them here." Kelly paused, deciding how to tell Jayleen what she'd learned from Burt earlier. "Maybe Hal is taking some time at home. He's got a lot on his mind, from what I've heard."

That statement caught Jayleen's attention right away, and she peered at Kelly, clearly curious. "What have you heard, Kelly? Have police charged Malcolm or something? From what Burt told me, it looked like old Malcolm was at the top of their suspect list."

Kelly reached for the carafe and began to

pour iced coffee into her mug. "Someone else has pushed Malcolm out of the number one spot on that list."

"Lord have mercy! Are they suspecting Big Barb now?"

"No, I'm afraid Hal Nelson has claimed that spot now."

Jayleen's eyes popped wide. "*What?* That's *crazy*! Hal Nelson couldn't kill anyone! What in hell is wrong with the police?"

"They have a witness who saw Hal talking to Rizzoli in his car that evening, right in the driveway in the same place Rizzoli was found dead the next morning. The temporary cook who replaced Pete also works at that new brewery café across the street. Burt told me this morning that the cops questioned Frank yesterday, and he recalled seeing Rizzoli's parked car in the driveway. Apparently Frank the cook recognized the car and he recognized the man talking to Rizzoli. Frank had seen Hal come into the café several times while he was substituting for Pete. Burt even said he described Hal's blue jacket."

Jayleen stared at Kelly, her expression half shock, half anger. "*Damnation!* What in hell would Hal Nelson be talking to Rizzoli for?"

"That's where it gets sticky. Burt told me police found a connection between Hal and

Rizzoli. Years ago, Hal's mother lost all her life savings in Rizzoli's Ponzi scheme."

"Oh, Lord . . ." Jayleen wagged her head.

"And what makes it doubly tragic, Hal's mother's breast cancer returned about a year or so later, and she died. Apparently Hal was one of the Fort Connor residents who wrote to the newspaper with the story. He claimed his mother's despair at losing everything she'd worked and saved for over a lifetime caused her cancer to return and kill her."

"Good Lord almighty . . ." Jayleen whispered, her face reflecting her obvious sorrow.

"It's simply awful. I still can't believe Hal Nelson would kill Rizzoli, but . . ." Kelly let her words drift away. She had nothing else to say.

Jayleen stared out over the golf course. "God have mercy on Hal Nelson. He's gonna need it."

SEVENTEEN

"I'm going to be out of the office until the middle of next week," Don Warner said. "Let me call you when I'm back and we'll find a time to meet. I want to go over some of my ideas for projects."

"Sounds good, Don," Kelly said, cradling her cell phone between her chin and shoulder as she gathered file folders together. "Knowing you, I'm sure you've got lots of plans already."

Warner's chuckle sounded over the line. "You can say that again, Kelly. I'll talk with you next week."

"You got it," Kelly said, then clicked off her phone and dropped it into her briefcase along with her laptop and files. Grabbing her empty coffee mug from the kitchen counter, she left the cottage and headed across the driveway toward Pete's café. At nine thirty in the morning, it was time for another shot of high-voltage caffeine. Her brewed coffee was good, but Eduardo's was way better. Another dimension of good.

As she walked across the driveway, Kelly spotted Hal Nelson standing in the doorway of the newly remodeled garage. She slowed for a second, wondering whether Hal would want to talk, then decided to simply ask.

"Hey, Hal, do you have a minute?" she called out as she gave him a wave. "I was going to have a cup of coffee in the garden here. Why don't you join me?"

Nelson glanced up, then smiled. "Sure, Kelly," he said, and walked over to her as she stood on the sidewalk beside the garden entrance.

Kelly noticed Hal Nelson had a haggard look to his face now that she hadn't seen before. Being a police suspect in a murder investigation could certainly do that to you, she figured. Dropping her briefcase on one of the wrought-iron tables, Kelly pulled out a chair for herself and gestured across the table for Hal to do the same. "I need some of Eduardo's high-octane brew. How about you?"

"Don't mind if I do, Kelly," Hal said, settling into a chair. He gave her a crooked smile. "I'm afraid my first two mugs of coffee have already worn off."

"I know just how you feel," Kelly said as

Julie walked up to them, pad and pen at the ready.

"You two going to have some breakfast?" Julie asked.

"No, we just want some of Eduardo's strong coffee," Kelly said with a smile. "Mugs would be better. Cups don't hold enough for the likes of us."

"You got it." Julie laughed as she scribbled, then hurried off.

Kelly looked over at Hal Nelson. "How're you doing, Hal? I mean, how're you *really* doing? Burt told me what happened with Frank the temp cook's statement to police."

Nelson glanced down at his big hands in his lap. "I kinda figured you had something on your mind, Kelly. I've been able to tell that about you while I've worked here." He looked up and met her gaze. "I'm doing okay. Not great, as you can imagine. It really knocks your legs out from under you to learn that police think you killed a man." He shook his head slowly. "Lord help me, I never intentionally hurt anyone in my life, Kelly. So, it's hard for me to even comprehend all of this."

"Well, for the record, Hal, I believe you. And so does Burt."

An unmistakable look of gratitude appeared in Nelson's eyes. "Thank you, Kelly.

That means a lot."

"Unfortunately, you were one of the few people who saw Rizzoli while he was still alive that night," Kelly continued. "We know that Malcolm was in the vicinity, but he'd been drinking. So who knows if he saw or spoke to Rizzoli."

Nelson shook his head firmly. "I never saw Malcolm anywhere around here that evening. So he couldn't be involved."

Kelly stared at Hal Nelson, still protecting Malcolm even at his own expense. Hal rose even higher in her estimation. Other men would have eagerly grabbed at the chance to incriminate someone else so they could shift attention from themselves.

"I was very sorry to hear about your mother's struggle with cancer," Kelly said in a quiet voice. "That must have been heartbreaking for you to watch. I watched my father battle lung cancer, only to lose eventually. So, I have an idea of the sense of loss you must have felt."

Nelson stared solemnly at Kelly for a long moment. "I can truthfully say that was the hardest thing I've ever done in my life. Watch my mother's life ebb away slowly . . . and I was unable to do anything to stop it." He looked out over the garden patio. Several breakfast diners were lingering over late breakfasts or brunches. "She was such a gentle soul. Wouldn't hurt a fly."

Julie appeared then with two large mugs of coffee. "I already know how both of you take it, so dive in and inhale that caffeine, you two."

"Thanks, Julie," Kelly said as the cheerful waitress scurried away to tend other customers. She looked across at Hal. "I know what you mean, Hal. My father was an easygoing, good-natured guy, a great dad, and a good friend to everyone who knew him. Part of me still feels cheated that he was taken away too early. But then . . . I have to admit that Dad did help that cancer grab hold of him. He was a lifetime smoker." She frowned. "I kept telling him to quit, but he couldn't seem to do it."

Hal exhaled a long breath. "Yeah, my mom couldn't quit, either. She said it helped calm her nerves." He wagged his head again. "Until she got cancer the first time. That scared her, and she stopped finally. And she beat it, bless her heart." His mouth tightened. "She'd beat it, then that bastard Rizzoli stole all her money. That's what broke her heart. You can never convince me that wasn't the reason my mother's cancer returned. It was Rizzoli's fault she fell into despair and died. *Damn him!*"

Kelly saw the remnants of anger flash through Nelson's eyes and realized that the memories of his mother's tragic death were still very much alive in Hal Nelson's heart and mind. That made Kelly a little uneasy, and she decided to probe gently.

"I can understand your feelings, Hal. I would feel the same if it had happened to my father. Is that why you went to talk to Rizzoli that evening?"

He glanced over at her, then out into the patio garden again. "Not at first. I saw Rizzoli pull into the driveway when I was getting into my car. I'd just left a remodeling invoice for Mimi and Burt in their mailbox so I was standing there as he pulled in. I decided to set Rizzoli straight about Malcolm. Tell him about Malcolm's struggles and how he'd turned his life around. And then . . . tell him about my mother." He shrugged.

"What did Rizzoli say when you told him all that?" Kelly asked, leaning her elbows on the table as she sipped from the large coffee mug.

Hal Nelson looked over at her with a jaded expression. "Nothing. He didn't say a word. He simply stared coldly at me as I told him about Malcolm and my mother. He just stared at me like I was wasting his time."

He scowled as he glanced away. "Cold-hearted bastard."

Kelly watched him carefully. "And you told the police all this, right?"

"Of course. I told them everything I just told you now. They asked me what I did after I spoke to Rizzoli, and I told them I walked away and got into my truck. I watched Rizzoli park his car. He was still sitting there when I drove off, like he was waiting for someone."

The "mystery text." The text sent from Jennifer's missing cell phone. The text sent to Rizzoli asking him to meet her in the Lambspun parking lot that evening at seven o'clock. That was why Rizzoli was sitting in his car, looking like he was waiting. He *was* waiting. But unbeknownst to him, he was waiting for the killer.

She looked at Hal. Clearly he was still angry at what had happened to his mother years ago. But was he angry enough to kill a man? The murder weapon was a knife that came from his toolbox. Could he have killed Rizzoli in a sudden act of rage? If so, Hal was a skilled liar. He appeared honest and sincere. *Was he?*

"I can't tell you how sorry I am about what's happening with you, Hal. I wish I could help in some way, but . . ."

286

Hal smiled at her. "I appreciate it, Kelly. Just knowing you believe in me is help enough."

Kelly wished that were true. But she'd been involved in too many murder investigations to believe it.

"One Wicked Burger with all the trimmings," Jennifer said as she set Kelly's lunch order on the café table.

"And all the calories," Kelly joked as she scooted her chair closer to the table. She'd moved inside when the clouds darkened and the wind picked up.

Maybe this afternoon's thunderstorm would bring rain. Yesterday's clouds brought only lightning strikes and rumbles of thunder. All of northern Colorado needed rain. The capricious weather pattern called La Niña had stolen away the normal spring snows and rain. Nary a flake nor a drop fell the entire month of March.

Kelly couldn't remember the last time that had happened. March was always Colorado's snowiest month. And April and May usually brought delightful warm spring temperatures and rain showers. But not this year. There was a smattering of rain in April; then high temperatures arrived and the drying heat continued throughout May. Now it was well into June, and they'd barely had more than a few sprinkles along the Front Range.

The high heat caused their usually healthy snowpack to melt even faster. Last year's plentiful snowstorms in the High Country left the Front Range with a snowpack that was more than 200 percent of normal. This year, even the High Country was short-changed because of capricious La Niña. Less snowfall meant a shorter ski and snow-board season. And the snowpack was only 25 percent of normal.

They were all in Deep Drought, and the forests were bone-dry kindling. That was a dangerous situation because thunderstorms had routinely rumbled throughout Colo-rado's Front Range every week since spring. They brought little to no rain but multiple lightning strikes. Brilliant, frightening lightning shows that lit up the night sky in dramatic jagged forks, flashing. Dramatic and dangerous. The majority of Colorado's wildfires were caused by lightning strikes.

"I saw you talking to Hal Nelson outside." Jennifer gestured through the window. "How's he doing? I heard that Frank saw him talking to Rizzoli that evening."

Kelly popped one of the fries into her mouth and savored before answering. "He

288

looks worn-out and ragged around the edges, as you can imagine. Being the number one police suspect for murder would make anybody depressed." She devoured another crispy fry. "This is the most heartbreaking murder investigation I've ever witnessed since I've been here in Fort Connor."

"You mean since you've been sleuthing around?" Jennifer teased as she leaned her hand on her hip.

"Yeah, I guess so. I mean, it's so awful. Every one of the police suspects is someone we know and care about. That's awful! I've known Barb the longest, and I guess Malcolm would be next, but I've grown really fond of Hal Nelson since he's been working here." Kelly stared off into the café, not even seeing the other lunch customers there. "I cannot picture any of them killing Jared Rizzoli. Especially in such a brutal, bloody fashion." She screwed up her face, picturing how Rizzoli must have been killed, according to the medical examiner.

"I know what you mean, Kelly. It makes my stomach hurt just thinking about it."

"Jen, your order's up," Eduardo called from the grill counter.

"Listen, try to forget about all of that for a few minutes and enjoy your Wicked Burger. I'll talk with you later." Jen hurried back to the counter.

Kelly took her friend's advice and took a big bite of the thick, juicy burger topped with melted cheese and grilled onions. *Yummmm!* Ohhhh, the calories, not to mention the fat. But today Kelly didn't even care. Her conversation with Hal Nelson had left her feeling disheartened. So, her usual willpower had disappeared. Besides, what had Eduardo once said? A little grease is good for you. Or . . . was it a little fat? Wasn't that the same thing? She couldn't remember, but it was close enough. The Wicked Burger might not make her feel better about bad things happening to good people, but it did taste good. Wickedly good.

Barb turned the corner of the alcove into the café and noticed Kelly. Kelly gave her a wave while she swallowed another large bite of yumminess.

"Hey, Barb, how're you doing?" Kelly beckoned her over. "Got a moment for coffee?"

"Just a couple," Barb said as she approached, an empty coffee mug dangling from her hand. "I have to get back to the doctor's office in half an hour."

"Did you come over to help Madge teach a class?"

Barb perched on the edge of the chair across from Kelly at the table. "No, I brought over another of Mom's fleeces to Mimi to sell."

"Oh, that's right. Mimi will be at the Wool Market this weekend with her booth. Will you be going? Do you have items that you're going to put up on consignment at Lamb-spun's vendor booth there?"

"I was thinking about it a couple of months ago, but then all this other stuff came along and distracted me, you know." Barbara glanced off into the café. "I was going to try to spin more of Mom's fleeces, but I never got around to it." Her voice drifted off.

Kelly put the rest of her Wicked Burger on the plate and leaned forward over the table. "I'm sorry about everything that happened, Barb. I can't imagine how frightening it was for you, having the police question you again and again. I can vouch from my own experience, being interrogated by a police detective is not a pleasant experience."

Barb's mouth twitched into a little smile, then was gone. "You've got that right, Kelly."

"Have the police spoken with you this week?"

Barb looked at her intently. "No, they haven't. Have you heard something?"

Kelly pondered how to phrase what she was about to share. "I'd heard that one of the temporary cooks saw Hal Nelson standing beside Rizzoli's car that evening, talking to him. That makes Hal probably the last person to speak with Rizzoli."

Barb's eyes widened. "No! I hadn't heard that. Why would Hal Nelson talk to Rizzoli? Did they have an argument?"

Kelly shrugged. "Who knows? I spoke to Hal this morning, and he told me he wanted to tell Rizzoli about Malcolm and how he'd remade his life. Then Hal admitted he wanted to tell Rizzoli about his own mother's struggles with cancer. It was clear that Hal still blames Rizzoli's robbing his mother's life savings for causing her cancer to return."

"Good Lord," Barb said, staring off into the café again. "I . . . I can't believe that. I knew about Hal's mother. She and Mom were good friends years ago, and Mom told me about her fight with cancer. But I never really knew Hal well. I'd seen him around town with some charitable organizations and such, that's all." She stared off. "Do you think police seriously consider Hal a suspect in Rizzoli's murder?"

"I'm sad to say that they do. Burt said so. Of course, that's awful news for Hal, but it is also good news for you, Barb," Kelly said. "It was obvious that police considered you as a suspect, even though no one ever saw you anywhere near Lambspun that night. Now that there's a witness placing Hal Nelson here, that certainly means you've dropped lower on the police radar screen. Along with Malcolm. Witnesses saw him there, but he was drunk."

Barb released a long breath. "Lord, I hope you're right. But I hate to tell Mom. This will really upset her. She was fond of Hal's mother, Bernice."

"Well, I'm sure that will be outweighed by her relief that police no longer are looking at you," Kelly said with an encouraging smile. "She's been so worried about you, Barb."

"I know. Bless her heart. She worries so."

"I remember her telling me how upset she was when you were out driving the evening of Rizzoli's death. She said she'd gotten a bad feeling when you came home and told her you were driving in the canyon."

Barb looked at Kelly sharply. "What? Mom wasn't there when I got home that evening. Why would she say that?"

Kelly shrugged. "Who knows, Barb. Your

mother's been under a lot of stress watching you go through this police investigation and interrogation. She probably just got confused."

"I guess you're right. She has been under a lot of stress with this investigation. No wonder she's forgetting things." Barb smiled. "She even forgot about the neighbors' sprinklers and walked right through them that night. Her dress was soaked when she got home." Glancing at her watch, Barb rose. "I'd better head to my office now. Don't want to be late. Patients will be stacked up in the waiting room. Thank you for bringing me some good news, Kelly. Good for me, that is. I appreciate that."

"That's what friends are for, Barb." Kelly returned her smile.

Barb hastened to the café doorway just as Jennifer walked up to Kelly's table. "Big Barb heading back to the doctor's office?"

"Yes, indeed. I made it a point to tell her the bad news about Hal Nelson, which is also good news for Barb. She's probably dropped off the police radar screen."

"Well, let's see what else turns up." Jennifer wiped off a nearby table. "I just heard from Bridget, the temp waitress who works three jobs. She's looking for a few extra hours, if you can believe. Anyway, she told me the police detective was finally able to schedule a time between all her jobs when he could ask questions. So, who knows if she saw anything suspicious. Maybe she saw Malcolm over here before he got drunk." She shrugged.

Kelly didn't even want to think about it. She was tired of all the different murder scenarios playing in her head. She stared at the remaining half of her Wicked Burger. She couldn't eat another bite. "Did Bridget say anything to you?"

"I didn't really ask. This whole murder in the parking lot has spooked all of us. I don't think I can handle any more details." She gave Kelly a rueful smile. "You gonna finish that burger?"

"I can't. Could you please box it up, and I'll take it over to the cottage fridge. I can have it for lunch tomorrow."

"Will do. Are you going back there now?" She picked up Kelly's plate.

"Yeah, I have some phone calls to make, then finish one of Warner's accounts. We've got a softball game tonight in Wellington."

"Knock it out of the park," Jennifer advised with a grin.

Kelly nosed her car into the ball field's parking lot as she reached for her ringing cell phone. She saw Burt's name and number flash on the phone screen. "Good timing, Burt. I'm arriving at the ball field right now. What's up?"

"Hey, Kelly. I won't keep you. I just wanted to bring you up to speed on the latest and probably last round of witness questioning."

"Oh, yeah. Jennifer told me that police finally were able to meet with that workaholic Bridget. Boy, I don't know how that girl finds time to sleep."

"I hear you, Kelly. She puts most college kids to shame. Apparently she impressed the detective as a real down-to-earth sort. She told him she went over to the driveway that evening to pick up her bike, which she'd locked in the café's bike rack. She thinks it's safer than the one at Big Box." He chuckled.

"Well, that's entirely possible. Plus, no people coming into the café. Did she see anything?"

"Nope. Bridget said she didn't see Rizzoli or his car because she never even went around to that side of the driveway that evening. She retrieved her bike and rode off along the edge of the golf course, heading to another restaurant job."

"A working fool, as Jayleen would say,"

Kelly observed as she closed her car door and popped open the trunk, which contained her softball gear.

"I'll say. So . . . I'm afraid that leaves the situation as it was. Hal Nelson is the main suspect with Barb and Malcolm tying for second place."

Kelly heard his tired sigh over the phone. "I know how you feel, Burt. It makes me sick to think of that."

"Yeah, it does. Listen, Mimi and I are going out to dinner tonight. Something to take this situation off our minds for a spell. You guys have a good game, you hear? And knock it out of the park for me, will ya?"

"I'll do my best, Burt."

EIGHTEEN

Kelly spotted Madge crossing the driveway beside Lambspun, her arms filled with two large bags. Kelly hurried down the sidewalk to help her. "Hold on, Madge, I can get the front door for you," she called to the slightly built older woman.

Madge turned at the steps leading to Lambspun's entry. Only her head was visible over the plastic bags stuffed full of cinnamon brown fleece. "Why, thank you, Kelly. I could use an extra hand," she said as she climbed the brick steps.

Kelly skipped up the steps ahead of her and pulled the heavy wooden door open, holding it wide. "It looks like you and Barb have been spinning. Are these for the Wool Market?"

"They sure are." Madge walked into the foyer. "Mimi said she'd be glad to take up any fleeces I brought, so Barb and I got to work last night and finished spinning Sweet

Georgia Brown's fleece. It's such a distinctive shade of brown, I think it will sell easily."

Kelly followed after her. "I imagine your spinning went faster now that you and Barb have that weight lifted off your shoulders. Here, let me take a bag."

Madge allowed Kelly to relieve her of one bag of fleece. "You're right, Kelly. I am relieved that police are no longer scrutinizing Barbara, but I'm heartsick to think that Hal Nelson is now in their crosshairs." She looked at Kelly, concern evident in her eyes. "I've known Hal Nelson since he was a boy. He could no more kill someone than Barbara could."

"I feel the same way, Madge," Kelly said in a low voice, so as not to be overheard by nearby customers. "But we can't escape the fact that someone killed Jared Rizzoli. I doubt he stabbed himself in the throat. So, police are naturally going to scrutinize anyone with a grudge against Rizzoli. And Hal admitted to me he still blames Rizzoli for causing his mother's cancer to return and kill her. He even told me that's why he talked to Rizzoli that night. He wanted to tell him face-to-face."

Madge frowned, her brows knotting together. "I knew his mother Bernice well.

She was my best friend in Fort Connor. So I know how her despair affected her. And how her death affected Hal. So I understand his resentment. But why, oh, why did he choose that evening to confront that awful man? Of all times . . ." Her words drifted off as Madge stared out the nearby paned windows.

"I don't know, Madge." Kelly sought something to ease Madge's worry. "Hal told me he was outside putting a remodeling invoice for Mimi and Burt into the Lambspun mailbox. Jared Rizzoli drove into the driveway while Hal was standing there, and it sounded like Hal decided to speak to him on the spur of the moment."

Madge wagged her head, worry still creasing her face. "That awful man, that awful, awful man is still hurting people," she said in a quiet voice.

"I know how you feel, Madge."

Madge looked at Kelly, doubt still clouding her face. "Have you heard any more about that roving gang of thieves? Police should be looking for them."

Kelly leaned closer, speaking quietly. "They did find them. In fact, they caught them in the act of stealing a car. And when they interrogated them, Burt said the cops learned that all those guys were at a party

300

that night. Plenty of witnesses can swear they weren't involved." She met Madge's disappointed gaze with her own. Not knowing anything else to say, Kelly fell back on one of her father's old sayings. "The truth will come out. It always does."

Rosa walked up then and addressed them both. "Are those fleeces for the Wool Market? If so, bring 'em this way, so I can tag them and get them in the new storage building." She beckoned them toward the front room and the winding table, where Kelly saw tags spread out next to a large notebook.

"Looks like you guys are all organized," Kelly said, setting the bag of fleece on the floor beside the table as Madge did the same.

"Burt and Mimi will start taking things up to Estes Park tomorrow to the exhibition hall of the fairgrounds. Connie and Mimi are up there today setting up the booth. Tomorrow we'll be taking things up in shifts all day to get ready for Saturday morning's opening."

"Mimi and Burt will be staying up there starting tomorrow night, right?" Kelly asked, as her cell phone's music sounded from her briefcase.

"You got it. Go ahead, Kelly. I've got it

covered here. You go back to work," Rosa said with a grin.

"Slave driver," Kelly teased, then gave Madge's arm a reassuring squeeze as she dug out her phone. "Don't worry, Madge," she repeated. "Things will work out."

Madge gave a pinched smile. "You're probably right, Kelly."

Kelly sent the older woman one more reassuring smile before answering her phone. Her client Arthur Housemann's name flashed on the screen.

Delicious aromas of tempting lunchtime selections tickled Kelly's nostrils as she turned the corner into the café from the knitting shop. She'd finished the Wicked Burger last night before going to her game. There was no way she'd succumb again, she swore to herself, ignoring the yummy plate sitting on the counter as she passed by. Deliberately turning her head away, Kelly walked into the front of the café, away from the grill. Less tempting, she figured.

Spotting a small empty table near the front door, Kelly plopped her briefcase on an empty chair and claimed a seat. She quickly scanned the daily lunch specials and decided on a healthy blackened chicken salad with lots of greens. Plus a slice of

Pete's scrumptious whole wheat bread.

A young brunette woman who looked college-age approached the table, notepad in hand. She looked vaguely familiar to Kelly.

"Hi, there. I'm Bridget. What can I get for you today? We've got a fantastic tomato basil soup on special for lunch. And the spinach and feta quiche also."

"Hey, Bridget, you're one of the temp waitresses. I thought I'd seen you before," Kelly said, smiling. "Jennifer said you're actually juggling three jobs and going to school, correct?"

Bridget smiled brightly. "Guilty as charged. I'm insane, I know. But I can't afford to finish in four years otherwise."

"Whoa, girl. I wonder when you sleep. Jen told me even the cops had to bow to your schedule," Kelly teased.

"Yeah, I felt bad about that, but, hey . . ." She laughed softly. "Two of my jobs are right next to each other at the university labs, so I go from one to the other. And there're no strangers allowed in the sterile rooms where I work on cataloging seeds. So, they had to wait for a break in my schedule."

"Boy, I'm impressed, Bridget. You make

the rest of us feel like we're moving in low gear."

Bridget laughed again. "I don't know about that. You're Kelly, right? I've heard Jennifer and Pete talk about you. You're certainly not moving in the slow lane."

"Coming from you, Bridget, that's high praise."

"What can I get you, Kelly?" She poised her pen over the pad.

"You know, I was about to have a salad, but those lunch specials enticed me away. Why don't you bring me that tomato basil soup and the spinach and feta quiche. That's a favorite of mine. Oh, and a refill of black coffee, too."

"I remember that part about you, Kelly," Bridget said, then winked as she took Kelly's mug.

Suddenly curious, Kelly ventured, "By the way, I confess I'm curious. Were you able to help the cops at all? Did you see anyone hanging around Lambspun that evening? Jennifer said you parked your bike over here."

Bridget shook her head. "Naw, I'm afraid not. I never even went around to that other side of the driveway, so I didn't see that guy in his car. I came across the street to this side of the shop, right here in the front."

She gestured out the window. "This bike rack is way safer than that one across the street at Big Box. I keep my bike here the nights I work at the store. I get off at seven."

Kelly glanced out the window and spotted the bike rack tucked between the adobe outside wall and a metal storage shed near the front entrance. "That makes sense. Way too many people walking around Big Box. It's too bad you didn't see anyone else walking around that evening. That nice builder guy who was remodeling the garage outside is in the cops' bull's-eye right now. Apparently he was seen talking to that Rizzoli in his car." Kelly stared out the window.

"Yeah, I talked to him a couple of times when I worked here last month. You know, when Pete was in Denver. He seemed a nice guy. I'm sorry I couldn't have been more help. But I didn't see anybody sneaking or lurking around the building. Only that little gray-haired lady who teaches spinning classes in the shop. She was around the back of the shop at the faucet washing her hands."

Kelly turned back to Bridget quickly. "Madge? You saw Madge outside washing her hands at a faucet?"

Bridget nodded. "Yeah. She was washing her dress, too. Weird. I guess she'd been pulling weeds again or working in the garden. I'd seen her outside pulling weeds from the patio gardens. They're so pretty. She must be a gardener at heart, as well as a spinner." Bridget smiled down at Kelly. "Well, I'd better get this order in so you can have lunch."

Kelly stared at her blankly and nodded. "Sure. Thanks." Kelly watched Bridget hurry off toward the grill; meanwhile her mind was going a mile a minute. Her instinct was buzzing, and thoughts were bombarding her, demanding her attention.

Madge was seen washing her hands at the faucet behind the back of the Lambspun knitting shop. In the back. Outside. Where no one could see her. Why would Madge be washing her hands at seven in the evening that Saturday? Had she been pulling weeds in the patio garden as Bridget suggested? Or had Madge gotten something else on her hands? Something else that needed to be washed off. Something like blood?

Other thoughts darted in and claimed Kelly's attention, dancing in front of her eyes. Barb said that Madge was not at their home when she returned from driving around the canyon. But Madge had told Kelly she *was* at home because she'd asked Barb where she'd been when Barb returned from driving. That was a lie. Barb clearly was surprised to hear her mother had claimed to be at home. Barb also said her mother came in later that evening, and . . . and her mother's dress was all wet. She'd laughed and told Barb she'd accidentally walked through the neighbors' sprinklers.

Kelly stared out the window without seeing, her thoughts darting and zooming, little bits of information she'd heard or learned coming forward now. Rosa saw Barb outside talking to Hal Nelson as he showed Barb his tools. But . . . Rosa also said that Madge was there in the garden beside the fence, pulling weeds.

Madge clearly was there to see and hear Hal talk about his tools. So, Madge knew exactly where to find the knife that was used to stab Jared Rizzoli in the throat. Violently stab Rizzoli in the throat. The medical examiner said the wound was jagged, indicating that the knife was jerked to the side, too. A large, bloody wound in Rizzoli's throat, which obviously resulted in a great deal of blood. Blood that obviously got on Rizzoli's killer . . . and on the killer's hands and clothes.

Kelly pictured petite Madge squatting beside the outside faucet at the back of Lambspun. Washing her hands, washing her arms, washing her dress. Of course she'd wash off the blood. There was no way she could walk into a store and use its restroom facilities to clean up. Even gas stations gave out keys for the facilities. And Madge certainly couldn't arrive home to greet her daughter while she was still covered in blood. No . . . she had to clean up first. Wash off all trace of Rizzoli's blood.

"Here's your soup. Enjoy," Bridget said, placing a steaming bowl of tomato basil soup in front of Kelly.

"Uhhhh, thanks . . ." was all she could manage. Kelly's thoughts had left mundane issues like lunch or hunger. They were slowing down now in the pattern Kelly recognized from all her earlier sleuthing efforts. Usually she'd taken some time to sit quietly and knit on a project while her thoughts sorted themselves out. But she didn't have her knitting with her now. Her almost-finished baby hat was still at the cottage.

Kelly stared at her soup, the enticing aroma drifting upward. She picked up the soupspoon and dipped it into the rich, creamy, red mixture. Her thoughts would simply have to sort themselves out over soup this time, she decided, and took a sip. Delicious.

She proceeded to slowly savor the soup

while her thoughts started arranging themselves in logical order. The conclusion they brought was shocking. Almost incomprehensible. How could such a sweet, slight older woman like Madge commit such a brutal murder? Was it possible? Was Kelly seeing things that weren't there? Drawing bogus conclusions? Maybe, maybe not. She would have to run all this by Burt and see what he thought. One thing Kelly had learned over these last few years of involving herself in murder investigations was that nothing was impossible when it came to murder. *Especially* when it came to murder.

Kelly listened to the last of Steve's phone message saying he'd be home later tonight because of a late meeting. Kelly leaned against the kitchen counter at her cottage and stared outside at Carl sniffing about the backyard. The sun was in the middle of the afternoon sky. She pondered for another minute, then scrolled through her phone directory. Pushing Burt's number, she listened to the rings. Again and again. Not surprising. Burt and Mimi were probably inside the loud exhibition hall setting up the vendor booth.

Kelly waited for the voice mail beep to come on. "Hey, Burt, Kelly here. When you get a chance, could you give me a call when you're in a quiet place. I need to share some information with you. Something I've just learned concerning the Rizzoli murder. Something important. I'd like your advice. I know you and Mimi are busy up at the Wool Market, so call when you can. I'll be heading for the house in a little while and I plan to be home this evening. So, give me a call. Thanks." She clicked off.

NINETEEN

Kelly heard a short staccato knock on her cottage front door. Burt was right on time, she thought, glancing at her watch as she hurried to the door. Eight fifteen in the morning.

She yanked the door open. "Hey, Burt. Perfect timing. The coffee is brewing now."

"Thanks, Kelly, but I'll take a pass," Burt said as he stepped inside. "I drank way too much of the stuff yesterday while we were setting up the booth."

"Well, I'm ready for my first mug of the day," Kelly said as she headed for the kitchen. "Have a seat, Burt. Try out that comfy new chair I bought."

"Don't mind if I do, Kelly. This may be the only time I get to sit down all day." Burt settled into the overstuffed armchair and leaned back. "Say . . . this *is* comfortable. I may sneak over here and steal a nap sometime."

"Be my guest, Burt," she said as she filled her mug. "You won't bother me or my accounts. Besides, you may need a break in between trips to Estes Park and back. Is the booth ready for the market opening tomorrow?"

"Almost. The shelves are nearly filled. Both Rosa and Connie are taking turns driving loads of stuff from the shop to the exhibition building. We should be ready by tonight. We're going to take both of them to dinner and pay for their hotel. We always need them during the market on Saturday and Sunday."

"You're bringing in the part-time help to run the shop tomorrow, right?" Kelly settled into another upholstered chair across from Burt.

"Yes, thank goodness, we have a deep enough list of temp helpers who've worked in the shop, so they know what to do and can answer customers' questions." Burt settled his hands in his lap, lacing his fingers, in what Kelly recognized as his "let's talk" pose. "Now, let's go over how we're going to handle this meeting with Madge. I called her earlier this morning and asked her if she could come in and discuss another spinning class we might have her teach. So we'll have some time before I have to drive back to Estes Park. I'm thinking we'll meet her in the remodeled storage building. That's where we've been keeping bags of fleece for the market. Plus, it will give us some privacy." Burt sighed. "I have to tell you, Kelly. I think you've really gone out into left field with this one. I know what you've told me sounds incriminating, but . . . I just can't picture Madge doing something like that. I don't even know if she has the strength to rip open Jared Rizzoli's throat. I just don't think she could. It's entirely possible Bridget thought she recognized Madge, when she didn't. Maybe it was someone else. Then again, why would some unknown woman be washing her hands behind Lambspun?" His familiar puzzled frown appeared.

Kelly took a deep drink of her coffee. She still had her doubts, too. Assuming Bridget was correctly identifying Madge, then everything Bridget told her sounded suspicious. Then add Madge's lies — to her daughter and to Kelly. Why would Madge lie about something so innocuous if she wasn't hiding something? Then again . . . Madge was slightly built, not big and muscular like her daughter Barb. Could Madge commit such a brutal murder?

"I know how you feel, Burt. That's precisely why I called you. Why I *always* call you. You're my sounding board. And I admit, I could be completely wrong about Madge. That's why we'll have to make this questioning sound innocent. I certainly don't want to accuse an innocent woman and have her mad at me forever." Kelly made a face.

"Same here. Madge is a valuable teacher, and a wonderful spinner, and a good friend of Lambspun. We don't want to lose her. So we're definitely going to have to tread carefully. As I said before, Bridget could have been completely mistaken."

Kelly glanced at her watch. "Maybe we should go over there now. She's coming in fifteen minutes, so we might as well get set up and comfortable in the storage area."

"I agree." Burt pushed himself out of the chair. "We've got a worktable and chairs in there now, so we can be working when Madge shows up. I've got some files with class schedules inside, so I'll go get those now."

"I'll bring my charity baby hat with me," Kelly said as she headed back to the kitchen for a coffee refill. "I'm almost finished anyway."

Burt stood in the open doorway. "Okay, grab your knitting and come on over. I think we should settle in now, so we look natural. Madge often shows up early."

"Got it. I'll be right over," Kelly said, but Burt was already out the door.

"Okay, that looks like Madge's car pulling into a parking space now," Burt said, as he leaned back in the metal chair to peer through a side window.

Kelly looked up from the almost-finished baby hat. She was working on the crown now, reducing the stitches row by row, so the circle narrowed and narrowed, until it was just a small opening that she would pull closed from a strand of yarn beneath the crown. She looked toward the door. "Okay, I'll follow your lead as usual. Have you figured out how you're going to make this sound innocent?"

"Kind of. I'll probably play it by ear. We'll see." Burt moved more of his class schedule papers around him on the table.

Suddenly Madge appeared in the doorway, and Kelly was astounded to see she was carrying another bag of fleece. A beige one this time. Instinctively, Kelly jumped from her chair to help the older woman. "Here, Madge, let me take that. I can't believe you've spun another whole bag of fleece."

"Well, I had some left over from my

315

Creamy Beige Beauty. She always throws the prettiest shades of beige and brown." She handed the bag off to Kelly. "Thank you, my dear. That's very sweet of you, but I can really manage, you know. I'm stronger than I look."

Burt stood and pulled out a chair on Madge's side of the worktable. "Hey, Madge. Have a seat, will you, and take a look at this schedule I've drawn up. I think I could use you for another class." He placed a sheet of paper on the table in front of her chair.

Madge looked up at the ceiling and the bigger windows on the walls. "Hal Nelson certainly did a good job with this old garage. Repaired the walls, brought in more light. Even patched up the stucco with new." She gave a satisfied nod. "He's a good craftsman."

"He certainly is," Kelly added as Madge sat down. "I kept track of his progress every day. His and Malcolm's, that is."

"Oh, yes. Malcolm. He seemed to be a good worker, despite his problems." Madge looked down at the paper in front of her. "Looks like you could use someone for a Thursday afternoon class, am I right?"

"You sure are. Do you think you could handle another class, Madge?" Burt asked, his pen poised over some other papers.

"Certainly, Burt. I'd be glad to," Madge said with a little smile. "Now, is that all you wanted to talk to me about?"

Kelly looked up from the knitted baby hat, surprised by Madge's question. Burt looked surprised, too.

"Well, I . . . I did want to get on your schedule so you could . . . plan ahead," Burt answered after a few seconds' pause.

"You could have asked me that question on the phone, Burt," Madge said, her little smile turning sly. "Are you sure you don't have some other questions?"

Kelly stared at Madge. She couldn't help it. Madge was acting like she knew what Burt was going to say before he said it. Kelly's little buzzer went off inside.

Burt seemed a little nonplussed for a second, then looked down and cleared his throat. He laid the class schedules aside. "Well, yes, Madge . . . there is something else I wanted to ask. I . . . We, Mimi and I, have noticed you doing some weeding in the garden lately."

Madge cocked her head and kept that little smile. "Yes, whenever I see an intrusive weed in a garden, I just have to yank it out. Why do you ask? Did you not want me to remove the weeds?"

"No, no . . . it's just that . . . Mimi planted some new flowers and she wanted to make sure you didn't mistake them for weeds. And someone said you were weeding at the back of the building Friday night, two weeks ago. And that's where Mimi planted her new flowers."

Madge folded her hands in her lap. "No, I wasn't weeding behind the building two weeks ago. That was the night Jared Rizzoli was killed."

Burt's expression grew somber. "Yes . . . yes, it was."

Kelly was watching this short exchange with fascination. Madge was carefully answering Burt's questions. But she also added information or asked a question of her own. Kelly's little buzzer got louder. Something was definitely up with Madge. She decided to jump in, if for nothing else than to distract Madge's attention.

"Don't be annoyed with Burt, Madge. It's all my fault for telling him that one of the café waitresses said she saw you that Friday night about seven o'clock. You were washing your hands and your dress beneath the outside water faucet. I just happened to mention it to Burt, and . . . well, he got worried about Mimi's flowers."

Kelly was quite pleased with her quick

subterfuge and even quicker lie. She'd noticed that lying in the midst of questioning suspects had come all too easily when she was sleuthing. She glanced at Burt and he looked slightly grateful.

Madge, however, eyed Kelly and her smile grew. "Just happened? Kelly, I doubt that you 'just happen' to do anything. You appear far more deliberate a person than that."

Kelly blinked. She wasn't expecting that response. "I'm not sure what you mean," Kelly managed after a few seconds' pause.

"Yes, you do. Burt didn't ask me to come in for a simple scheduling question. There's something else he wants to ask me. Why else would he be sitting here in this nice quiet room, where we cannot be disturbed? And why else would you be sitting next to him, Kelly?" Madge gave her an almost maternal smile. "You really should finish that hat, dear. Those little babies could use it." She pointed to the knitted hat in Kelly's lap.

Kelly stared back at Madge, who was sitting in the chair, calm, cool, and collected — asking *them* questions.

Burt cleared his throat again, and leaned forward over the table. "You're right, Madge. We do have some other questions to ask you about the night Jared Rizzoli died. Kelly said you told her you asked Barbara where she had driven when she returned to your home that Friday evening. Yet, Barbara told Kelly that you were not there when she came home. You came in later, and your dress was wet. Barbara said you told her you walked through a neighbor's sprinklers. Now, those seem to be innocuous lapses from truth, except for the fact that you were seen outside Lambspun within the time frame that Jared Rizzoli was killed." Burt's voice dropped lower. "So, Madge, would you like to tell Kelly and me exactly where you were during the hours of six o'clock and eight o'clock the evening that Jared Rizzoli was killed?"

Madge looked first at Burt, then at Kelly, her little smile still in place. She leaned back into her chair and folded her hands again. "I'll be glad to. I met Jared Rizzoli here in the Lambspun driveway. I spoke to him for a minute, then I stabbed him in the throat with the knife I took from a tool-box in this building."

Kelly stared at her. She couldn't help it. *What the heck?* Madge calmly admitted murdering Jared Rizzoli like she was describing a new spinning technique. Kelly quickly glanced to Burt, who looked equally stunned at Madge's brazen statement.

"Madge . . . do you know what you're saying?" Burt asked, looking startled. "Are you feeling all right?"

"Of course I'm all right. And I know exactly what I'm saying. I borrowed Jennifer's cell phone overnight so I could send a text message to Rizzoli that he would respond to. I figured he would definitely show up later in the evening if his real estate agent asked him to." Her smile turned smug. "Of course he did. If it had to do with money, Rizzoli would come running. So, I waited until Hal Nelson and Malcolm left for the evening, and I took one of their work knives. I purposely chose one that was old and worn. But the blade was still sharp enough to do the job." She gave a self-satisfied nod. Job well-done, obviously. "I gave it an extra yank to make sure he died quickly. Got all those important veins and arteries. I didn't want him trying to get out of the car and attracting attention. Of course, that made quite a mess. That's why the waitress saw me. I had to wash off all that blood, for goodness' sake."

For goodness' sake. Kelly stared at Madge, mesmerized by her calm recitation of a bloody, brutal murder. *For goodness' sake.* Goodness had nothing to do with it. She looked at Burt and their gazes met. Burt looked as shocked at what he'd heard as Kelly felt. What was it the night watchman would cry out in warning as he walked London streets two centuries ago? *"Murder! Bloody murder! Murder most foul!"* Murder. *For goodness' sake.*

Burt leaned forward a little more. "Did you know Hal Nelson was going to talk to Rizzoli that night? Had the two of you discussed —"

"No such thing!" Madge snapped angrily, sitting up ramrod straight in the chair. "I was shocked when I saw Hal outside talking to that awful man. Hal Nelson had nothing to do with my plans. I'd already decided to kill Rizzoli the day after Barbara went to his seminar and confronted him in public. Rizzoli was an evil, evil man who caused great pain and suffering and death. Yes, death! Good people sickened and died like Hal's mother or committed suicide like my dear husband. All because of Jared Rizzoli's greed and hateful schemes. He was an evil man and deserved to die. And I'd kill him all over again if I had the chance!" She gave a firm nod, as if saying, "That's that."

Kelly watched Madge, sitting tall and proud in her Righteous Anger. She looked to Burt, who was watching Madge with a mixture of astonishment and sadness. Burt took a deep breath and spoke. "Madge, you realize I will have to report this conversation to the police."

"Of course I do. I knew you two had figured it out when you asked me down here."

"You also need to speak with an attorney. Do you have someone you've used and can trust?"

"Yes, I've used Lawrence Chambers for years. He's excellent and as trustworthy as the day is long."

Kelly sat up straighter at that. At last she could do something to help Madge. "Lawrence Chambers is my lawyer, too. I have his number in my directory. Would you like to call him now?" She dug her phone from her pocket.

"Why, thank you, Kelly. I'm not surprised you have Chambers as your attorney. He's sharp as a tack. Like you." Madge gave her another of those disconcerting maternal smiles.

Kelly found the number and handed over her phone as Madge pushed away from the table. "Is it all right if I speak to him outside, Burt?" she asked politely.

"Of course, Madge." Burt gestured toward the door. Then he sank back into his chair and looked over at Kelly. "Well, that is the damnedest thing I've ever heard. I've had criminals confess before, but nothing like this. I'd better leave a message for Dan. I can talk to him while I'm driving back to Estes Park." He shook his head. "Mimi's never going to believe this."

Kelly could barely believe it, either. "What do we do with her? I mean, after she finishes talking with Chambers?"

"Oh, I'm going to take her to Chambers's office, then I'm going to notify the investigating officers in this case and tell them what we just heard and inform them that Madge is presently with her lawyer. I assume that good attorney Chambers will personally take Madge to the police department to turn herself in."

This time, Kelly wagged her head in Burt fashion. "I swear, Burt. If you'd told me yesterday that we'd be having a conversation like this today, I would have thought you were crazy. Good Lord! She was so . . . so calm and collected and cold-blooded about it. Just sat there smiling, like she was pleased with herself or something. Talk about bizarre."

"I've learned over the years to never say 'now I've heard everything.' Because sure as shooting, you'll hear something even stranger later on."

"I'll take your word for it, Burt." Then she

couldn't resist saying, "For goodness' sake."

Burt just rolled his eyes as he pulled out his cell phone.

TWENTY

"Man, I forgot how big this event is," Steve said, looking around at the colorful vendors' booths, crammed cheek-by-jowl into every aisle of the Wool Market exhibition building. "Look at all these people."

"I know. Fiber arts have surged in popularity these last few years," Kelly said as they slowly maneuvered their way toward the Lambspun booth ahead.

People crowded every aisle in the large building on the county fairgrounds where the Estes Park Wool Market was held every June. Knitted, spun, woven, crocheted, tatted, sewn, and felted creations beckoned from every booth; some even spilled over the sides. Spun yarns of every fiber imaginable and in colors that would put a rainbow to shame enticed passersby. Kelly would have given in to the temptations as she moved through the aisles, but today she was looking for information, not fiber.

"Hey, I think I spotted the booth," Steve said, craning his neck. "Yeah, there's Burt."

"Good. He's the man I want to see," Kelly said, sliding sideways around a woman who had stopped in the middle of the aisle. Kelly sped up in front of a gaggle of women who had stopped to admire a weaver's exquisite handiwork. Now there was a clear shot to the Lambspun booth.

"Slick move," Steve said with a chuckle as he caught up with her.

"I learned to walk in big East Coast cities," she joked, heading straight for Burt, who was placing books on a lower shelf of the booth. She called out as she sped up, "Hey, Burt. How're you folks doing?"

Burt glanced up and smiled as Kelly and Steve approached. "Hey, there, you two. Good to see you both."

"How's business so far?" Steve asked, shaking Burt's hand as he scanned the crowds. Lambspun's booth was filled with customers.

"Great, so far. We're nearly sold out of the Lambspun hand-dyed yarns. I'll run back tonight and ransack the basement for more."

"Did you hear anything more from Dan?" Kelly asked. "Last night you said that Madge would go before a judge on Monday to hear charges. Did she spend the night in the county detention facility?"

"No, Dan said the detectives in the case took her statement, then conferred with the county prosecutor about charges. Meanwhile, she was allowed to post bail. But I'm fairly certain she'll be heading to the detention center on Monday after she's been charged with murder."

Steve shook his head. "Brother, that is so hard to believe. I've never met Madge, but listening to Kelly describe what this sweet little grandmother did . . . Wow. Scary."

"I know what you mean," Burt agreed. "Kelly and I were stunned. But, at least she's got a good attorney. Larry Chambers is one of the best in town. He'll take good care of her."

"Yes, he will, and that makes me feel a little better."

"Thank goodness Chambers called Barbara and told her what was happening. I did *not* want to be the one to do that."

"I'm glad you didn't have to, Burt. Keep me updated, okay?"

"Will do, Kelly."

Just then, Cassie came around the corner of the booth, spotted them, and raced over. "Hey, Kelly and Steve. Mimi's selling tons of stuff today! Boy, I've never seen so many people and yarns and stuff all around," she bubbled.

"You got that right, Cassie," Steve said with a grin. "Whole bunches of stuff."

"I'm so glad you came up today, Cassie," Kelly said. "This Wool Market is fantastic, don't you think?"

"Oh, yeah, awesome," Cassie said, watching the people pass.

"Have you been to the livestock barns yet?" Steve asked.

"We did that first thing when got here," Burt said. "I went down early and picked her up from the café. Pete and Jennifer were already hard at work." Burt reached over and gave Cassie a hug. "Saturday morning is always packed for breakfast, right, Cassie?"

Her eyes went wide in agreement. "Oh, yeah. People are there every morning when Pete opens the doors. It's amazing."

"I bet you've been a big help to Mimi and Burt in the booth," Kelly said. "There are tons of people here today."

"Cassie's been a great helper," Burt agreed.

"Can we go over to the alpaca barns now?" Cassie asked. "I haven't seen Jayleen yet. She said she was bringing eight of her alpacas today."

"I'll take her, Burt," Kelly offered. "You're

probably needed here."

"Well, I don't know about needed, but I'm reasonably useful," Burt teased. "You tell Jayleen hello for me. And Curt. I spoke with him earlier. He brought up one of his trailers to help transport the alpacas back to her ranch Sunday night."

"Will do, Burt," Steve said, as he and Kelly and Cassie turned into the aisle. Pointing toward the side of the building, Steve beckoned. "Let's go out this exit because it's closer to the livestock areas."

Kelly and Cassie followed as Steve carved a path through the crowded aisles and headed for the exit door. As soon as the hot sun hit Kelly in the face, she blinked and slipped on her sunglasses.

"Alpaca stalls used to be over in that direction," Kelly said as they walked past new crowds of people eating hot dogs, smoked turkey legs, barbecue, corn dogs, cotton candy, ice cream, popsicles, even hot apple pie. Kelly marveled at the variety of food vendors were selling to lines of eager customers, standing in the hot sun.

Since Estes Park was higher in altitude than Fort Connor, 7,500 feet as opposed to 5,000 feet, the heat was not as intense up here. Only the high eighties instead of high nineties. Kelly was grateful for the difference in temperatures. It was a welcome relief.

"Hey, isn't that Jayleen at the end of those stalls?" Steve said, pointing ahead as they approached the larger livestock area.

"Yeah, it is. Hey, Jayleen!" Cassie called, then broke into a run, heading for the last stalls.

Kelly saw Jayleen turn quickly at the sound of her name being called. Curt was standing beside her, talking to a couple who were obviously admiring one of Jayleen's alpacas.

Cassie raced up, and Jayleen reached out and gave her a big hug.

"Cassie's adopting grandparents all over the place," she said with a laugh. "Isn't that great?"

"Sure is," Steve agreed. "Both Jayleen and Mimi need grandkids, don'tcha think?"

"Ohhhh, yeah," Kelly said in a low voice as they approached the stalls. "Hey, there, Jayleen, Curt. We thought we'd see how you're doing."

"Nice to see you two up here," Curt said, touching the brim of his Stetson.

"Well, well, it's good to see you up here with Kelly, Steve. You haven't been to one of these markets in a coon's age," Jayleen said with a wide grin, her arm still around

Cassie's shoulders.

"You're right about that, Jayleen. Denver keeps me pretty darned busy." Steve reached out and gave Curt a handshake. "You got any livestock here, Curt? Or just helping out Jayleen?"

"I'm helping out. Less work, actually," Curt said with a lazy smile.

"Can I go inside with the herd?" Cassie asked, blue eyes wide.

"Sure, you can, girl," Jayleen said, tousling Cassie's hair. "Curt's grandson Eric has been helping clean up after them. I reckon he'll be glad to have some help with pooper-scooper detail."

Curt laughed. "He sure would. He's getting some sandwiches for us, but he'll be back in a minute."

Kelly watched Cassie effortlessly climb over the metal stall fencing and drop to the hay-strewn floor inside the stall. Two gray alpacas approached her, extending their graceful necks to sniff her. Cassie stood still and let them sniff, Kelly noticed.

"She's learned fast," Kelly observed.

Jayleen nodded. "Cassie's a fast learner. Picks up stuff right away."

"Speaking of picking up stuff, here comes the chief scooper, back with our lunch," Curt announced. "Hey, Eric. We've recruited a helper for you on the waste removal patrol."

A skinny, sandy brown–haired boy walked up with a box filled with sodas and wrapped sandwiches. The boy glanced over at Cassie and smiled. "Hey, Cassie. Did Grandpa trick you into that job?"

"Heck, no, Eric," Jayleen said with a laugh. "Cassie volunteered. She already got an idea of the job this week when she came out to my ranch."

Kelly thought she scented barbecued chicken, and her stomach growled. Lunchtime already. Looked like she and Steve would have to join the crowded lines. "I saw some folks talking to Curt when we walked up. Are they interested in buying one of the herd?"

Jayleen shrugged. "They're thinking about it. People need to take time before they jump into buying livestock. Especially if they've never done any —"

A man in a black tee shirt and a Colorado Rockies baseball cap suddenly called Jayleen's name as he raced up. "*Jayleen!* I just heard on my short wave there's a fire over in Bellevue Canyon! Started near Stove Prairie, but it's spreading fast! Firefighters are out there now!"

Jayleen stared at the man, her face draining of color in an instant. She grasped his arm. "Stove Prairie? That's . . . that's down the other side of the mountain!"

"Where's it spread to?" Curt demanded.

"I don't know . . . It didn't say . . . just that it's spreading and firefighters are already there! I know your place is in the canyon, Jayleen. Who else is here? I'd better tell 'em, too." His head swiveled around, as he scanned the stalls.

"Uhh, Mary and . . . Tom Robbins . . ." Jayleen clutched at her throat. "Oh, no, God, no . . . my ranch!" She reached out and Curt caught her hand.

"We have to get back, Jayleen. *Now!* Eric and Cassie can watch over the animals until I come back. But we've got to get the rest of your herd out now." Curt put his other hand on Jayleen's shoulder.

Kelly's heart had gone to her throat. *A wildfire!* Oh, no. Not in these dry forests.

"Jayleen, Kelly and I can help," Steve said. "We can get trailers from my parents' place and go over to your ranch and get your animals out. Kelly can drive my truck, and I'll drive one of my dad's."

"Steve, why don't you take Jayleen's truck right now," Curt said. "It's already got a trailer on it. We'll take mine. That way you can drive to her ranch with us. We could use your help getting the animals out."

Jayleen still looked in shock, too stunned to speak, as she stared at Steve. "I've got to go . . . I've got to go," she repeated.

Burt raced up then, white-faced and panting. "Jayleen! I just got a call from a firefighter friend. An alarm went out. Wildfire in Bellevue Canyon!"

"We just heard," Curt said, moving Jayleen away from the stalls. "We're heading back now. Eric and Cassie can look after the animals. *Eric!*" He turned to his grandson, who was standing stock-still, as was Cassie, both young faces stunned. "Give out Jayleen's cards to anyone who's interested and tell them to call her for information. I'll be back later. Don't worry, I'll call your mom. Cassie, help out Eric. He needs you now."

"I'll stay with them here, Curt," Burt offered. "Mimi's got it covered inside. I'll stay with the kids and make sure everything's okay. Keep us posted, *please*!"

"I've gotta go, I've gotta go, I've gotta go . . ." Jayleen repeated, staring out toward the mountains. "My ranch, oh, God, my ranch . . ."

"C'mon, Jayleen, let's get to my truck. You'd better not drive right now," Curt directed as he took her arm.

"We'll help you, Jayleen, I swear, we will," Steve promised as he and Kelly fell in step with them. "Kelly will get another trailer from my dad and meet us up at your ranch."

"And I'll call Lisa and Greg and Megan and Marty," Kelly said. "They can borrow some trucks from Marty's family and head to your ranch. We'll load up everything you need. We'll get your animals out. I *promise!*"

Curt used his big frame and broad shoulders to create a path for them through the throngs of people filling the fairgrounds. They were all happily enjoying the summer weekend in this gorgeous mountain setting. Exactly like Kelly and her dear friends had been doing only minutes ago. How quickly everything could change. Someone's entire world could change. Jayleen's world was now threatened — in an instant.

Wildfire. The one thing that everyone who lived in Colorado's beautiful mountain areas dreaded. There had not been a wildfire in the northern Colorado mountains and canyons near Fort Connor for as long as any of Kelly's friends could remember. And now — when their forests were thick and filled with pine-bark-beetle-killed trees. Bone dry. Drought dry. Kindling. Waiting for a spark.

Kelly felt her stomach clench at the fearful thoughts bombarding her as they pushed through the crowd. Steve had parked on the edge of the parking area. It would take another five minutes or more for her just to reach his car.

"Here are my keys," Steve said, fishing them out of his jeans. "Be careful driving back into the canyon with that trailer." He reached out and drew Kelly close for a quick kiss.

"I'll try to meet up with Greg and the others. Maybe they'll have the trailers by the time I reach Fort Connor. If so, we can all drive up together."

"C'mon, Steve," Curt called as he and Jayleen broke free of the crowd and started to run.

Steve ran after them, quickly disappearing behind people heading toward the livestock barns. Working her way through the crowds, Kelly pulled her cell phone from her jeans pocket and began to call her friends . . .

AUTHOR'S NOTE

The next Knitting Mystery takes place as Kelly and friends try to help Jayleen save her ranch. I don't usually set my stories so close together in time, but I was revising *Close Knit Killer* in early June 2012, almost ready to submit the eleventh in the Knitting Mysteries to my editor. And then, the High Park wildfire broke out in Rist Canyon just northwest of Fort Collins, Colorado, where I live. I call that canyon Bellevue Canyon in the mysteries.

Life as normal changed in Fort Collins and the entire area of Northern Colorado at that moment. Even though Fort Collins was never in any danger of the wildfire spreading into our city (there is a large and very long lake — Horsetooth Reservoir — that stretches almost the entire length of the western side of Fort Collins), we were all riveted by the fast-moving, wind-whipped wildfire as it jumped and darted about our canyons, leaping from Rist Canyon into the Buckhorn Canyon area, and briefly into Cache La Poudre River Canyon and several other mountain communities. Smoke filled the air, and those of us who lived on the western side of Fort Collins sought shelter with our friends on the north or eastern edges of the city. My dear friend Joey Waltz very generously let me stay in the house she had just moved from and was preparing for resale. And it was Joey who told me during the first week of the fire, as we watched from her wide windows looking toward the mountains, "You have to include this in the mysteries." I knew immediately that she was right. So, I totally revised the entire manuscript. Interestingly, I already had the novel taking place during late May and early June of last year. And the day the story ended, with Kelly and Steve in Estes Park at the Wool Market, was the actual day the wildfire started.

The next mystery in the series will be out June 2014, and the High Park wildfire will definitely play a large role. I will not pretend that I will write a newscaster's account of how the High Park wildfire affected all of Fort Collins, but I promise I will try to include real-life details of those life-changing, dramatic events of June 2012 as seen by Kelly and her friends and all of the folks at Lambspun. Jayleen Swinson has her alpaca ranch up in Bellevue Canyon, so everything she's spent the last twelve years building is at risk. Kelly and all of the characters — and new ones, too — will come to Jayleen's aid. And — don't worry, mystery readers — I won't forget that I'm writing a murder mystery. So, a dead body will definitely be part of the story. ☺

PATTERNS

Author Note: Kelly used the easy Collapsible Cloche hat pattern with size-eight needles for the baby hat she knitted. That pattern is found in book five of the series, Dyer Consequences. *Here's a more challenging hat pattern for tiny babies.* ☺

SWEETHEART BABY HAT

Fits Newborn–4 Months

Materials:

Main Color (MC) — 2 ounces cotton yarn of your color choice. Can double to obtain gauge

Set of 4 #6 double-pointed needles, or size needed to obtain correct gauge

Set of 4 #8 double-pointed needles, or size needed to obtain correct gauge

Tapestry needle or crochet hook to weave in ends

Gauge:

In MC on larger needles, 4 1/2 sts = 1 inch

Hat:

On smaller needles, loosely cast on 60 sts with MC.

Join work, being careful not to twist sts.

Work in modified twisted rib as follows:

Rnd 1: (K1, P1) around.
Rnd 2: (Kb1, P1) around.

Repeat these two rounds until piece measures 1″ from beginning. Change to larger needles and work for ten (10) rounds in stockinette stitch.

Work in seed stitch for 3 rounds as follows:

Rnd 1: (K1, P1) around.
Rnd 2–3: Knit the purls sts and purl the knit sts.

Decrease as follows:

Rnd 1: (K2 together, K8) around.
Rnd 2: (K2 tog, K7) around.
Rnd 3: (K2 tog, K6) around.
Rnd 4: (K2 tog, K5) around.

Continue in this manner for a total of 8

decrease rounds.

Rnd 9 and 10: (K2 tog) around.

K in the round on 3 remaining sts for about
1 1/2 inches for nubbin.
Break yarn, leaving a 4-inch tail. Pull tail
through remaining sts, then through nubbin with tapestry needle or crochet hook
and weave securely into crown on wrong
side of hat. Weave in all other loose ends.
Tie a knot in the nubbin if desired.

*Pattern courtesy of Lambspun of Colorado,
Fort Collins, Colorado.*

RECIPES

Here are the Best Cold Appetizer recipe winners from my Knitting Mysteries Appetizer Contest.

CAPRESE ON A STICK

Contributed by Julie Dewar.

Ingredients: 1 pint grape tomatoes; 24 small basil leaves; 1 container ciliegine (small fresh mozzarella balls); balsamic vinegar. Marinade: 1/4 cup extra virgin olive oil. Finely grated zest of 1 lemon; 1 1/2 tablespoons fresh lemon juice; 1 tablespoon dried thyme leaves or basil; 2 garlic cloves, minced; kosher salt and freshly ground pepper to taste. In a large bowl, whisk olive oil with lemon zest, lemon juice, thyme, garlic, and a generous pinch of salt and pepper. Add tomatoes and ciliegine to bowl and turn to coat. Let stand at room temperature for 30 minutes. Skewer grape tomato, basil leaf, and ciliegine ball onto toothpicks and place on a serving dish. Drizzle with balsamic vinegar.

DILL DIP

Contributed by Judy Seeley.

Ingredients: 1 cup sour cream; 1 cup mayonnaise; 1 1/2 tablespoons dried onion flakes; 1 1/2 tablespoons dried parsley; 1 1/2 teaspoons dill weed; 1 1/2 teaspoons beau monde or bon appetít (whichever one your store carries). Pinch of accent. Mix all ingredients together and chill before serving.

TZATZIKI DIP WITH RAW VEGETABLES

Contributed by Liz Veronis.

Mix thoroughly: 8 ounces of plain, whole milk Greek yogurt (American yogurt requires draining excess liquid through cheesecloth); 2 cucumbers, peeled, seeded, and diced, with excess liquid squeezed out; 2 tablespoons olive oil; juice of 1/2 lemon; 1 tablespoon chopped fresh dill; 3 cloves garlic, peeled. Some recipes call for salt and pepper to taste, but we are salt free. Refrigerate, covered, for 1 hour.

CHUTNEY MOLD

Contributed by Maryfrances Charnley.

Ingredients: 12 ounces Philadelphia Cream Cheese, softened; 1/2 jar bacon bits; 1/2 can cocktail peanuts; 3 heaping tablespoons sour cream; 1/2 cup chopped scallions (green onions) — fine; 1/2 box raisins (I use golden raisins). Mix all ingredients. Shape into a log wrap in plastic wrap and foil and freeze overnight. To serve: Pour one jar of Major Grey's Chutney over log and sprinkle with coconut. Serve with crackers.